PRAISE FOR SOMEONE ELSE'S LIFE

"Well-developed characters and plenty of local color add to the slowly simmering plot, which builds to a strong and unexpected climax. Alfred Hitchcock fans will be satisfied."
—*Publishers Weekly*

"Chilling from page one, *Someone Else's Life* is an unputdownable descent into two women's parallel lives. With genuine jaw-dropping twists and enough seeds of doubt to populate a very wicked garden, Butler's debut thriller is a breath of fresh Kauai air."
—Eliza Jane Brazier, author of *If I Disappear*

"Lyn Liao Butler has mastered the art of full-body-tense suspense in this fresh take on the 'stranger in the house' concept, which will have you racing to the end even as your blood pressure increases and you have to remind yourself to breathe."
—Amanda Jayatissa, ITW Thriller Award–winning author of *My Sweet Girl*

"A chilling and immensely readable psychological thriller, *Someone Else's Life* simmers with menace as an unsettling encounter reveals the darker side of paradise and the fractures in a seemingly perfect life."
—Heather Chavez, author of *Blood Will Tell*

"*Someone Else's Life* is the read that every thriller lover needs. Atmospheric and character-driven, this story of two women's parallel lives at times disturbed me, then brought me to tears within the same page. The slow build that Butler executes seamlessly translates into a satisfying ending that took me by wine-soaked surprise."

—Elle Marr, Amazon Charts bestselling author of *Strangers We Know*

"Get ready for the storm, and brace yourself! Lyn Liao Butler's psychological and suspense-building thriller packs a punch with provocative prose, layers of heart-racing conflict, and so many plot twists and turns that I read it in one sitting."

—Samantha Verant, author of *The Spice Master at Bistro Exotique*

"A captivating and atmospheric thriller with twists and turns that kept me guessing until the very end. There's so much to love here: the Hawaiian setting, an animal shelter with adorable doggos, a female MC who isn't perfect but is striving to find her footing after a mysterious accident, and an ever-increasing creep factor with the backdrop of a tropical storm. Eager to see what Lyn Liao Butler writes next!"

—Kate Lansing, author of *Killer Chardonnay*

"Gripping, twisty, and clever, *Someone Else's Life* unfolds in a tantalizing slow burn, building to a heart-thumping, tense, breakneck crescendo. With astonishing twists and a pulse-pounding plot, this is a thriller that will leave you gasping for breath."

—Samantha M. Bailey, *USA Today* and #1 national bestselling author of *Woman on the Edge* and *Watch Out for Her*

"I couldn't put this book down. A masterful story of sorrow, secrets, and unexpected romance. Ms. Butler writes with humor, compassion, and honesty. Simply wonderful. I can't wait for more from this gifted author."

—Kristan Higgins, *New York Times* bestselling author of *Pack Up the Moon*

"Lyn Liao Butler does it again! I was anticipating Butler's second book after devouring The Tiger Mom's Tale, and Red Thread of Fate did not disappoint! With a poignant tale and beautiful prose, Butler once again whisks us onto a powerful journey of loss, sorrow, but ultimately a journey of quiet strength."

—Jesse Q. Sutanto, critically acclaimed author of *Dial A for Aunties*

"Lyn Liao Butler is quickly becoming a go-to author for heartfelt, complex stories. Red Thread of Fate has everything—family secrets, mystery, identity. The rare blend of suspense and humor makes this story hard to put down. I can't wait to read what Butler writes next!"

—Saumya Dave, author of *What a Happy Family*

"A heartfelt contemplation on the course of our lives—what is fate, what is the result of the choices we make—coupled with a central mystery that will keep you reading late into the night. It seems Lyn Liao Butler's fate is to entertain with absorbing stories and compelling characters that linger long after the final page."

    —Steven Rowley, *New York Times* bestselling author of *The Guncle*

"*The Tiger Mom's Tale* is a heartfelt, delightful read. Lyn Liao Butler's story of Taiwanese and American identity had me turning pages and laughing (and drooling over the delicious descriptions of food)."

—Charles Yu, author of *Interior Chinatown*, winner of the 2020 National Book Award

"Unembellished and forthright, *The Tiger Mom's Tale* is a touching story that illuminates intricacies of race, ethnicity, traditions and stereotypes...Filled with potential book club discussion topics and perfect for fans of YA novels by Jenny Han, *The Tiger Mom's Tale* will unleash timely dialogue about identity, family secrets and cultural divides."

—BookPage

"Sharp and humorous, *The Tiger Mom's Tale* is a scenic, debut novel with a cast of complicated characters sure to bring laughter and discussion to your next book club. I can't wait to read what Lyn Liao Butler writes next!"

—Tif Marcelo, *USA Today* Bestselling author of *The Key to Happily Ever After*

"An absolutely absorbing story...*The Tiger Mom's Tale* grabbed me from page one and never let me go. I highly recommend this book to fiction readers, especially those who like plucky, get-back-up-again female leads, stories set in New York City, and those with settings on less familiar terrain."

—Fresh Fiction

"*The Tiger Mom's Tale* is a breathtaking debut from a compelling new voice in women's fiction. With captivating characters and vivid descriptions of mouth-watering meals, Lyn Liao Butler whisks us from the bright lights of New York City to the bustle of Taichung. A story of belonging, betrayal, and the bonds between family that can never be broken, *The Tiger Mom's Tale* is a deeply emotional and satisfying read."

—Kristin Rockaway, author of *She's Faking It*

"*The Tiger Mom's Tale* has it all—family drama, scorching love, vivid transcontinental settings, and culinary scenes that made me drool. A charming, engrossing debut from Lyn Liao Butler."

—Kimmery Martin, author of *The Antidote for Everything*

"With a keen eye for detail and a lush appreciation for the joys and comforts of food, Lyn Liao Butler delves into the complicated bonds of family, the endurance of sisterhood, and the fundamental yearning to connect with our heritage."

—Allie Larkin, internationally bestselling author of *Swimming for Sunlight*

"This is a story of complex family relationships, standing up for oneself, and the power of forgiveness."

—Bookriot

"Butler's riveting debut follows a half-white personal trainer who reconnects with her Taiwanese family after her biological father's death...Butler weaves in convincing descriptions of Lexa's navigating of the dating scene and the fetishizing of Asian women, and depicts a fascinatingly complex antagonist in Pin-Yen, who by the end must contend with the effect of her past actions. Butler breathes zesty new life into women's fiction."

—*Publishers Weekly,* starred review

"Filled with mouthwatering descriptions of food, a messy family, and a bit of mystery, this is a heartwarming story of one woman's search for her place in the world."

—Bust.com

CRAZY BAO YOU

LYN LIAO

ALSO BY LYN LIAO BUTLER

The Tiger Mom's Tale

Red Thread of Fate

Someone Else's Life

ISBN-13 Print: 979-8-9876860-0-3

ISBN-13 Ebook: 979-8-9876860-1-0

Cover Illustration by Sean Walsh

Cover Design by Janice Rossi

*For my agent, Rachel, who believed in me
when I didn't*

and for anyone doubting yourself, you CAN do it

MyCraftyBao

Handmade Purses and Accessories
Osage County, OK
758 Sales
Contact Shop Owner: Kim

The Meaning of Bao . . .

I've been asked, What does "bao" mean and why did you name your Etsy shop that? "Bao" means "precious treasure" in Chinese. It can also mean a steamed bun, often filled with vegetables and meat (and they are delicious!). So why "bao"? Because my creations are precious treasures to me, and my shop literally means, "My Crafty Treasure." Also, baos were one of my parents' favorite foods and since they passed away thirteen years ago, I wanted something to remember them by. I also love food, and this double play on words represents everything I'm passionate about in life, hence my logo of a steamed bun.

I hope you enjoy the purses and accessories I have created in My Crafty Bao. I love custom orders, so if there is something you want that you don't see in my shop, please convo me. I might be able to make it for you.

Thank you for stopping by and taking a look!

Be daring, be bold, be you.

xo, Kim

ONE

Kimmie

There was nothing like having a very public breakdown and insulting my boss (well, ex-boss) at my place of work to bring my best friend and beloved aunt flying to my front door. I sat on the couch where I'd planted myself for the past forty-eight hours and didn't move, listening to them pound on the door and ring the bell repeatedly.

"Kimmie! Open this door right now or I'm going to kick it down." Aunt Hana's voice was sharp, and I groaned. Hana was petite, two inches shorter than my five-four frame, but she was the toughest person I knew. I had no doubt she really would kick the door in like the Terminator, so I reluctantly got off the couch and shuffled to the front door.

I flung it open and stared at Hana and Alicia. "You're supposed to be in New York," I said to my best friend, Alicia Colgan. I pointed to Hana. "And you're supposed to be in London. What did you do, meet up in New York to fly in together?"

Hana nodded, her short bobbed hair swinging. "Yes, we coordinated it."

I sighed. "I guess you've heard, since you're on my doorstep?"

"Kimmie," Alicia said, her eyes wide. "*Everyone* has heard. Didn't you read my texts?"

"And listen to my messages?" Hana added as she wheeled two suitcases into the foyer with Alicia trailing behind.

"No." I stepped aside and watched them take note of my faded yoga pants and the ratty T-shirt I wore with the tomato stain on the front where I'd dribbled pasta sauce last night. My frizzy black hair was shoved into a topknot anchored by a scrunchie and I was pretty sure I had potato chip crumbs stuck to my lips.

Hana's eyes swept over me from head to toe. "Michelle called me. She's really sorry."

"Michelle?" My forehead wrinkled in confusion. What was my co-worker sorry about? She wasn't the one who'd gone off on our boss. And why would she call Hana in London?

"Why didn't you answer us? We've been trying to reach you for the past two days." Alicia dragged her two suitcases, a carry-on, and a backpack into the living room and turned to survey me.

"I threw my phone in the garbage." I hadn't really, but I wanted to. I walked back to the couch and flung myself onto it, staring at the TV, where I'd been binge-watching cooking shows for the past two days. I preferred food over people. Food never let you down. Food didn't disappear from your life, leaving you to fend for yourself. I ignored the looks Alicia and Hana were exchanging.

Alicia walked over and threw her arms around me,

hugging me tight. "What happened?" she asked. "This isn't like you at all." We'd known each other since we were little because our mothers were in the same book club. Alicia's family lived on the ranch where her father worked, about twenty-five minutes from the town where I lived.

I shrugged in her embrace. "I just kind of lost it. I couldn't take that jerk anymore."

"But you . . . danced. You don't dance." Alicia pulled back to study me.

I buried my face in my hands. "I don't know what happened. It was like something inside me snapped. And he was being so mean to Hallie, the new girl."

By "he" I meant my pig of a boss, Rip (yeah, that was really his name; who named a baby Rip?), owner of a boutique in town called Let Her Rip (what a stupid name) that carried clothing, accessories, and home décor. I'd been working there for the past five years. I'd always loved to sew and thought it would be a fun place to work and gather inspiration. Well, it would have been, if not for Rip.

"You twerked. I didn't know you could twerk." There was awe in Alicia's voice and I peeked between my fingers at her.

"I do not twerk." I dropped my hands and met her gaze dead on.

"Kimmie. You twerked." Alicia pulled her cell out of her purse. "Look." She scrolled through her phone and then shoved it at me.

I took it and stared at her screen. My mouth dropped open in shock. It was a video of a woman twerking. She was shaking her butt and thrusting her hips, legs bent, tongue hanging out of her mouth. And that woman was . . . me.

"Where did you get this?" I dropped the phone as if it was a hot potato.

"It's all over the internet. You went viral." There was no mistaking the admiration in Alicia's voice.

I glared at her. "The fuck?" Alicia took social media very seriously. She was always posting gorgeous photos of herself. Me, not so much.

"There's more," Hana said, walking to my side. "Michelle got you yelling at Rip, calling him all kinds of names." She tousled the top of my head as if I were a little girl. "I didn't know you had it in you."

"I don't understand." I sputtered, trying to form coherent thoughts.

"Michelle took that video. She posted it because she wanted people to know what a jerk Rip is and that you're her hero for standing up to him. She doesn't have much of a following so she thought only people she knew would see it." Hana paused for breath as I stared at her, speechless. *Michelle* had taken that video?

"She didn't mean for it to go viral," Alicia said. "But some YouTube sensation saw it and shared it and it just went nuts from there." Alicia picked up her phone. "Want to see the whole thing?"

"No. I do not." I turned and fell facedown onto the couch. This was bad. How could a video of me losing my shit be all over the internet? First of all, it was so unlike me. I was a rule follower. I didn't make waves. I hated drawing attention to myself. I was a private person. And second, how was it that the one time I lost control, it would end up on the internet?

I sat up suddenly and grabbed Alicia's phone out of her hands.

"I thought you said you didn't want to see it," Alicia said.

"I don't." I scanned the video, my stomach dropping

when I saw how many views there were. "How is this possible?"

"The video has been shared millions of times," Alicia said in a helpful voice.

Millions? How? Who cared about me, Kimmie Park, who'd lived in the middle of Oklahoma all my life? The most interesting thing about me was that I thought I was Korean until my parents died and I found out I was adopted and was actually Chinese. But that had nothing to do with a video of me screaming at my boss. How could this have happened?

"Michelle feels so bad. She's been trying to reach you and thinks you're mad at her." Hana broke into my thoughts. "When you didn't answer, she called me."

"I'm not mad at her. I just haven't looked at my phone since that day." I shook my head.

"They gave you a nickname," Hana said. "They're calling you Let Her Rip."

I lifted my head, face scrunched in horror. "No."

"Yup." Alicia pushed her long dark brown hair behind one ear. "I've been telling everyone that Let Her Rip is my best friend."

"Alicia!" I sat up and smacked her on the arm. "It sounds like I farted or something. I'm now known as the farting girl?" I flopped back against the cushions, wondering what the hell I had done.

They were quiet for a moment, but I could see Hana biting her lip to keep from laughing, while Alicia actually stuffed her fist in her mouth, rocking with silent laughter.

Hana sat in the love seat catty-corner to the couch. "What happened, Kimmie?"

"I don't know." My voice came out really small. "Rip is always yelling at us for no reason. He still calls me the 'little

Asian girl' when I've told him a million times that it's racist. He made Hallie cry that day. She's still in high school and had made a mistake." I sat up because thinking about that day made my blood boil again. "He yelled at her in front of the customer. And then later, he called her into his office to yell at her some more. And if that wasn't bad enough, he shoved his chair and it fell, making Hallie run out in fear. And I just lost it."

"I'm proud of you." Hana's lips twitched. "But the twerking?"

I moaned and closed my eyes. "This fury just built inside me. I screamed at him, telling him exactly what I thought of him. And I guess my body took over . . . like something bottled up inside me all these years. I . . . it just started moving by itself."

"Rip couldn't get a word in at all. You took over, voguing and moonwalking all around him." Alicia's voice was filled with awe, and I opened my eyes. "It was like Robin Williams in that scene from that old movie . . ." She broke off, looking at Hana for help.

"*The Birdcage*," Hana said.

"Yes! That's it. You were so amazing that it shut Rip up!" Alicia shoved her phone at me. "Here, just look at it."

I scrunched up my nose but took it. I watched the woman on the screen. She started off by making giant movements with her arms as she yelled out, "That's it. I've had enough of you!" She pointed at Rip, telling him he was a bully. Then when she said he wasn't as great as he thought, she started twerking. And damn, her butt looked good. It was curvy and full and the way the woman was shaking it had me mesmerized.

"That's my butt?" I asked without taking my eyes off the screen.

"Yup," Alicia said. "Told you, you look good."

I watched as the woman on the screen started doing the running man, saying "Adios, I quit. I'm out of here." And then she started voguing, framing her face with her hands as she said his employees were better than him. At that point, Rip tried to cut her off but she gave him the hand and did some sort of interpretive dance complete with head banging and hair flinging. She spun and got in his face when he again tried to stop her, making a "shut it" motion with her hands. The woman moved with a grace that was ingrained. When she picked up her purse and then moonwalked out of the store, shouting, "Sayonara, au revoir, zaijian!" I dropped the phone and clapped with everyone else in the video, except for Rip. Rip looked like he was about to have a coronary.

"Oh my god, that was me?" I turned to Hana and Alicia, horrified yet oddly proud.

"See? But it's so out of character for you. We knew something was up." Hana picked up the phone and watched the video again, chuckling to herself. "I had no idea you could dance."

"Me either." I was the most awkward person I knew. Always walking into furniture or walls and stammering when people I didn't know talked to me. But the woman in the video wasn't awkward at all.

"You're amazing," Alicia said.

"I'm really not. I'm so embarrassed. I can never show my face in town again." I buried said face back in my hands. "If I had known Michelle had recorded that, I would have left town."

I suddenly jumped up and went into the kitchen, which was at the back of the house, connected to the living room. I could feel Alicia and Hana watching me as I opened the fridge, rummaging around inside. Then I flung open cabinet doors, one after another.

"What are you doing?" Hana came up to me.

"Checking to see how much food I have. I think I can last another few days." I looked over my shoulder at my aunt. "Then I'll have to drive at night to the next state and get groceries so no one recognizes me."

"Um, Kimmie. This video went viral *internationally*. People in China have seen it." There was glee in Alicia's voice, and I suddenly wanted to stab her in the eye with a fork.

Oh my god, what was happening to me? Not only had I lost my job and yelled—no, *screamed*—at my boss, it was now all over the internet for the world to see. I couldn't even move to Timbuktu. I'd have to move to another planet. And I just had a violent urge to hurt my best friend. My best friend who'd left her dream trip to New York City early to come to my rescue. This was so not like me at all.

Hana put an arm around me and guided me back to the couch. She deposited me next to Alicia and then sat down so that I was flanked by the two people I was closest to in the world. They were all I had, since my parents died when I was sixteen. And just like that, the floodgates opened and I was weeping.

And not weeping prettily like Alicia would have done, but full-on sobbing, gasping for breath as snot shot out of my nose and my hair fell out of its knot and stuck to my face and neck. I made these awful honking sounds, as if I was a dying goose. Grief that I didn't know I had shook my body. I couldn't control the tears or the heaving. I couldn't breathe. Alicia and Hana murmured and one of them got up and pressed tissues into my hand. But all I could focus on was this swell of pain and hurt that I'd tamped down deep within me surging up, wanting to be let out of my body like a hungry beast.

When I caught my breath, words started pouring out without my permission. It was as if I'd lost all control of my mouth, just like that day with Rip. I was horrified, but at the same time, a rush of relief washed over me.

"Everyone I love leaves me and no one wants me and I quit my job and now I have no way to make money and I'll starve because I have no money to buy food and I love food so what am I going to do and I'm turning thirty in a couple of months and I'm still living in the house where I grew up and I haven't had sex in years and I don't have anything or anyone that I'm passionate about and I have no idea what I'm going to do and even though Let Her Rip was a dead-end job at least it was a job and now I have nothing and I'll never find my soulmate because I'm afraid to leave home but I know I won't find my soulmate here and I'm going to die all alone!" That last word ended in a high-pitched wail and then I collapsed against Hana.

She patted my back while Alicia fluttered around us. They stayed with me until the tears finally stopped. I hiccupped and blew my nose with the wad of tissues.

"You're going to be fine." Hana rubbed my back with one hand.

"No, I'm not." My lower lip trembled. "I think I might have blown up my life."

"You think?" A laugh sputtered out of Alicia. "You sure as hell caused an explosion. Sweet, agreeable Kimmie Park told Rip van Patten to fuck off in the most public way possible."

Hana laughed with her. "Look at it this way. Maybe you can get a job as a dancer. Anyone would hire you after that video."

A laugh-snort came out of me. And then when Alicia whispered, "We need to fix your no-sex status ASAP," I was laughing as hard as they were.

I'd messed up. Bad. Thank goodness Hana and Alicia were here. Maybe they could help me fix my life. Then I remembered the other thing that had pushed me over the edge and said, "Oh, and my birth mother reached out to me. She wants to talk to me."

Both Hana and Alicia froze, but I kept cackling, tears leaking from the sides of my eyes. Because I wasn't just Let Her Rip. I was the farting girl who'd completely lost her shit.

TWO

Matt

I hurled myself off the elevator into the lobby, cursing the renovation work being done in 7D that had held up one of the elevators again. I was going to be late for work. Again. The guys were going to break my balls. Again.

I'm an FDNY firefighter. I couldn't have just run down those fifteen flights instead of waiting for the elevator? I rushed through the lobby, bypassing Mrs. White, whose two giant white poodles were taking up most of the space as she blathered with Junior, the doorman on duty. The building had a one twenty-five-pound dog policy. Somehow, Mrs. White had "grandfathered" herself into two giant llamas while complaining about the twenty-six-pound beagle in 12B.

"Hey, Matt," Junior called out as I ran by. "You got a package."

I skidded to a halt. I should have just told Junior to hold it until I got off my straight night tour tomorrow morning, but I'd been waiting for the tote bag that I'd bought on Etsy for my grandmother. The package had gotten lost in the mail and tomorrow was Nana's birthday.

Junior went to the desk by the front door and handed me a package.

"Thanks." I ripped it open. I could feel Mrs. White's nosy eyes on me as I pulled out a gorgeous round-bottomed tote in a colorful floral pattern. It was perfect.

"That's beautiful," Mrs. White said. "New girlfriend?" Her eyes glittered in anticipation.

I shook my head, suppressing a grimace. "It's for my grandmother." Mrs. White spent most of her days in the lobby collecting gossip on the residents of the building. I did my best not to give her any material to share.

Junior held the door open for me. I put the tote back in the plastic bag and thanked him as I rushed out. I hailed a cab, asking the driver to drop me off a block away from the firehouse. Ever since becoming a probational firefighter eight months ago, I'd tried to blend in. I usually took the subway to the firehouse in the Bronx from my one-bedroom on the Upper East Side. But I was really late today, not just because of the elevator but because my father had called, lecturing me about coming back to work for him.

My jaw tightened and I vowed again not to let my father get under my skin. I'd made my decision over a year ago and I wasn't going to let anyone talk me out of what I wanted to do. Not the guys, and certainly not my father.

I called the firehouse from the cab, and Bill, who was on house watch, picked up.

"I'm running late, sorry." The words rushed out of my mouth. "Let whoever's waiting for me know that I'm coming."

"Hurry up, West." Bill's voice was gruff. "It's all senior guys."

Oh, shit, I'm fucked. I hung up and slumped back against the seat. To distract myself from whatever fate awaited me at the firehouse, I fired off a quick message to Kim, the owner of the Etsy shop, to let her know the package had finally arrived. She'd been great to work with. Her products were beautiful and, judging by the tote I'd received, well made. Plus, she'd offered a full refund if it didn't show up by my grandmother's birthday. I wouldn't have taken her up on it since the postal service was out of her control.

The taxi crawled along, making me jittery. By the time I got to the Bronx, I was sweating bullets. I was now twenty minutes late for my tour.

"Shit, fuck, fuck," I muttered as I ran the last block from the taxi to the firehouse. As a probie, I should be early to work, not twenty minutes late. The guys were really going to give me shit. Especially since I hadn't been on time last week either.

As soon as I walked up to the front door of the firehouse, a five-gallon bucket of water was dumped on me from the second floor. On instinct, I clutched the plastic bag with the tote inside to my chest. Gasping for breath from the ice-cold water, I stood there dripping as I was bombarded with a hail of jeers and insults.

"Fucking probie, it's about time."

"Thanks for coming in."

"Your limo break down or something?"

"Hey, probie, what you think this is, a high-society event?" This from Frank, a guy two years my junior who hated me. "You fashionably late?"

"You just earned yourself the doggie car wash. And it's your turn for the night watch." Jack, one of the senior men, pointed at me before walking into the firehouse.

I groaned inside as I stood there and took it. I deserved it. Once a month, we tried to wash all the local dogs, especially those belonging to the homeless. They usually stunk to high Heaven, and were matted with Lord knew what. It was a dirty, smelly, and wet job. Plus I'd be the one up all night manning the computer, while everyone else tried to sleep between calls.

"Time to break out the doggie shampoo, probie." Frank sneered, his thick neck bulging with veins. "What's that you got?"

And before I could stop him, Frank had snatched the package from me with his meaty hands. I knew better than to try to get it back. My own hands fisted by my sides and I took deep breaths, trying to tamp down my anger. I couldn't do or say anything. It would only make things worse.

"Well, look-it here." Frank held up the floral tote for everyone to see. "Our late probie has a purse."

Amid catcalls and whistles, I clenched my teeth. I knew if I made a lunge for the bag, it would only spur Frank on. I brushed the water out of my eyes and wrung my T-shirt, feigning indifference until Frank slapped the tote against my chest. "Better get to work with your murse."

I snatched the bag back from Frank and turned without another word, sloshing my way upstairs to put my stuff away. I dried off with my towel and changed my clothes. Once done, I went down to my locker and got my bunker gear and set it next to the rig, ready to go when a call came in. Dave, the other junior guy on tonight, called down from the engine. "Thanks for making me check the rig by myself."

I ran a hand through my still wet hair. "Sorry. I'll finish." When I took a deep breath, the familiar smell of diesel fuel hit my nose.

Dave hopped off the rig. "You just have to check the masks and the radios. I did all the equipment and tools already." He mumbled something about privileged rich boys and disappeared.

I shook my head, trying to let Dave's comment roll off me before climbing up. I made sure the SCBAs, the self-contained breathing apparatus that we needed to go into a fire, were working properly before moving on to check the radio. Then I did one more check of all of the equipment and tools just to be sure. The last thing I needed was to make a mistake.

Once I was done, I found the guy I was relieving. "Hey, Tom. I'm ready to ride. Take up."

Tom, who had twenty years on the job, raised his eyebrows at me. He gestured with his chin for me to follow him into the bunk room.

"Listen, you can't keep coming in late like this." Tom crossed his arms over his chest, standing in front of a row of twin beds. "The guys will make your life even more miserable if you keep this up."

I nodded. "I'm sorry. My father called and wouldn't let me go, and then the elevator . . ." I stopped and bit off my words. "Not your problem. Won't happen again."

"Good." Tom gave me a brief smile and then left to get his stuff. I stood there alone, burning with embarrassment. I liked Tom. The older man was one of the nicer ones, who didn't give me as much grief as everyone else. Which made his disapproval sting even more.

You knew what you signed up for when you quit your cushy job at your father's company to become a firefighter at twenty-eight. I took a breath, ready to plunge into this straight night tour. I'd have preferred to do a twenty-four hour, but again, as a probie, I got the worst shifts.

With a shake of my head, I walked out of the room where we slept. It was time to do the grunt work—cleaning the firehouse, doing the laundry, not to mention the doggie baths. I could do it. Only four more months before I got the patch for my helmet with my company number on it. Four more months before I would no longer be a probie and would earn my spot as a full-fledged firefighter. It would all be worth it then, this switch in career, in memory of my mom. I vowed not to be late again. Tom was right. I needed to get my shit together if I was going to survive.

THREE

Kimmie

As happy as I was to have Hana and Alicia here, guilt ate at me all night, making me toss and turn. Hana, a novelist, had been living in London for the past six months researching her latest book. Alicia had finally saved up enough money to go to New York City, where she'd always wanted to visit. And they'd both dropped everything and hopped on a plane and flown back to Oklahoma, all because I'd gotten the urge to dance in public.

The next morning, I sat at my desk in the corner of my sewing room and looked around. Hana had helped me convert my parents' bedroom into my sewing haven when she came to live with me. This room was my sanctuary. Sewing was the way I escaped from the harsh realities of life. Losing my parents and then finding out by accident that I was adopted . . . well, it was a lot. And now my birth mother wanted to talk to me.

The early morning light bounced off the big white custom-built sewing table that stood in the center of the room. It was huge, five feet by five feet, and housed both of my sewing machines and three workstations. Plus, it had all these drawers and cabinets underneath to store my supplies. I loved it so much. I'd been practically in tears when Hana surprised me with it for my college graduation.

I turned to my laptop, where I'd pulled up my Etsy site. There were two orders awaiting shipment and a lost package that I'd finally tracked down. I was hoping it had made it, since the man who bought it wanted it for his grandmother's birthday.

There was a message in my inbox that had come in yesterday, from matte194nyc.

Hey Kim, wanted to let you know the package finally arrived. And just in time for my grandmother's birthday tomorrow. It's beautiful. Did you go to design school? I know she's going to love it! Thanks for working with me, Matt

Phew. I let out a sigh of relief. I'd been worried that I would have to replace the bag or issue a refund so that he didn't leave a negative review. But more than that, I was glad he got it since he was so nice. Some customers weren't as understanding.

I fired off a quick reply to Matt, thinking about his question. I hadn't gone to design school. Before my parents died, I had wanted to be a designer and hoped to attend FIT, the Fashion Institute of Technology in New York. My parents fully supported my plan. But then they'd gone on that camping trip on the Colorado Trail, something they'd always wanted to do, and died in that freak accident.

I'd developed a phobia of leaving Oklahoma ever since. When Hana had tried to take me to New York my junior year to visit FIT, I'd had a panic attack at the airport. I was convinced I was going to die like my parents if I got on that plane. We never made it. Instead, I enrolled in a local college only thirty minutes away and commuted from home, forgetting about my dreams. Dreams were fine in your head. In reality, dreams killed you.

"You're awake. How'd you sleep?"

I looked up to see Hana in the doorway. "Good. Just checking on my Etsy shop."

Hana smiled. "I'm glad you started that, what, eight years ago?"

I nodded. "At least I have my shop now. I guess I can devote more time to it since I no longer have a job and can't show my face in public ever again." I scrunched up my nose, thinking about that blasted video.

Hana chuckled. "It's not that bad. Some people would be loving the fame."

I shook my head, sending my hair flying out in every direction. "Not me."

We both turned when we heard Alicia climbing the stairs. "What're you guys doing?" she asked when she came into the room.

Even with her eyes half open and hair a mess, she was gorgeous. Her father was half white and half Mexican, while her mother was Japanese. She'd gotten the best of both her parents, with long dark brown waves hanging almost to her waist, big brown eyes, and a dimple in her chin.

"Checking my Etsy shop. It's my only source of income now." I closed the laptop and banged my forehead on top of it a few times. "That stupid video."

"But it gives you a chance to focus on your shop until things die down." Hana reached over and picked my head up off the laptop.

"I don't make enough in sales to live on." I rubbed my forehead.

Alicia came to our side, her eyes twinkling. "You should

totally use your fame to promote your shop. I bet it'd blow up."

"No way." I shook my head. "People already either think I'm a weird freak who wigged out on her boss or that I'm some sort of farting phenomenon. I'm not linking that to my store."

"But this could be huge." Alicia's eyes widened as she warmed to her idea. "Take advantage and let her rip!"

I glared at her. "Do you even know me?" I pointed to myself, the one who'd only gotten an Instagram account under the name Kim because of my Etsy shop.

"Yeah, you." Alicia smirked. "Everyone is wondering who you are. Michelle didn't tag you since you have no social media presence as yourself."

"You know I hate pictures of me." For some reason, I always looked like I had a double chin in photos (and for the record, I don't have a double chin, so what the heck?). And my head looked ten times the size of my body, as if I was a bobblehead or something.

"Come on, Kimmie. You looked great in that video." Alicia's voice was cajoling. "Think how much business you could drive to the store if you told everyone who you are. And hashtag your posts with #letherrip."

"Nope." I shook my head vehemently. "Not happening." I had absolutely no intention of associating myself with that meme. I knew I was cute in an America Ferrara kind of way (people always told me I looked like an Asian America —ha, get it?). But that didn't mean I wanted pictures of my private life all over the internet. And I certainly didn't want that video associated with my Etsy shop.

"Whatever." Alicia muttered under her breath about "wasted opportunities." Out loud, she said, "I've been taking some business and marketing classes. Maybe I can help you figure out how to drive more business to your shop."

I stared at her. "You've been what?" Alicia had been modeling and waitressing in Austin, Texas, where she'd moved with her boyfriend, Josh, two years ago. She hadn't gone to college, having hated school.

She made a face. "Oh, and Josh and I broke up. I'm moving in with you until I figure out what to do."

"Wait, what?" My head was spinning. Alicia and Josh had been together for six years. "Why didn't you tell me?"

"I was going to, after my trip to New York."

"Oh." I felt bad. She'd probably asked me to go with her because she'd needed a friend. But even if I'd known why, I wouldn't have had the guts to go. And *that's* why she'd gone to New York without Josh. I'd been wondering.

"I shouldn't have moved to Austin with him. I knew things weren't going to work out but I just wanted to get out of Oklahoma so bad." Her perfect nose wrinkled. "And I thought I was ready for New York City, but . . ." She trailed off. "To be honest, New York was too intimidating by myself. I was glad for an excuse to leave early."

"Really?" She was usually fearless and had been dying to go to New York for years.

She shrugged. "It's no big deal."

"But still . . . I'm sorry I cut your trip short."

Alicia waved a hand. "Don't worry about it. You're more important."

My throat clogged at her words. I'd missed Alicia the last two years.

"And my sublet in London is about up, so I'm moving in too." Hana gave me a sunny smile. She'd never married, perfectly content with her nomadic lifestyle, traveling the world writing her novels.

"But . . ." I looked back and forth between the two of them. "You don't need to babysit me. I'm fine."

They exchanged a look. "Sorry to break it to you, but you're not fine," Alicia said.

I gave her a doleful look before remembering what she'd said about classes. "And what's this about business classes?"

Alicia sat in the chair in front of my Bernina sewing machine. "I got bored with modeling. I almost fell asleep at the last shoot." She made a face. "I just wanted to try something new." She gestured to the sewing machines. "I can help you sew too."

I was silent for a moment. I did love to design and make things. And now I'd finally have time to do that. I didn't want to admit it yet, but a flicker of hope ignited in my chest.

"Thank you," I finally said. "I would love to have both of you move in with me." And that explained why they had so much luggage with them.

They surrounded me for a group hug. I swallowed, not wanting to cry again. Something had been building up in me for months now, something I couldn't explain. And when I'd gotten that letter from my birth mother, it all exploded in one gloriously fucked-up meltdown of epic proportions.

Alicia pulled away first. "We're here if you want to tell us about your birth mother."

"Thanks. I will." I sniffed. "Just . . . not yet." I needed to process the letter before I could talk about it.

"Anytime you're ready." Hana gave me a gentle smile. "How about I make us breakfast?"

Alicia walked to the door. "I need to change. See you downstairs?"

"Okay." I nodded and opened my laptop again. "I'm going to see if I can come up with ideas for my Etsy shop. Maybe take new pictures."

"That's good." Hana gave me an encouraging smile. "You might want to text Michelle back too."

"Right." My shoulders drooped as I pulled out the drawer in my desk where I'd stashed my cell phone. "I guess I should check my messages."

Hana left and I turned on my phone and couldn't believe how many missed calls and texts I'd received. I quickly texted Michelle and she answered right away, relieved to hear from me. Then I sat down at my laptop. The rest of the messages could wait.

I pulled up my Etsy page and scrolled through my shop, looking at the products I had listed. An idea began to take shape in my head. I sat back, studying the cabinet with the glass doors where I kept my fabric collection. Bold colors popped out at me and I narrowed my eyes.

My heart lifted as it always did when the creative juices were flowing. I went over to the neatly folded stacks of fabrics and flipped through them, trying to visualize the ideas in my head. A sense of calm overtook me. For the first time in a long while, I was inspired to create. I might be sex deprived, and I might be known as the farting girl now, but one thing I could do was sew. And if that was all I had going for me, then I was going to throw myself completely into my Etsy shop.

FOUR

Matt

The next morning, after being up all night on late watch, I was busy in the firehouse kitchen. It was a big utilitarian-looking room with an industrial range and oven, and a large beat-up table in the middle where we gathered to eat. A flat-screen TV was mounted on one wall and another held a large bulletin board where football pools and bets were posted, as well as our firehouse calendar.

I had made a large panful of scrambled eggs and fried the bacon while Dave made a fresh pot of coffee. We'd laid out the food so the men could grab whatever they wanted. A few guys were already seated at the table eating and talking shit, but I tuned them out. I was tired. I couldn't wait to get out of here, go home to catch a nap before taking my grandmother out for a birthday lunch. Then I had to be back at the firehouse in the early evening for another straight night tour like last night. And this time, I would make damn sure I was early.

Frank sauntered into the kitchen and plopped his big

frame in a chair next to Jack. "Hey, probie, get me a cup o' coffee, will ya?" He gestured to me.

I gritted my teeth. But before I could speak, Jack turned to Frank with a frown. "You too lazy to get your own coffee?"

"Nah." Frank smirked. "Figured Richie Rich there needed something to do." He gestured to me with his chin. "You know I like it with milk and sugar."

Jack shook his head at Frank and grunted in disgust while the other men in the room turned their attention to Frank.

"West isn't your servant, Frankie Boy."

"Lazy ass."

"You have hands, use them."

And other profanities that made me bite my bottom lip to keep from smiling. It was good to see Frank get back some of what he dished out.

I pointed to the coffee maker as I leaned against the counter eating my breakfast. "There's a fresh pot right there. Get your own coffee."

Frank shrugged, ignoring the jeers from the other men, and got up to pour a mugful. "Hey, you guys see that video of the woman losing her shit at her boss? It's so funny."

Some of the guys chuckled, nodding. Frank walked back to his seat and pulled out his cell. "I was just watching it again. She's got a nice ass. Cute body too. You know I like my women with a little meat on them."

I watched him as I ate and frowned at the way he was ogling his phone. He looked up and caught my eye. "Wanna see it, probie?"

I shook my head, but he held up his phone and I had a quick glimpse of a woman twerking. Man, she could dance.

Before I could see more, Frank had pulled his phone back, staring at the video again.

Jack spoke up. "Still can't find a girlfriend, Frankie?"

Frank ducked his head, his face flushed. Good. Let him take the heat for once.

"Still looking," he mumbled. "Got to keep my options open, ya know?"

One of the other guys laughed. "You mean you need to find some options. Who'd have you? You're a slob and you stink up the whole bunk room with your smelly socks."

As the others joined in giving him shit, I looked around and, seeing that everything was in order, decided to slip out for a minute to call my grandmother to wish her a happy birthday.

I made my way to the apparatus floor, where it was quiet. We'd had a run in the middle of the night, which had turned into a good job—a two-room fire that we'd been able to contain quickly. The smell of smoke lingered in the air from our bunker gear, mingling with the diesel fuel from the rigs. It was familiar to me now and made me feel a part of something bigger than myself. I leaned against the truck and pulled out my cell.

"Hello?" Nana's voice was loud over the phone.

"Nana. Happy birthday!"

"Matt!" My grandmother's cheerful voice brightened my mood. "You remembered."

"Of course I remembered. I'm still taking you out for a late lunch, right?" Affection for my grandmother made me grin widely.

"Yes, I can't wait. How's your tour?" At eighty-three, Nana was still very much young at heart and had learned all the lingo. She knew to call my shifts "tours," because that's how the FDNY referred to them. She knew what "up-and-down" meant (going in in the morning and working until the next morning), that "rigs" referred to both the truck (the ladder) and the engine, and that "job" meant catching a fire.

"It's fine." I gave a low laugh. "Can't say I'm not looking forward to not being a probie anymore though."

"The guys still giving you shit about your life?"

"Nana!" It always made me smile when she cursed. "But yeah."

She chuckled. "Well, you knew that was going to happen."

I hadn't told anyone when I started that my father was the CEO of one of the largest retail stores in the country. I didn't want to alienate myself that way. I'd certainly not told anyone that not only was I a trust fund baby, but I'd worked for my father with a very nice salary, which had paid for my apartment on the Upper East Side. I knew most of the guys lived in the other boroughs in more affordable housing and that very few actually lived in Manhattan. There was no reason to point out that I was different. Which was why I didn't engage on social media and kept my accounts private. I also stayed out of pictures at social events if I could help it.

But a month after I finished probie school, an online publication had run a picture of me and my father, captioning us as "retail mogul Robert West with his son, Matthew West" at a fundraising gala for organ donations. One of the guys had seen it and that was when my anonymity ended. The guys in my house hadn't let me live it down. The real assholes like Frank had made it their mission to make my life miserable. But I could take it. I'd wanted to be a FDNY firefighter since my mother died in that horrific accident and I'd be damned if anyone was going to take that away from me.

"You're almost there." My grandmother's voice brought

me out of my thoughts. "Lily would have been so proud of you."

"Yeah." I paused at the mention of my mother. It'd been three years since she died. I looked around to make sure I was alone and dropped my voice. "I still miss her every day." I'd never admit that to anyone but Nana. Certainly not to my father. He couldn't bear to even say her name.

"Oh, Matty." Nana sighed. "Me too."

"Do you ever wonder . . ." I trailed off and shook my head. The firehouse wasn't the place for this.

"What?" Nana asked.

"Nothing."

We were quiet for a moment and I imagined Nana was picturing her daughter the way she'd been when she was alive. Full of life, kind—a real sweetheart, everyone said—and the only person my father would listen to. I clenched my jaw. With her gone, there was no one to act as a buffer between me and my father. Our family had fallen apart when that accident had taken her life.

"I'm looking forward to our lunch." Nana's voice broke through my thoughts.

I smiled, even as I yawned. "Me too. I'll meet you at Sarabeth's at one thirty, okay?"

"I'll be there. Can't wait to see my favorite grandson." Nana laughed and I joined her. She had six grandchildren, but I was her only grandson.

After we hung up, I stayed where I was for a moment, even though I knew I should get my butt back in the kitchen. Yesterday, I'd cleaned not only the bathroom but also the kitchen, as well as five filthy dogs, as punishment for being late. I'd had to bite my tongue and take it when Frank and the others poked fun at my rich-boy status and asked why I had toted a floral murse to the firehouse.

Just four more months. I could hold out that long. When I'd quit my job in my father's business, I'd been tired of having everything handed to me. I wanted to do something meaningful, like the firemen who'd been with my mom when she took her last breath. My own breath caught as I remembered what the firefighter had told me about my mom's last moments. That was why I'd quit my job over a year ago. That was why I was willing to put up with shit from guys like Frank.

To distract myself from my dark thoughts, I scrolled through social media quickly. When I opened Instagram, I saw that one of the "suggested for you" accounts to follow was Kim from mycraftybaokim. Clicking on the profile and noting that it was mostly pictures of the merchandise from her Etsy shop, with a few scenic shots of what looked like a prairie, I idly wondered what Kim looked like. In my head, I pictured a kindly older woman, maybe a grandmotherly type who was nurturing and caring.

Well, whoever she was, she had great customer service skills. And a sharp eye for what would sell. After being immersed in the retail business all my life, I knew what was going to trend before it did and always trusted my instincts. Just because I'd gotten tired of a desk job and itched to do something more physical, something that mattered, didn't mean I didn't recognize quality and appeal when I saw it. And I had a feeling about this Etsy shop. I clicked the Follow button before heading back to the kitchen to clean up.

FIVE

Kimmie

Later that day, I got out of my car at the grocery store, pulling my hood up over my head to try to stay as inconspicuous as possible. We were out of milk and eggs and bread and just about everything fresh. When I'd looked at what food I had in the house yesterday, I hadn't taken into account two extra people. I'd hoped Alicia or Hana would go to the grocery store, but they insisted that I should be the one to go. Hana claimed she had a great idea for her book and Alicia was creating a profit and loss statement for my Etsy shop. I was horrible with numbers and Alicia had been appalled at my pathetic attempt at keeping track of my sales and expenses.

I hoped to get in and out of the store without anyone noticing me, but people were pointing. A guy actually cheered when he saw me and said, "It's Let Her Rip! Right on, dude!"

I gave him a peace sign and ducked my head so that my chin was practically attached to my chest as I took a shopping cart. Zipping up one aisle after another, I grabbed things that we needed, trying to get this over with as fast as possible. Thank goodness the Let Her Rip shop wasn't near the grocery store, so hopefully I wouldn't run into Rip. I'd just finished with my list and was heading to the checkout lines when I heard someone call my name.

"Kimmie, is that you?"

Oh, crap. But at least whoever it was hadn't called me by that atrocious nickname. I looked up and saw that it was Mila Yang, a girl I'd gone to high school with. She'd been a year behind me and the only other Asian in our school at the time. Alicia hadn't gone to our school—she'd been home-schooled.

"Hi, Mila. You visiting from New York?" I knew she'd moved there after graduation to become a dancer.

"Yup, home for a few days. How are you?" Her smile was friendly but she looked tired and there were dark circles under her eyes. I wondered if she was okay.

"I'm fine." I wasn't sure if she'd heard about my video and wasn't about to bring it up if she hadn't.

"I saw that video of you." What sounded like sympathy tinged her voice.

Right. She'd seen it. Of course she had. "Yeah." I cleared my throat. Mila was a *real* dancer. She'd probably laughed her head off at my little performance.

"It was amazing. I didn't know you could dance." Her eyes lit up. "You should have tried out for the school plays back in high school." The genuine admiration in her voice had me raising my eyebrows in surprise. Maybe that hadn't been sympathy I'd heard in her voice.

You'd think we would have been friends back then, given our token Asian kid status, but we hadn't really clicked. She ran with the theater crowd and was the second lead in *Oklahoma!* (yes, they really did *Oklahoma!* in Oklahoma) her sophomore year, which was unheard of. There'd been an uproar among some mothers who'd complained that Ado Annie wasn't Asian. Her parents had been born in Taiwan. The music director, Mr. Valentino, had shut down those moms fast. Mila had gone on to become the lead in her junior and senior years.

I shrugged at Mila now. "Theater wasn't really my thing back then. I wasn't talented like you. I remember how much Mr. Valentino loved you." Meanwhile, Mr. Valentino wouldn't have even cast me as a tree in the play. His loss. I would have made an amazing tree.

"I'd love to get together, but I'm leaving tomorrow." Mila gave me a friendly smile. "Maybe next time? Or if you're ever in New York City, let me know. I'll take you around."

"Sounds good." I smiled back at her as she waved and walked away. I stared after her. Sometimes I wished I could be like Mila, confident enough to move to New York City to follow her dreams.

Then I shook my head and rushed to the checkout lines. No sense in looking back.

I made it home without anyone else accosting me. As I pulled into the driveway, Alicia came outside. I noticed she had on the bright pink belt I'd made for her.

"Hey. Don't move." I jumped out of my car and motioned for Alicia to stop.

She halted. "Why?"

I leaned into the car and grabbed my cotton wristlet printed in bold aqua and emerald green with geometric shapes. When I'd first seen the fabric, I knew exactly what I would do with it. I'd pleated the top into a border with a rounded bottom, giving it a unique shape, rather than a boring old rectangle. I handed it to Alicia.

"I love this pattern." She held up the wristlet, admiring the wide pattern creating almost diamond-like shapes. She held it up to the pink belt. "And it looks good with this color. I'd never have put them together."

"That's going to be my next Instagram post. How to not coordinate and put unexpected colors together. Can I take a picture of you with them?" I fiddled with my iPhone. "I call it un-coordinate."

Alicia struck a movie star pose. "Sure. Have at it." She had an amazing figure and literally turned smart men into blathering idiots with one flutter of her lashes.

I fired off a few shots and then studied them on my phone. "Wow, you look great. And you make my products look amazing." I showed them to Alicia and then had her pose for a few more. "Okay, one of these should work. Help me get the groceries inside?"

She handed me back my wristlet and we lugged all the grocery bags to the kitchen and unpacked them. I sat on a stool at the island and scrolled through the pictures I'd taken again. They were really good.

"I'm going to post one now." I picked the best and uploaded it to Instagram.

"You sure you don't want to hashtag it #letherrip?" Alicia popped open a can of seltzer and threw me a hopeful look.

"No." My voice was firm. "My Etsy shop is the one good thing I have in life right now. I'm not going to taint it with that video."

Alicia made a face but I ignored her and focused on typing in the caption that had popped into my head when I saw Alicia wearing the belt. I added hashtags but not the infamous one Alicia wanted me to use. My Etsy shop would either succeed or fail based on the merits of my products.

Not on some embarrassing footage of me losing my inhibitions.

"There." I looked up. "Posted it. Thanks for letting me use your picture."

"Anytime." Alicia headed out of the kitchen to her room on the main floor. "I'm staying at my parents' tonight. My mom made me promise to come. I have to pack a bag."

"Okay." I got up and went to the fridge. Since Alicia wouldn't be home for dinner, I should put something together for Hana and me. She was off somewhere writing and it wasn't like I had anything else to do. I had already filled all the orders so far for my Etsy shop.

By the time Alicia came back with a bag, I had pulled out the ingredients for a simple udon noodle soup and was chopping the vegetables to make it easier to throw together once Hana came home.

"I'm off," Alicia said. "Any likes on the post?"

"I haven't looked at it." I kept my eyes on the mushrooms so that I wouldn't accidentally chop off a piece of my finger.

"Give me your phone." From the tone of Alicia's voice, I didn't have to look up to know she was rolling her eyes at me. "Oh my god."

That made me look up. "What?"

She thrusted my phone at me, holding it in front of my face. My eyes widened. "OMG."

Alicia snorted. "Did you really just say OMG?"

"Yeah. OMG." My eyes were glued to the phone. I wiped my hands on a towel and grabbed it from her. Together, we watched the Likes count adding up, faster than I could keep up with.

"Look how many people are liking this post." There was glee in Alicia's voice.

"No way." I'd had an Instagram account for Kim from My Crafty Bao for years now but hadn't had much engagement on it. According to the Likes and comments piling up, people were loving the picture of Alicia.

I looked up, a smug smile on my face. "People love you!"

Alicia gaped at me. "I can't believe this. We're blowing up IG!" She reached out to give me a high five, and I slapped her hand, hard.

I looked at my phone and the numbers were still going up. We were for real blowing up IG. This was the best idea I'd ever had. I was a genius.

Instagram Post

1,423 likes

mycraftybaokim Be Bold and Color Un-Coordinate! Add a pop of color. I know, I know. I'm the first to admit that I used to go with neutrals 'cause I wanted to blend in. I'm super awkward in real life, always walking into furniture and stammering when someone talks to me. So why draw attention to myself?

But the real Kim LOVES bright colors. Bold colors. Colors that don't conventionally go together. That's why my new collection for this fall features bright colors. Most stores are selling fall tones. Not me. I don't want to be like everyone else.

Here's a bright pink belt I came up with over the summer. I love the intricate braid I put into it, but I left the ends full and free so you can tie it in a bow. Pair it with this aqua and emerald green wristlet and see how well they go together. You don't have to color coordinate—

in fact, I think you should color un-coordinate. Just be you.

Be daring, be bold, be you.

xo, Kim

VIEW all 156 comments

melissabegood35 I don't believe it that you're awkward in person. I mean look at you! You look so graceful. But love the message, just be you!

nicoleloveswine Thank you for this. I'm one of those that wears black to blend in and disappear. But I secretly love the color red. You've inspired me.

tomkennedy My girlfriend loves your Etsy shop. I now have a go to place to get her gifts so thank you.

abentley

ambersmalley8 You're really not all that, you know? I don't know why everyone loves you. You look kind of fake to me.

melissafoster I just love your new collection! I've already bought the daisy tote, and now I'm going to get the belt. Can you make me a custom order? I'll convo you on Etsy. I want to combine two colors. Love it!

SIX

Matt

When someone finally relieved me at the firehouse, I walked the few blocks to the subway. This part of the South Bronx was not one where I'd ever have a girlfriend or my grandmother meet me. The rate of violent crimes here per capita was greater than that of the city as a whole. And the incarceration rate was higher than that of the entire city. It was populated with drug addicts and notorious for prostitution. On my short walk to the subway, I passed no less than two prostitutes, one drug dealer, and four pit bulls. I had a soft spot for them (the dogs, not the drug dealers or prostitutes), knowing they weren't the violent creatures they were portrayed to be. In fact, if I could have a dog again, I'd rescue a pit bull in a heartbeat.

And not that I had a girlfriend whom I could tell not to take the subway to my firehouse. My last serious girlfriend had been the year my mother died. Melanie had broken up with me the month before my mother's accident. She'd wanted a ring, but at twenty-six, I hadn't been ready for marriage. Melanie had contacted me when she heard the news about my mother, but by then, the grief of losing my mom had hardened me. I'd dated a few women casually since then, but my heart hadn't been in it.

As I got on the subway, a part of me wished there was someone waiting for me at home. Someone I could share my life with, and who could tease me about the way I was being treated at the firehouse. But there was no one. Not even a dog.

My phone dinged and I looked at it. It was a text from my oldest friend, Jason Powell. We'd gone through school together, all the way from kindergarten to senior year of high school. He'd moved to Connecticut with his wife last year when they had their first child.

Hey, Bro. Still planning on coming in next Saturday. You good to grab dinner?

I smiled as I sent back a reply. *Yup. Glad Mandy is letting you out.*

His reply came fast. *Haha, very funny. I have Ollie myself this weekend so she can go on a spa trip with her sister. Want to come help change diapers?*

I made a face. Although Ollie was really cute and always smiled when he saw me.

Wish I could man, but I'll be at the firehouse most of the weekend.

They still breaking your balls? At least I could count on Jason to make fun of me. Not quite the same as a girlfriend, but he'd have to do for the time being.

I tapped back a response. *Yeah. Almost done.*

Better you than me. I'll stick to law. There was a pause and the three dots that said he was typing jumped around. And then: *I admire you though.*

Thanks.

He gave me a thumbs-up in return.

Yawning as the train swayed, I closed my eyes for a moment. I dozed on and off, one eye always open to my surroundings. I'd grown up in New York City and was street-smart enough to never let down my guard even for a moment. But I was tired and was looking forward to that nap before I met Nana.

Two stops before mine, I touched my phone to check the time. It opened right to Instagram, to Kim's page. And I saw she'd posted a new picture. I tapped on it to make it bigger, and my eyes almost popped out of my head. Holy shit, Kim was smoking hot. Long dark hair, big brown eyes, a slender body. She'd posted a picture of herself wearing one of her belts, a wristlet dangling from her arm. But it was her smile that caught my eye. She was looking right into the camera, a mischievous look on her face, as if she knew something I didn't. This was not the older, kindly matron I'd pictured in my head earlier. This was a woman about my age who suddenly made me sit up taller. Reading the caption under her picture, I smiled even wider. She was beautiful and clever. I'd always had a thing for witty, clever women.

With a grin spreading over my face, I couldn't help myself and typed a comment in answer to her post. I never engaged on social media. I was more of a lurker. And I'd certainly never slid into anyone's DMs before. But I couldn't fight the urge to do so now. It was overpowering. Before I could think it through, I sent her a DM. I was already being humiliated at the firehouse. What could I possibly lose in reaching out to Kim?

Kimmie

Alicia and I were still squealing over the popularity of the photo when I saw that I had a few DM requests. I scanned them quickly, expecting the usual rando saying "hello, beautiful" or fake celebrity, and I was right. But then a username caught my eye. It was from matte194nyc.

Hey Kim. Just found you on social media. That picture and caption are amazing. Love it!

A smile took over my face. Someone thought I was amazing. Without thinking, I accepted the request and DMed him back.

Hi, Matt. Glad you found me over here. And thanks!

I waited to see if he'd respond, vaguely aware that Alicia was hovering next to me.

Matt answered right away.

You're a beautiful and talented woman. And so clever too.

OMG, he thought I was beautiful! I grinned, but then I realized he'd never seen me before. In the next breath, my eyes widened. He thought Alicia was me. He thought *Alicia* was beautiful. I scanned the post again and the other comments. Holy crap, everyone thought Alicia was me. I looked up at her, my mouth open.

"What?" Alicia cocked her head to the side.

"People think you're me." I showed her my phone.

"No way." Alicia read some of the comments and then looked up to meet my eyes. "They love me. I mean you. I mean . . . me as you?"

I looked back at Matt's message. He did say I was clever too. The smile crept back on my face and I chose to think about that rather than the fact that everyone thought Alicia was me. We'd figure that out later. I might not be as beautiful as Alicia, but yes, I was smart. Except when it came to math and talking to people in real life. But online and DMs I could handle.

"What are you smiling at?" Alicia's voice broke through my thoughts.

"Nothing." I couldn't quite wipe the grin off my face.

"Come on, tell me." She nudged me in the side with an elbow.

"Just—some guy said I was clever." I didn't mention the beautiful part, since he thought *Alicia* was beautiful. Which was kind of awkward, come to think of it.

I turned back to my phone and responded, *Thanks! I finally decided to bite the bullet and start posting pics.*

I'm glad you did. 😄 *Smart marketing decision.*

A shot of confidence went through me. I'd always been really good at DMs and texts, since I had time to compose witty comebacks. Not like in real life, when I would freeze up around people I didn't know. Now I typed, *What do you look like?*

Was I flirting with him? I didn't even know I knew how to flirt! And what if he was an old creepy guy? But he bought something for his grandmother, so unless his grandmother was really old . . .

I guess you'll have to follow me back to find out.

I squinted at his profile picture. It was of a white dog. Well, that didn't give me much of a hint. His profile was private, so I clicked on the Follow Back button and waited to see if he'd accept my request. Within seconds, he had, and I eagerly clicked on his posts, expecting to see an average-looking man or the creeper I'd imagined.

What I saw instead took my breath away. Holy crap, Matt was hot with a capital *H*! I couldn't take my eyes off his toned forearms and the way his biceps strained against short sleeves in one photo. I scanned his bio, trying to figure out what he did for a living, but it didn't give me a clue. And then I scrolled down to his earlier pictures and what I saw had me puckering my lips as an "aw," drawled out of me. There were many photos of him with the white dog in his profile picture. My eyes landed on one of him laughing as the dog licked his face.

I was a sucker for men with dogs. I'd always thought dogs were smarter than humans and had better instincts. And the way the dog was staring adoringly at Matt said so much to me. My eyes found another of the two of them mugging for the camera, and yet another where the big dog sat on his lap, partially obstructing Matt's face. And when I finally saw a close up of Matt, I sucked in a breath. He had dark wavy hair and the kindest but smolderest eyes I'd ever seen. Was that even a word, "smolderest"? I didn't care. All I knew was that there was something about Matt and his interactions with his dog that made me see heart eyes and caused a shiver to run through my body.

And I hadn't even met him in person. This was so unlike me. I, who had always scoffed at "love at first sight." I, who hadn't had a serious boyfriend in five years because, let's face it, all I'd done the last few years had been go to work and come home to my empty house to binge-watch TV shows.

"Kimmie? Are you okay?"

Alicia's voice floated toward me as if from far away. But I was lost in Matt's eyes and my heart melted because I knew here was a man who was kind to animals, and that was my undoing. My ears rang as I sighed and my heart pounded out of control. I'd never reacted this way to a man before, much less some *pictures*. I was literally vibrating, my cheeks warm and my palms suddenly sweaty.

"Kimmie? Answer me. You're scaring me." Alicia grabbed me by the arms and gave me a shake.

"Hm?" I blinked until my eyes focused on her. "What?"

"What's wrong with you?" She was staring at me, her eyes wide with concern. "Are you having a seizure or something?"

I slowly shook my head. I blew out a breath as I gave her a tremulous smile. "No. I'm fine." But I wasn't. I was a goner.

Matt

I was still smiling when I walked into my building, opening the front door myself since the doorman was helping someone with a large package.

"Good morning, Matt West. What are you smiling at?"

I looked up from my phone to see Mrs. White and her two poodles staring at me. She always called me by my full name for some reason. I'd saved her dogs a few months ago when they got away from her and ran out on the street, chasing after another dog. Ever since then, she seemed to have developed a soft spot for me.

"It's a nice day out, isn't it?" I deflected her question.

"Are you sure you don't have a new girlfriend?" She peered at me from over the top of her glasses. "You have that glow young people get when they're in love."

Glow? I was glowing? FDNY firefighters did *not* glow. Thank god Frank wasn't here to hear this. Otherwise, I'd never live it down at the firehouse. I'd be known as the glowing probie with the murse who was always late.

"I'm sure." I gave Mrs. White a big smile, patted each of

her dogs on the head, and got on the elevator when the doors opened.

I looked down at my phone and a smile spread over my face when I saw Kim had messaged me after I accepted her follow request.

K: *Wow, I have no words. You're not the old creepy guy I was expecting. You're actually quite*

She hadn't finished the sentence. My thumbs moved over my phone rapidly as I typed a response.

M: *Quite what? And do you think all your customers are old creepy guys?*

K: *No, not the female ones.* 😏 *And you're quite hot.*

I let out a laugh. I'd thought the same about her.

M: *Why thank you. I think you are too.*

I expected her to answer but there was nothing. I got off on the fifteenth floor, walking the short distance to my door. I let myself in and she still hadn't answered. I hoped I hadn't offended her.

Kicking off my shoes and leaving my backpack on the floor, I walked to my brown microfiber couch and sat, staring at my cell. Just as I was about to type something, she finally responded.

K: *But you said I was clever too. That's more important, right?*

I let out a sigh of relief.

M: *Of course. I love clever, witty women.* Shit, I shouldn't have used the word "love."

But she responded right away.

K: *Then you'll love me, ha ha.*

I smiled again.

M: *Clever, witty, talented, and beautiful. What a combo.*

K: *Why thank you, sir. What do you do? Your profile doesn't give much away.*

M: *I'm a firefighter.*

K: *No shit! Oh, sorry, language. Wait, your address is in New York City. You're FDNY?*

M: *Yup.*

K: *No way. That's so cool. And hot!* 🔥

M: *Ha. Thanks?*

K: *You're the first FDNY fireman I know. I mean, not that I know you.*

M: *Would you like to? Know me, I mean?*

I couldn't suppress a grin as I waited for her response. This DM exchange was making my day. I'd missed having someone to flirt with like this.

K: *I'd definitely like to get to know you. In a strictly professional way of course. You know, I have to make sure my customers are satisfied.*

I pressed my lips together at her response.

M: *And how do you satisfy them?*

K: *I have my ways. Stick around. Maybe you'll find out.* 😂

I laughed and put the phone down so I could take off my T-shirt. I'd showered at the firehouse before leaving and I really needed to lie down and get some rest before meeting Nana. Stripping down to just my boxers, I walked into the bedroom with my phone and got in bed before responding to Kim.

M: *I'm definitely sticking around. I'm intrigued.*

K: *What're you doing now?*

M: *I just got in bed. Need a nap before I take my grand-mother for lunch and give her the tote you made.*

K: *Ooh. Ok, question. Do you sleep in pjs, just boxers, or naked?*

M: *Who says I wear boxers?*

K: *You wear tighty-whities?* 😱

I barked out a laugh, balancing the cell on my chest.

M: *No tighty-whities. And my, ahem, boys thank me.*

K: *Ha. I'm sure they do. So boxers to bed?*

M: *Maybe.*

K: *Oh.*

M: *LOL*

K: *Well, with that image seared in my mind, I hope you have a nice nap. And say happy birthday to your grandmother from me. I hope she likes the tote.*

M: *I'm sure she will. Thanks, Kim. It was great chatting with you.*

K:

I put my cell down on the night table and rolled to my side, closing my eyes with the smile still firmly on my face.

NANA and I sat at a table for two at Sarabeth's on Central Park South. It was one of her favorite lunch places and she'd taken a Lyft (yes, my nana Lyfts) from her brownstone in Brooklyn to meet me in Manhattan. We'd just ordered and she was opening my present.

"What is this?" She pushed the tissue paper aside and pulled the floral tote out of the gift bag I'd put it in (that was the extent of my gift-wrapping abilities). "Matty, this is beautiful!"

She held up the large round-bottomed tote, admiring the outside pockets and the magnetic snap that closed the main compartment. There were more pockets on the inside, some with zippers. Nana liked to have a place for all her stuff, and I knew she would appreciate the pockets in this bag.

She reached out her arms and I stood to give her a hug.

"I love this floral fabric." She looked up with shining eyes. "Where did you get this?"

"From a shop on Etsy. The owner makes beautiful products." I couldn't keep back the smile that popped onto my face at the thought of Kim.

"I love it. It's perfect." Nana clasped the tote to her chest.

"I knew I had to get it for you the minute I saw it." I was so happy she loved it. I wanted to pull my phone out and send Kim a message that it was a hit, but I didn't want to distract my attention from my grandmother.

Nana tilted her head and looked at me. "What's going on with you? There's something . . . You look like . . ."

"Please don't tell me I'm glowing." I shot her a look.

"That's it." Nana snapped her fingers. "You're glowing."

I groaned and slapped a hand over my forehead. What was it with older women telling me I was glowing?

"What is it?" Nana placed the tote back in the gift bag and set it aside, focusing on me.

I met her eyes and my lips quirked. "Nothing."

She fixed me in her stare, her blue eyes unblinking.

"Fine, it's just the shop owner. She's h . . . I mean, she's gorgeous and we had a fun conversation earlier."

"Oh." Nana nodded knowingly. "And where does this gal live? In New York?"

"No." I shook my head. "She's in Oklahoma." That was a problem, but it wasn't as if I wanted to date her. I'd just enjoyed my conversation with her.

Nana studied me and then picked up her glass of iced tea, taking a sip. When I didn't respond, she said, "Well, go on. Text her and tell her I love it. And that I said hello."

With a grin at Nana, I pulled out my phone and tapped

on the Instagram app. Going to my messages, I found Kim and sent her a message that my grandmother loved the bag.

"Hold up the bag, Nana. I'll take a picture and send it to her."

"Oh, good idea." Nana pulled the bag out and struck a pose, making me laugh.

I sent the picture to Kim, not expecting her to answer right away. But before I could put my phone down, a message came through.

So glad she loves it! That just made my day. And thanks for the picture. Would she mind if I posted it in my stories?

I looked up at Nana. "She wants to know if she can post the picture of you to her stories."

"Sure." Nana fluffed her short silver hair. "I'm flattered. Tell her to tag me."

Yes, my nana had an Instagram account and knew what an IG story was. She was more active on Instagram than I was. I had the coolest grandmother ever.

I replied to Kim and gave her Nana's IG handle.

K: *No way! That's so cool that she's on IG! I'll definitely tag her.*

I shot Nana a look. "She thinks it's cool that you're on IG and she's tagging you."

"Oh, good." Nana pulled her iPhone out of her purse. "I'm going to follow this young woman who is putting that smile on your face." She peered at her phone and then tapped it a few times. "There it is. Okay, got her." Then she looked up at me. "It's good to see you smile, Matt."

The waiter placed our lunches in front of us just then, the seafood Cobb salad for her and the lobster roll for me. Once he left, she went back to her phone and started typing.

"What are you doing?" I asked, picking up my roll and taking a bite.

"Messaging your friend." She finished typing and raised her eyebrows at me.

I gave her the side-eye. I knew that look. "What did you do?"

Nana picked up her fork and dug into her salad. "Nothing. Simply asked the young woman, who is gorgeous by the way, if she's single."

My mouth dropped open. "You didn't."

"I did." She took another bite of her salad, swallowing before continuing. "I also asked her why her shop is named My Crafty Bao."

I shook my head. I knew Nana wanted to see me with someone. But Kim lived in Oklahoma. No matter how fun our exchanges were, that wasn't exactly the ideal situation.

Nana glanced down at her phone. "Look, she answered. She says that baos remind her of her parents, who passed away." Nana looked up at me, her expression concerned. "Did you know she lost her parents?"

"I read that in her bio on her Etsy site." We had that in common.

Nana looked down at her phone again. "Oh, and she says she's single."

"Nana." I couldn't help but laugh. "You're such a matchmaker."

She tapped something into her phone before replying. "Is it so wrong to want to see my handsome grandson with a good girl? I haven't seen you like this since Lily died."

I put the lobster roll on my plate and reached for my iced tea. "Like what?"

"Light. Lighter. Not so bogged down." Nana reached across the table to grab my hand. "You're young,

Matty. Only twenty-nine. You're doing something you want, going for your dreams. But you're lonely. I can see it."

I squeezed her hand and then let go. "I know. I was thinking of getting a dog. But who'd watch him when I'm on the overnight tours?"

Nana laughed. "I meant a girlfriend. Or boyfriend if that's what you're into. Not a dog."

I laughed with her. "I know what you meant." I gave her a sly grin.

Nana resumed eating, shaking her head. "Life's too short. You know that. Look at your mother. I was lucky to have my Charles for almost fifty years . . ." She trailed off. My grandfather had died seven years ago. "But your father and mother didn't get that time. If someone makes you feel the way you look right now, what's the harm in seeing if there's something there?"

"Nana. She lives in Oklahoma. I don't know anything about her. I've never even talked to her on the phone. There's nothing there."

"That's not how I see it." Her eyes twinkled and she raised her eyebrows at me. "And distance doesn't matter. All I'm saying is, have fun. See what happens."

My mouth twitched. I couldn't believe my grandmother was giving me dating advice. But I'd been out of the game for years now. Maybe I should listen to her.

"Okay, Nana. I'll take your advice."

I looked at my phone and saw that I had a message from Kim.

K: *Your grandmother looks so cool! I wish I had a grandma like that.*

M: *She is the greatest. And in case you're wondering, I'm single too.*

K: *Ohh!* 😊 *But how is that possible? Smoking hot fireman with a cool grandmother?!*

M: *Haha—no idea. Can I message you later? We're having lunch now.*

K: *Sure. Look forward to it. Have a good lunch!*

M: *Thanks!*

I put my phone down and met my grandmother's knowing look. When she wiggled her eyebrows at me, I laughed out loud. She was right. Life was too short.

EIGHT

Kimmie

It had been three days since Matt followed me on Instagram, the day of his grandmother's birthday. We'd been flirting over DMs every day since. I fell back on my bed, clutching my phone to my chest. I found myself looking forward to seeing if I had an IG message and hoping it was him. Most of the time, it was. Me, awkward Kimmie, had been flirting with a really hot guy. Like, hot like those fireman calendar models. I fantasized about him at night. Dark, smoldering, wearing only his bunker pants with a thumb hooked at the waist pulling them down slightly, showcasing a set of ridged abs, his chest and biceps so firm I wanted to bite them. A five-o'clock shadow on that chiseled face and those eyes staring at me as if they could see into my soul. Yum.

But Matt was so much more than his looks. He was kind, just like I imagined when I first saw the pictures of him and the dog. He'd told me that was his mom's dog Cleo, who'd passed away several years ago at the age of eleven.

The way he talked about Cleo made me sigh with longing, that someone would ever speak of me with so much love and affection.

If I ever met him in person, I'd probably faint at his feet. But over DM, I was the smooth Kimmie I imagined in my mind, and not the klutzy Kimmie who inevitably tripped and fell in a heap in front of the hottest guy in school, underwear showing because my dress had ridden up my thighs. Yeah, that really happened senior year of high school.

And the things I'd asked him! Whether he slept in boxers, in pj's, or naked? I mean, who was that? And that thing about making sure my customers were satisfied? We'd gone on to debate thongs versus bikini underwear (definitely bikini for me) and chocolate versus vanilla (him, chocolate; me, vanilla). He was a pleasant way to pass the time between sewing more products and posting new items to grow my shop. Talking to him had lightened my mood. I decided it was finally time to tell Hana and Alicia about my birth mother's letter.

"Kimmie, are you home?" I heard Alicia calling from downstairs as she came into the house. Oh, good, now I could tell them both before I changed my mind.

"Up here." I pushed myself off my bed. Walking to the door, I saw Hana poke her head out of her room as Alicia thundered up the stairs. I beckoned to them. "Come in here. I want to show you something."

They followed me into my sewing room. I could practically hear them questioning each other with their eyes.

"You won't believe how busy Rip's store is, all thanks to you." Alicia sat down at the sewing table. "People are driving from miles away to see the asshole from the video."

"No way." I hadn't gotten the courage to stop by and pick up my last paycheck. I wasn't even sure if Rip would give it to me.

"He should totally thank you for all the attention his store is getting." Alicia looked at me. "You should see him. He's acting all pleasant now to his employees. I don't know if it's all an act or if the attention is making him realize he can't behave like that."

I shrugged, leaning against the sewing table. I didn't want to talk about Rip. I had more pressing issues on my mind.

"So, I'm glad you're both here." I reached to pull out a drawer in the sewing station. "I wanted to show you the letter I got from Ruby."

"Your birth mom." Hana nodded, her eyes on the letter I took out of the drawer.

"Yes." I held the cream stationary in my hand.

"What does it say?" Alicia pointed at it and I handed it to her.

"She wants to get to know me. You can read it." I leaned against the table again. "I've gotten two cards from her since my parents died. On the milestone birthdays. Eighteen, twenty-one, and now this letter."

"Your birthday's not for another two months," Hana said.

"She reached out early. Hoping I'll want to connect." I started pacing. "I haven't before. Not because I'm angry at her or anything. She's just not a part of my life. I never thought about her." I turned and looked at Hana. "My parents are still my parents. And because they didn't want me to know I was adopted, it felt like a betrayal to reach out to Ruby. So, I never did."

"And now she wants you to." Hana's voice was quiet. "Do you?"

I sighed. "Yes and no. I'm curious. And that breakdown with Rip made me realize that something needs to change." I looked from one to the other. "I feel as if I'm missing out on life. Staying here, safe at home, but not accomplishing anything of value. I didn't go to New York. I didn't become a designer. I was working for an asshole and then coming home to this big house all by myself every night. Because it's safe."

Neither of them said a word, so I took a deep breath and continued.

"I want to find someone, someone who gets me and laughs at my stupid jokes." My cheeks flushed as my thoughts immediately jumped to Matt. "I want to go places, do things. I want to see New York. I want to get over my fear of leaving home."

"That's good, Kimmie." Hana gave me a gentle smile and I thought to myself how pretty my aunt was. I always wondered why she never married, but it seemed kind of rude to ask.

"Have you ever looked her up on social media?"

Alicia's question had me spinning around to face her. "No," I said, my voice incredulous. "Why didn't I ever do that?"

"Everyone is on social media these days." Alicia pulled out her cell. "Do you want me to search for Ruby?"

"Yes." I was suddenly nervous. I knew nothing about her. It had been an open adoption, but my parents hadn't given Hana many details. Who was she? Where did she live? Did she have a family? Did I look like her?

"Okay. I'm going to look on Instagram first. What's her full name?"

"Ruby Tzi-Yi Chen." I had her name memorized. I didn't even have to look up the spelling of her middle name.

"No Ruby Tzi-Yi Chen. But there's a bunch of Ruby Chens." I watched Alicia's eyes sliding back and forth, reading and scanning. "Nope, too young . . . this one has posted nothing . . . I don't think this is her . . ."

Disappointment stabbed through me. I hadn't realized until now that I wanted to know something about my birth mother.

Suddenly, Alicia said, "Aha! I'm pretty sure this is her. You said she was a ballet dancer, right?"

"Yes." That was one of the few details I knew about Ruby.

Alicia looked up and studied me. "You kind of look like her."

I jumped up and ran to her. "Let me see!" But Alicia was hogging her phone.

"She's a yoga instructor now. She's so pretty." Alicia finally held out her phone to me.

And there she was. My birth mother, Ruby Chen. And she really was beautiful. I scrolled through her feed, looking for a close-up picture. She was much skinnier than me, ballerina skinny with sculpted arms and a small waist. But she had my face. Or I had her face. I couldn't think. I could only stare at the picture. It was like looking at a more polished version of me. We had the same wide forehead and small nose that kind of tilted down. And the same full lower lip with a thinner upper lip that I'd always hated but looked right on her. In one picture, she had her hair down, and it was long and silky straight, not like my coarse hair. I must have gotten my hair from my father, whoever he was.

I couldn't stop staring at her pictures, and Alicia, Hana, and my sewing room faded away as I devoured picture after picture. There she was, performing onstage in a tutu, her back leg lifted up. There she was in mid-leap on a beach, soaring high above the sand. There she was with a group of friends, her hair flying long behind her. And there she was hugging an older Asian woman, a woman who looked like her. It must be her mother. My grandmother.

I looked up at Hana and Alicia and couldn't stop the tremor in my voice when I spoke. "I look like her. And I have a grandmother." For some reason, I never thought beyond my birth mother. I knew she didn't know the birth father. She'd told my parents that she'd had a one-night stand with a man in college whom she never saw again. She didn't know his last name. Only his first name. Hana had told me when I discovered I was adopted.

"Can I see?" Hana's voice was gentle, and I nodded, unable to control the way my chin wobbled. It always did that when I was about to cry.

I handed her the phone and heard her soft exclamation of awe. "She's so graceful and beautiful." Hana's eyes moved along Ruby's page. Her mouth opened into a surprised O and her eyebrows rose.

"What is it?" I asked.

"Did you see her bio?" She pointed at the phone.

"That she's a ballet dancer and yoga instructor?"

"No, further down." Hana handed me the phone. "Look."

I took it from her and scanned the bio. And then I saw what had surprised Hana. It said, "Made in Taiwan" with a Taiwanese flag next to it.

"OMG." I clapped a hand over my mouth. "I'm Taiwanese? Not Chinese?" The adoption paperwork had listed my ethnicity as "Chinese."

"It looks like it." Hana had an equally shocked look on her face.

"No way. First I thought I was Korean all my life, only to find out at sixteen that I'm Chinese. And now at almost thirty, I find out I'm actually Taiwanese?" I sank into a chair and blew out a breath. Hello, what? Talk about an identity crisis.

NINE

MyCraftyBao

Handmade Purses and Accessories
* Star Seller Osage County, OK
816 Sales ⭐⭐⭐⭐⭐
Contact Shop Owner: Kim

Kimmie

The next day, a Monday, Alicia and Hana were both helping me sew for my Etsy shop. Sales had been coming in fast, faster than I could believe, and I'd had to recruit Hana to cut out the patterns while Alicia and I sewed. I was now a Star Seller, which meant my shop consistently provided excellent customer experiences. I'd posted more pictures of Alicia with my products, and they did just as well as the first one. I should have corrected everyone's assumption and clarified that the pictures were of my friend Alicia, but I *really* didn't want anyone to know I was Let Her Rip. It was amazing how those posts were helping to increase the shop's reach.

"Did I cut this out right?" Hana handed me the dachshund fabric that she'd just cut out of the pattern I'd made for the double-frame purses. They were flying out of the shop. It was a purse frame within another purse frame, so there were three separate compartments. I'd sewn a detachable wristlet strap to it, so that you could just hook it over your wrist, put your phone, money, and cards in the separate compartments, and go. Perfect for people who didn't like to carry big, bulky purses.

I took it from her and examined it. "Yup. Looks good. I think you're now officially part of the shop." I handed it back with a grin.

Hana laughed. "I guess you recruited a new employee. This is actually fun." She'd been skeptical when I first asked if she could help, saying she couldn't sew. But I put her to work with the scissors, and she actually cut the patterns more precisely than I did. I was always going too fast and cutting off part of the paper patterns I made, giving me more work because I'd have to make new patterns eventually.

"I can't believe how many orders you've gotten just from the few IG posts you put up," Alicia said, positioning the fabric in her hands under the foot of my second sewing machine.

Alicia kept talking as she stepped on the pedal of her machine. It hummed in response, sewing the pieces she pushed through it together.

"What?" I shouted over the thrum of the sewing machine.

"People still think I'm you though," Alicia shouted back. She took her foot off the pedal and turned to me. "Are you going to set them straight?"

"I should but I don't know. I don't want anyone to know

who I really am." I looked up from the fabric I was pinning together. That stupid video was still being circulated. I'd thought it would have died down by now.

"What if you just posted that the pictures are of your friend Alicia?" Hana said. "You don't have to post a picture of yourself."

"But then they're going to ask what I look like." I pieced two more fabrics together and then brought them all to my Bernina workhorse of a sewing machine. I didn't say out loud that I was worried about what Matt was going to say when he found out I didn't look like Alicia. If I confessed the truth, he was going to want to know who I really was. And no way in hell did I want him to know that I was Let Her Rip.

Ugh. I shook my head, not wanting to think about him finding out I was *that* girl.

"Are you okay, Kimmie?" Hana asked. "Thinking about Ruby?"

"Oh, um, yeah." I couldn't tell them I was obsessing over a guy I'd never met. And I was still trying to decide whether or not to respond to Ruby.

"Are you going to reach out to her?" Hana was focused on the fabric she was cutting, but I caught the look she and Alicia exchanged before she looked down.

"I want to. But it still feels like a betrayal to Mom and Dad." I stepped on the pedal of the machine.

"Kimmie, no." Hana put the scissors on the table when I lifted my foot off the pedal. "You know Min and I had a lot of discussions when you first came home. She wanted you to grow up knowing you were theirs. They didn't keep your adoption from you to hurt you. They really believed that not telling you was the best thing for you. I told her you had a right to know, but she and Ben were so adamant. They would never begrudge you a relationship with your birth mom. That's why they chose an open adoption, and someone who didn't want constant contact. They wanted you to have that info, just in case anything ever happened and I became your guardian."

I knew Hana had told my parents that if she ever was my guardian she would tell me the truth, and they had been okay with it. But none of them had ever thought it would happen.

"You really think they wouldn't mind if I talked to Ruby?" I finally asked.

"I think they'd be happy that you have as many people in your corner as possible. If that means connecting with your birth mother, I know that would make Min and Ben really happy."

Alicia had been quiet, but she spoke up now. "I know they'd be okay with it. I think you should reach out to Ruby."

I looked at them and my heart filled. "Okay, I'll think about it."

LATER THAT NIGHT, I sprawled on top of my bed and pulled up my Instagram account. I wanted to stare at Ruby's profile again and stalk her feed, as one does when one has just discovered one's birth mother.

I saw that I had a few DMs, one being from Matt.

M: *Where've you been? Everything okay?*

I felt bad. I hadn't answered any of his DMs yesterday, after I told Hana and Alicia about Ruby's letter. I needed to think. And Matt distracted me—in a good way—but I couldn't focus on my feelings about Ruby when I literally started vibrating every time I got a DM from him.

K: *Sorry I disappeared. Kind of crazy here. And kind of heavy.*

M: *I'm a good listener if you want to talk about it.*

Huh. Hot and a good listener. This guy was really getting to me. And I did want to talk to someone about Ruby, someone who didn't know me.

K: *Okay. So, long story short, I found out when my parents died when I was sixteen that I was adopted. I never knew my birth mother but she's sent a couple of cards over the years. And she just sent a letter a couple of weeks ago. Asking if we could talk on the phone or via Zoom.*

M: *Oh, wow. That's a lot.*

K: *Yeah.*

M: *That's great though, right? Are you going to reach out?*

K: *I don't know. I've been fine without her all these years.*

But had I really been fine? Was I hiding out here at home instead of finding out what life could be like if I just let go of my fears?

M: *How old are you?*

My mouth twitched. What did my age have to do with anything?

K: *Why do you want to know?* 😗

M: *When you said "all these years," I just wondered if you were ancient or something.*

K: *Oh, ha ha. I'm very old. I'm going to be thirty in two months.*

M: *You are ancient!*

K: *What?! How old are you? Please don't tell me you're eighteen or something.*

Because that would make me a cougar, bordering on illegal thoughts about a minor.

M: *Don't worry, I'm legal. I'm twenty-nine too. But I'm six months younger than you. I've never dated an older woman before.*

Even though we weren't dating, my heart hitched and the smile on my face could have lit up the entire state of Oklahoma.

K: *Would you like to?*

M: *Hm, maybe.* 😁

K: *LOL*

I collapsed back on my bed. I was dead. This was the most flirting I'd done in the past five years. What had I been doing all these years? I couldn't remember feeling so alive.

M: *You want to FaceTime? You can tell me more about your birth mother.*

I froze, not sure how to respond. I *did* want to talk to him. But we couldn't FaceTime. Because then he'd know I didn't look like Alicia. I'd been having so much fun with him, and part of it was because of the anonymity of our situation. I was able to flirt freely over DMs because I had time to think out my responses and didn't have to worry about someone watching me for my reactions. I hadn't smiled so much with a guy in so many years.

I guess I paused too long, because he messaged again.

M: *We don't have to talk if you don't want to. I just thought maybe you could use a sympathetic ear.*

OMG, I loved this man. And I hadn't even met him in person.

K: *No, I do. That's nice of you. But can we not do Face-Time? I didn't brush my hair today.*

I didn't brush my hair? I was so lame. But it was the best I could come up with on such short notice.

M: *Ha ha. I don't care. But that's fine, we can do a voice call. Give me your number.*

I sent it to him, then held my breath, waiting for the phone to ring. When it did, I jumped. I hadn't really expected him to call. I'd been in a dating drought since I broke up with my college boyfriend two years after we graduated. I suddenly couldn't remember how to talk to a man on the phone.

"Hello?" My voice squeaked, just like Minnie Mouse. Great.

"Kim! This is Matt. So happy to meet you." His voice was deeper than I'd imagined and sent shivers down my back.

"Me too. Um, thanks for calling." I had enough wits to say that, but then my mind went blank. Absolutely blank. I started sweating. Why was I sweating? I pulled at my shirt to fan myself while willing my mouth to open and say something, anything. I'd been so witty with him in our DMs, but true to form, Kimmie in real life had turned into a petrified statue who was currently saturating her T-shirt faster than if someone had poured a bucket of water over her head.

"Of course." Matt's voice held a hint of laughter. "I've really enjoyed getting to know you the past few days."

"Um, me too?" Why did that come out sounding like a question? I smacked myself on the forehead. I couldn't think. I couldn't even breathe. All I knew was that I was on the phone with Matt, the fucking hot guy that I'd like to . . . um, never mind.

"Tell me about your family."

Oh, thank goodness. Matt could make conversation, unlike me. My mouth flapped open, but nothing came out. I slapped myself on the cheek this time. *Wake up, Kimmie. Say something. Anything.*

"That must have been such a shock when you found out you were adopted." Matt to the rescue again.

"Yeah, it was." I closed my eyes for a moment, relieved that I'd remembered how to speak. "My parents hadn't wanted me to know." I told Matt about it and placed a hand to my chest, willing my heart rate to slow down. I was so revved up I wanted to tear around the house like a crazed puppy doing zoomies.

"How did you find out, then?" I could hear the curiosity in Matt's voice.

"By accident. When my aunt and I met with the lawyer about the will, he let it slip that they'd left almost everything to their adopted daughter. I guess he forgot or they never told him I didn't know. I thought I had a sister no one ever told me about at first."

"Wow. Were you angry? Shocked?" His voice washed over me, and I just wanted to drown in it. Was that weird? Wanting to drown in a guy's voice?

"Not angry, no. I was still so sad about my parents."

"What happened to them?" The sympathy in Matt's low voice made me want to leap through the phone and hurl myself into his arms. His strong, sexy arms, the muscles hard, just like his . . . I shivered.

How was it possible to feel this way about someone I'd never met? I shook my head and focused on his question. "They were camping on the Colorado Trail and a tree fell on their tent while they were sleeping." I heard a soft gasp, and somehow, his dismay felt like a balm over the hole my parents had left in my heart when they died. "Hana had come to stay with me so they could hike the trail, something they'd both wanted to do for a long time. We were told it was quick, that they never knew what hit them. But I can't tell you how many nights I've lain awake, wondering if they'd known the tree was about to fall, or if they hadn't died right away." I gave a short laugh. "I know, morbid."

"It's not morbid." Matt's voice was gentle. "I get it. I know what it's like to want to know what someone you love's last moments are like."

"Did you lose someone too?" I held my breath, already sad for whomever he'd lost.

"My mother." He cleared his throat. "Three years ago."

"Oh, Matt. I'm sorry." Maybe this was why I felt such a connection to him. We'd both lost our mothers.

"It was a really bad accident. She was on her way to our house in the Hamptons. I don't know what she was doing by herself. She doesn't usually like to drive, and I've wondered . . ." He cleared his throat again.

"I'm so sorry." I didn't know what else to say.

Matt sighed. "Thanks. It was a horrific accident. A tractor trailer had overturned and people behind it couldn't stop in time. A massive pileup. My mother's car was in the middle and she got it from both ends. She was pinned, and the firefighter . . ." He broke off.

"Oh, Matt."

"Anyways, that's why I wanted to be a firefighter. The guy who was with her, who held her hand as she died, found me after. She'd ask him to tell Robert and Matthew that she loved us. And he actually found us and delivered her final message." He coughed and then tried to laugh. "So, yeah, I know what it's like to want to know every detail."

"You get it," I said softly.

"I do."

"How long have you been a firefighter?"

"I just got out of probie school about eight months ago. I have four more months before I'm official." I listened as he told me about the shit he got as a probie and laughed when he told me about the murse he brought in the day it came.

There was a pause and then he asked, "What happened to you after your parents passed away? You were so young."

"Hana ended up staying with me. She's my mom's younger sister." I told Matt about how Hana had given up her travels to get me through college.

"I'm glad you had your aunt with you." Matt's voice deepened and I was glad I was already lying down, because otherwise I would have fallen.

Was it possible to fall in love with a voice? Because I thought I just had. There was something about him, and our shared experiences only made the connection deeper. Looking at his picture literally had me swooning, wanting to run my hands over his sculpted body. Yet at the same time, I understood him and he understood me at a level that I didn't think was possible. He'd lost a parent in an accident, just like I did. We got each other.

"Hana is great. She was planning on telling me I was adopted, when some time had gone by after my parents' death. But she knew I was Ch—" I cut myself off. I'd been about to tell him that she knew I was Chinese. But then I realized Alicia didn't look Chinese. She looked more like her father than her mother. Crap.

"Ch . . . ?" Matt's voice questioned.

"Uh . . . cheeky." *What? What the heck did that even mean?* But it was the first "ch" word I could think of.

Matt laughed. "Cheeky? What, you talk back to her or something? And what does that have to do with you being adopted?"

I shrugged and then realized he couldn't see me. "I don't know. I lost my train of thought. My brain gets scrambled sometimes." *Oh my god, someone, help me.*

"You're funny, Kim." He let out a low chuckle.

"Uh, thanks?" Was that the proper response when a guy you were crushing on said you were funny when you weren't trying to be funny?

"Are you going to reach out to your birth mom?" And he got extra points for changing the subject because I was starting to flounder for words again. I couldn't understand what was happening. One minute, I was so comfortable with him that I was able to speak freely, just like I would with Alicia. But the next minute, he made me so flustered that I couldn't speak or think.

"Kim?" His questioning voice made me realize I'd never answered him.

"Um, I think so." My voice shook and I sat up.

"It's a lot. And a big deal." He paused, and when I didn't say anything, he asked, "Where does she live?"

"Manhattan." And it hadn't escaped me that Ruby and Matt both lived in the one city I had always yearned to go to. Was the universe trying to tell me something?

"No way. If you ever come visit her, we should meet up." His voice was so strong, so positive, that it made me feel like I really could get over the fear of not only leaving Oklahoma, but actually *meeting* Ruby.

"That would be great." My heart gave a thump at the thought of seeing this beautiful man in person. But then it sank. I'd have to tell him who I really was first. If it weren't for Matt, I'd be happy to let people continue to think Alicia was me. It wasn't hurting anything.

I shook my head. I was getting ahead of myself. This was just a fun flirtation over DMs and now a phone call. It was never going to turn into a "thing," so I didn't have to worry about what Matt thought I looked like.

"Keep me posted. Now that you have my cell, call or text anytime."

"Thanks, Matt." My voice was steady, but inside, I had melted into a puddle of goo. And how was I supposed to believe that this was just a fun flirtation when he'd just implied that he wanted to keep talking to me in the future?

"No problem."

We were both silent, but neither made a move to hang up. I breathed in deeply and held my breath. Something was happening here. As if to belie my thoughts that nothing would come of this, I could practically hear the electricity crackling between us, right through the phone. It was insane to think I was having this kind of connection with someone I'd never met. But my life hadn't exactly been sane lately. I wanted to embrace the insane, since the alternative hadn't gotten me anywhere.

"I'm glad we connected," I said, my heart pounding wildly.

"Me too, Kim." Matt's voice was husky.

I loved the way he said my name. Kim. Not Kimmie, like everyone called me.

"Bye." My voice was faint.

"Bye."

And I sat there on the bed, not moving for a long time after we hung up.

TEN

Matt

A few days later, I was at the firehouse when my phone rang. I looked down and stifled a groan when I saw it was my father again. I'd ignored his two calls earlier because I'd been texting with Kim. We'd been texting every day, sometimes multiple times a day. We'd also talked on the phone again since that first phone call a few days ago. I didn't want to admit to myself how much I looked forward to our exchanges. There was something about her. Not just her looks, but the way she kept me on my toes, made me smile, and once made me laugh so hard I choked. Plus, there was the shared experience of having lost a parent, or both in her case, that strengthened our connection.

I picked up the phone before it could stop ringing and walked outside the firehouse.

"Matt. I've been trying to reach you all day." My father's voice was irritated like it always was these days.

"I'm working." I leaned against the outside wall, deciding not to elaborate. The best way to avoid confrontation with Robert West was to keep my answers short.

"I need you back at the company." Without waiting for my response, he launched into a long list of reasons why. He needed my eye for trends and my recommendations for long-range growth initiatives. No one had brought on any good fresh ideas in the year I'd been gone. He couldn't operate without me. "We were a good team, Matt. Please, come back to work."

"I am at work. I have a new job now."

"Matt. Matthew. What are you doing there?" I could hear the impatience in my father's voice. He was used to getting his way and I'd basically gone against all his wishes in the last year and a half. "If you needed to prove something, you did. Now come back to where you belong."

"I belong here, Dad. This is what I want to do." And it was. Despite the grief I got and the extra work and nights when I was assigned to late watch, I loved being a firefighter. Not only was I doing something, a service, but the camaraderie with the guys and the sense of having one another's backs (even with the shit probies got) was something that I hadn't realized I needed.

"What do you want? You've proven your point. Why are you working at the FDNY when you're so good at your job here? It's certainly not for the pay cut."

"It's not about the money. It's like a . . ." I was about to say "calling" but knew my father wouldn't understand. He was a statistics man. A cut-and-dried, "by the books" kind of person. He understood numbers and profit and loss statements. He wouldn't understand about sentiments or a pull to do something that I felt I needed to do. And he'd especially not understand if I said it was because of Mom.

"Matt." He sighed. His exasperation was clear in that heavy exhale. "Stop this. Quit the FDNY. You belong in this world."

"I don't know how else to make it clear to you, Dad. I'm not quitting my job. This is where I belong." I gave a grunt of frustration. Our conversations had been like this ever since I gave him notice that I was leaving and going to probie school.

"Matthew, you need to—"

"I gotta go. Bye." I cut him off and then hung up before he could go into another tirade.

A noise made me look up. Tom stood just inside the firehouse.

"Trouble with your father?" the older man asked.

I nodded. "He wants me to go back to work for his company. He can't understand why I want to be a firefighter." I pushed myself off the wall and walked back inside.

"I guess you make more money at his company." Tom's voice was mild.

"It's not about money. It's . . ." I didn't know how to explain it.

"You're right. It's not all about money. We do this because we want to. To help." Tom clapped me on the shoulder. "You gotta do what makes you happy. It's your life."

I nodded again. "I wish he'd understand that."

Tom took his hand back. "You can't control how other people feel. You can only do what's best for you."

We stood there in silence, looking out at the street, at the people hurrying down the sidewalk, either heading out for the evening or rushing home for dinner. I was waiting for someone to relieve me and then meeting Jason for dinner at our favorite barbecue place in Harlem. I was grateful for Tom's advice.

"Thanks," I finally said.

He smiled at me and turned to walk back into the firehouse.

———

JASON WAS ALREADY THERE when I got to the restaurant. I found him at a booth with a pint of beer in front of him, near the back of the noisy and crowded restaurant. Wooden beams crisscrossed the ceiling and the brick walls and dark décor everywhere gave it a rustic feel. The smoky smell of barbecue wafted in the air and my stomach grumbled. When I approached the table, Jason looked up with a wide grin.

"Good to see you." He stood and slapped me on the back. I was just under six feet and Jason loomed over me. His parents had thought he'd play basketball, but he'd been more interested in making music. He'd played in bands all through high school and college and still jammed with a few musician friends several times a month.

I slid into the dark wooden booth across from him. "I need a beer."

"Tough day at work?" Jason shot me a sympathetic look.

"Kind of." I picked up the menu even though I knew it by heart. Jason and I always shared a half pound of the spicy shrimp boil, and then I had the brisket while he got the barbecue pork ribs.

The waitress, a woman with bright blond hair, probably in her fifties, stopped by the table.

"What're you drinking, hon?" She had a friendly smile and an impressive sleeve of tattoos up one arm.

"Whatever lager you have on tap," I said.

"Brooklyn Lager okay?"

I nodded and she winked as she turned on her heels.

"So, what's up?" Jason leaned back and picked up his pint glass.

I waved a hand. "First, how's Mandy and Ollie?"

"Great." A big smile spread over Jason's face. "He's walking. And has two teeth." He brought up some pictures on his phone and handed it to me.

Ollie grinned back at me. His skin was lighter than Jason's, because Mandy was of Irish heritage. But he had the same wide eyes as Jason, and the same full lips.

"I need to get out to you guys soon." I handed Jason's phone back to him.

"Let's get in one last barbecue before it gets too cold. You won't believe how big Ollie is." He looked down at the picture of his son and then turned his phone around on the table. "So, what's going on?"

"My father."

That was all I had to say. Jason's face screwed up. He knew my father well. We were both only children, having met at private school on the Upper West Side. His parents were doctors, so Jason often came home with me after school. My mom was a stay-at-home mom and used to make us the best snacks and helped with our homework. Once we got older, Jason still liked hanging out with my mom.

"Giving you a hard time for leaving still?" Jason's eyebrows rose.

"Yeah." I sighed. "He seems to think I'm just 'getting this out of my system' and will be quitting the FDNY soon."

The waitress deposited my beer in front of me and took our order. Before she left, she leaned in and whispered, "The two of you are stirring up a lot of attention over there."

She pointed at the bar, where a group of twenty-something women were giggling and staring at us. Jason grinned at them and took a sip of his beer, making sure they could see his wedding band.

He turned to the waitress and pointed at me. "This one is single though."

She winked at me before turning away. "I'll let them know."

I glared at Jason as I took a healthy swallow of ice-cold beer. "Thanks for that."

"What?" He put his glass down and turned up his hands. "Just trying to help you out here. You haven't had a girlfriend in a while."

I looked down, not wanting him to see the smile on my face when I thought of Kim. She was *not* my girlfriend. Not even close. I'd never even had a conversation with her where I could see her face.

But Jason knew me well and he planted his elbows on the table, leaning toward me. "What? You meet someone?"

"No."

"Come on, West. This is me. Your oldest friend. You're not getting away with that. I know something's going on." He narrowed his eyes at me. "Who knew you when you were a gawky teenager with braces and had a crush on Marilou Stevenson? We've been through it all together."

We had. He was tall with dark skin, handsome in a Denzel Washington way. Girls flocked around him and whenever I was with him, I often felt like his sidekick. Until I started to fill out in junior year, and then we'd made quite a pair. My mom had joked more than once that the two of us left broken hearts behind everywhere we went.

"Just this woman I've been texting with. I've never met her." I took a sip of my beer.

"Then how do you know her?" His forehead was creased.

"She has an Etsy shop and I bought something for my grandmother. Then I found her on Instagram and we just kind of started talking." I looked away and noticed the group of women at the bar were still looking our way.

"She live around here?"

"No. Oklahoma." I turned back to Jason. "So, no, nothing is going to come of it."

"Okay, okay." Jason started nodding to himself. "Oklahoma's not that far. What's she look like?"

I raised my eyebrows at him and then took out my cell. I pulled up Instagram, and when I found Kim's page, I showed it to him.

"Shit, man." Jason's eyes grew wide. "She's hot."

"I know. But it's not just that. She's funny. And smart. And a lot of fun." I took my phone back from Jason and looked down at Kim's latest post. She sat on the back of a horse holding a tote bag like the one I'd bought for Nana, only with a bold bright yellow print that looked like sunbursts. I hadn't seen this one yet. She must have just posted it.

Jason gave a low whistle. "My boy has it bad."

I gave him a half toast because yeah, I did. There was no sense in denying it to Jason. He knew me too well. "We're just talking. And we've never met. Not even on FaceTime."

"Dude, why?"

"I've only known her for over a week. We've talked on the phone a couple of times though." I cocked my head to the side. "I did suggest FaceTime once but she made some excuse about her hair."

"Hm." Jason tapped his fingers on the table. "Well, it's not because she's afraid of you finding out what she looks like."

"We're just having fun."

"Have you never heard of planes? Or even cars? It's not like she lives on another planet. You like her. You should see if there's anything there." Jason pointed a finger at me.

"I'll keep that in mind." I slanted him a look.

As if she knew we were talking about her, a text popped up on my cell from Kim.

Jason caught the way my eyes went straight to my phone when it dinged. "That her?"

I nodded, opening Kim's text. And laughed out loud when I saw she'd sent me a picture of her holding a giant burrito up to the camera, about to take a bite. I couldn't see her face. Just parts of her cheek and a glimpse of dark hair. She'd told me she loved to eat when we texted earlier and I'd told her to prove it.

"Let me see." Jason leaned toward me.

I turned my phone around and he gave me a look. "What's that?"

"Just . . ." I shook my head but didn't elaborate. As the waitress came back and put our plates in front of us, I sent Kim a text.

M: *Nice picture. Was just talking about you.*

The waitress handed me a piece of paper before she left. "From the blonde over there."

I looked over at the bar and the tall blonde fluttered her fingers at me. I glanced down at the paper, which read: *Call me. xo Katy* and her phone number.

Jason hooted as my phone dinged.

K: *Oh? To whom? And why?*

M: *I'm having dinner with my best friend Jason.*

K: *You told your friend about me?*

M: *Yup.*

"You are so whipped." Jason's voice had me looking up at him. "You're disappointing that woman over there."

"What?" I glanced over at the blonde again, who pouted her lips when she saw me looking. I gave her a quick smile before averting my eyes.

"You got it bad. Tell her I said hi." Jason smirked at me.

"Tell her yourself." Jason had always been my sounding board with women in the past. He could tell from one conversation with someone I liked if he thought they were "good people," or "nope, don't get involved with that shite." I dialed Kim's number and held the phone up to my ear.

"Dude. You're calling her?" Jason cackled and rubbed his hands together.

I nodded just as Kim picked up.

"Hi, Matt. I thought you were having dinner with your friend." Her voice brought a smile to my face. I couldn't help it. There was something about her that just made me happy.

"I am. Jason wants to say hi."

"Wait. What? He wants to talk to me?" The panic in Kim's voice only made me smile bigger.

"Yes. Hold on a second." And I held the phone out to Jason.

He took it with a lift of his eyebrows and a smug look on his face.

I shrugged and sat back, drinking my beer. I didn't know where any of this was going, but I hadn't felt this happy since my mother died.

ELEVEN

Kimmie

I clutched my cell in my hand and sat down on the wide bench on the front porch that my mom had bought at an estate sale years ago. It was a beautiful fall day and I'd been outside finishing the burrito I'd texted to Matt. The sun felt good on my skin.

"Kim?" A smooth male voice came over the phone.

"Here," I squeaked. *Here?* What was this, elementary school? I was nervous. Why did Matt's friend want to talk to me?

"I'm Jason. I've known Matt since he still had accidents at school. I hear you've captured the heart of my boy here." Jason laughed and I could hear Matt's voice yelling at him in the background.

"Um, yeah." *Get it together, Kimmie. Don't lose your cool just because Matt's friend told you Matt likes you.* "I do have a way with men." *I do?*

Jason's laughter rumbled over the phone. "What do you do, Kim?"

"I'm a . . ." I hesitated for a moment. "I'm a designer. Of

bags and accessories. I used to work for this asshole but I told him off and quit. Now I work for myself." Which was all true.

"Interesting. So what you're saying is, you can do your job from anywhere?"

"I guess?" I had nothing tying me down to Oklahoma anymore, now that I no longer worked for Rip. Alicia and Hana would go back to their lives soon and I'd be stuck in Oklahoma all by myself. Again. "You're right. I can work from anywhere."

"Great," Jason practically crowed. "And how do you feel about barbecue?"

"How do I feel about it? I'm from Oklahoma. Of course I love it. If you ever come here, I'll take you to the best ribs joint in the whole state. Smokies in Broken Arrow. It's about an hour away, but totally worth the drive." The minute the words were out of my mouth, I wanted to swallow them back. I'd just invited Matt's best friend to Oklahoma. Not only did I not know Jason, I didn't really know Matt either.

"Deal. My wife loves barbecue too. As long as Matty here doesn't screw things up with you, we'll meet in Oklahoma one day soon. Here, your boyfriend wants to talk to you." I heard some shuffling before Matt came back on the line.

"Kim. Sorry about that." Matt sounded flustered, which made me feel better since I was about to have a freak-out that Jason had called Matt my boyfriend.

"No worries. He sounds like a nice guy." I took shallow breaths, trying to calm my heart, and then realized I should be taking deep breaths, not this puffing out of air that wasn't doing anything for my revved-up body.

"He's a pain in my ass." But I could hear the affection in Matt's voice.

"Anyone who likes barbecue is okay in my book." I made an attempt to sound normal, and not like I'd just done a mad dash around the neighborhood.

"You seem to have worked your magic on him. He is right now encouraging me to get on the first flight to Oklahoma so we can meet in person."

"Oh, fuck." He couldn't come here! This wasn't supposed to turn into anything. We were just flirting, having fun over DMs and phone calls.

"Fuck?" There was laughter in Matt's voice. "Um, sure. But I was thinking of taking you out on a date first."

"No! Oh my god, I didn't mean it that way." I closed my eyes, mortification flooding me as I heard both Matt and Jason laughing. And did he just say he would take me on a date? My heart flip-flopped even as heat flooded my cheeks.

"I know, I'm just teasing you," Matt said, when he could talk again. "But no one has ever said 'oh, fuck' at the thought of meeting me before."

"That wasn't what I meant . . . I just . . . I mean . . ." I was so flustered I couldn't form a whole sentence.

"Don't worry." His voice was still full of laughter. "I won't be appearing in front of you in Oklahoma."

"That's too bad." I finally gathered my wits.

"Listen, our food just got here. Can I call you later?" Matt asked.

Well, considering I had nothing on my agenda for tonight, a Saturday night, except to sit at home by myself because both Alicia and Hana had disappeared earlier, saying they wouldn't be home for dinner, I guessed I could talk later. But I wasn't about to tell him that.

"Text me when you can." That sounded much better than *I'll be waiting by the phone.*

"Okay, talk to you later."

"Bye, Matt." And I hung up, staring at the vacant lot across the street.

I wanted to dwell on what was happening with Matt, but a movement caught my eye. A deer peered out from a stand of trees next to the lot. I held my breath, not wanting to scare it away. It walked out into the clearing and took a few steps toward me. My house was at the end of a cul-de-sac and there was nothing but land and trees on that side of the street. I often saw wildlife if I sat on the front porch. The deer walked out and I saw she had two fawns with her. By this time of the year, the fawns had started to lose their spots and I could see that was true with these two. One frolicked at the doe's side, while the other stood still, watching me like his mother. They came right up to my property. I held out a hand. The doe met my eyes, and then turned and ran back into the woods, her fawns at her tail.

I sighed and let my hand drop. It was natural to want to stay by your mother's side, like the two fawns. And my birth mother wanted to know me. With no parents in the world, shouldn't I want to get to know the woman who had carried me and given me life? And what was I going to do about Matt?

THE NEXT MORNING, I woke with a smile on my face. Matt had texted and then called me after his dinner with Jason. We'd been on the phone for over two hours. He'd told me about working for his father's company for years, and then quitting over a year ago and joining the FDNY because of the firefighter who had been there for his mother. And I'd told him about my job at Let Her Rip (except I didn't tell him the name of the boutique) and how

I'd quit recently too, and was now trying to make a go of it with my Etsy shop before I decided what to do next. I knew he had the day off today, and that he planned on sleeping in before tackling chores like laundry, grocery shopping, and cleaning his apartment.

I picked up my phone and scrolled through our texts from last night. We'd debated the merits of brisket versus ribs, shrimp you had to peel by hand or already peeled, and baos. I couldn't believe it when he said he'd never had a bao. I told him he had to fix that, ASAP. He lived in New York City after all.

Matt had also told me that Jason had given his approval, deeming me "good people." I'd laughed.

"How does he know I'm good people when he only spoke to me for a few minutes and has never seen me in real life? I could be a serial killer who likes to stalk my Etsy customers and then hack them into little pieces once I get my clutches into them, for all that he knows," I'd said.

Matt had made a noise of mock terror. "Is that what's going on here? I'm just a victim?"

"Yup. And now you're mine." I'd given an evil laugh, thrilled that we could joke like this.

"I'm scared." Matt then told me Jason was always right about people. All their lives, he'd take one look at someone and been able to say if they were "good people" or not. Jason had never been wrong.

I jumped when my phone dinged in my hand.

M: *Good morning, beautiful. How'd you sleep?*

I hadn't expected him to text so early. It would be nine in the morning his time. When he'd said he was sleeping in, I'd thought he meant until eleven or so. My heart lifted to see his text, but I paused at him calling me beautiful. How was I going to tell him that it was *Alicia* who was beautiful?

K: *Don't call me that. And good morning to you too.*

M: *Call you what? Beautiful? But you are. Don't you have any idea how gorgeous you are?*

I frowned. We were getting to a point where it felt like I should tell him the truth. This wasn't just a brief exchange with a friendly stranger anymore. I'd only known him for eleven days (yes, I'd counted), but he had already become the person I wanted to talk to most as soon as I woke up, and the person I wanted to talk to before I went to sleep. And he seemed to feel the same way.

M: *Hello?*

K: *Oh, sorry. I don't want to be reduced to how I look on the outside. What about the me on the inside?*

M: *I like the you on the inside too.*

I let out a breath. He just validated that he liked *me*, not just what I looked like. This was the perfect time to tell him. I started typing, deleted it, and typed something else. And then deleted that too. What should I say? And then I just typed what popped into my head.

K: *I have something to tell you.*

That was good, right? To the point. And a good lead-in.

M: *What? You're really a serial killer who's going to kill my pets?*

I sputtered out a laugh.

K: *No!*

M: *You're really a Disney princess who was beamed into the modern life by accident and you need my help finding your way back?*

I rolled my eyes but I couldn't keep from rocking in laughter.

K: *Believe me, I'm no princess.*

M: *Yes, you are. Are you in still in bed?*

K: *Why do you want to know?*

M: *Get your mind out of the gutter.*

K: *You're the one who brought up beds.*

M: *FaceTime with me and I'll prove that you're beautiful to me no matter what you look like. Even first thing in the morning.*

I sat up suddenly. I should do it. Get it over with. Just show him who I was and then explain. I swiped my phone to pull up my camera, flipping it around to face me. When I saw my image, I yelped, dropping the phone on the comforter.

I looked hideous. And I wasn't trying to put myself down, because I usually liked the way I looked. But I had slept on my hair when it was still damp and it now stood up on one side, while the other was matted down. There was some sort of rash on my face (I had really sensitive skin and anything could give me a rash) and I also had hives under one eye because I'd forgotten to take my allergy medicine last night. The hives were large angry welts that puffed up my face. I was about as attractive as a monkey's butt.

K: *Yeah, no. I look seriously scary. You'd run away if you saw me now.*

My phone rang a few seconds later.

As soon as I picked up, I heard, "But that's exactly why we should. I don't care what you look like. I always have fun talking to you and I look forward to it every time."

I scoffed. "That's great, but no. I'm not FaceTiming with you while I'm in bed."

"I'm starting to think you're not who you really are." Matt's voice was teasing, but his words made my heart sink. Because he was right. I was *not* who he thought I was.

I had to tell him the truth. "I'm really not—"

"Oh, hey. I forgot to tell you." Matt cut me off. "I found

a bao place in the Fifties and I'm going down there to pick some up for lunch."

A mixture of dismay and relief rushed through me that he had changed the subject. "I'm so jealous." What I wouldn't give to be in Matt's bed with him right now, about to go on the search for baos. Talk about a dream come true.

"What are you doing today?" he asked.

"Probably sewing by myself. Alicia's waitressing at the diner she used to work at and Hana is off somewhere writing." They had both promised to help me the next day. Orders for my shop were still pouring in and I was going to have to hire someone if it kept up like this. Even with Alicia and Hana's help and the stock I had, I was behind.

"What about your birth mom? I keep forgetting to ask if you've reached out to her yet."

I puffed out a breath. "No. I'm a chicken."

"You're not." I could hear the sympathy in his voice.

"I'm going to text her. Maybe this week. Ruby gave me her cell number."

"Is that her name?"

"Yes, her name is Ruby Ch . . ."

I stopped because I'd almost said "Chen." *Shit, shit, shit.*

"Ruby Ch? That's a strange last name." Matt's laughter literally shot right to my ovaries and made them do whatever it was they were supposed to do.

But now I had to come up with a last name that started with "Ch." And of course, my mind went blank.

"Um, yeah . . . it's Cheeky." *WTF?*

Matt laughed again. "Her last name is Cheeky? Isn't that what your aunt calls you or something?"

Okay. Kill me now. I wanted to die. I'd just told Matt my birth mother's last name was Cheeky. WTF was wrong with me? *"Ch" names, come on, think, Kimmie, think.*

"Ha, um . . . no. Yes, that's what my aunt calls me, but no, that's not Ruby's last name. Her last name is Chen . . . apov." And I died just a little more, because really? That was the best I could come up with? What kind of name was Chenapov?

Matt must have thought the same thing. "That's an unusual name. What is it, Russian?"

"Yeah, I think so." Open mouth, insert foot. "Um, but I'm not sure. I'll ask her when I talk to her." *Shut up, shut up, shut up, Kimmie!*

I couldn't believe I'd just told Matt I was Russian. Bad enough that I thought I was Korean, then Chinese, and then Taiwanese. Now Matt thought I was Russian. My identity crisis was getting worse. I was lying to a man I was starting to care about a lot. And I had no idea how to get myself out of this predicament.

"It must be nice to find out more about your heritage."

"It is." I closed my eyes, letting his voice soothe my nerves.

"I'm happy for you, Kim." His voice lowered and it was the sexiest thing I'd ever heard.

And then all I could picture was him lying in bed with no shirt on. The thought of seeing him bare chested was enough to send me into a tailspin. I turned on my side, imagining that I had my cheek on his broad, firm chest, running a hand down his tight abs. The sheets would be pulled up to his navel and my hand hovered at the edge. I'd look up to see his eyes flash at me, daring my hand to wander lower. His dark hair would be tousled, one arm hooked behind his head, his biceps straining. He'd smile slowly, his smoldering eyes gazing into my own, igniting the heat in my core and—

"Kimmie?"

I blinked, disappointed when I realized I was in my own

bedroom and not in bed with Matt. I fanned a hand over my face.

"Um . . ." I had completely lost all track of the conversation.

"Are you okay?"

I blew out a breath. "I . . ." My head was still snuggled on Matt's chest in my mind and I couldn't focus. "Yum."

He laughed. "Are you hungry?"

Oh, shit. Did I say that out loud? "Uh . . ." I swung my body so that my head was hanging off my bed, hoping the blood would drain into my brain and away from where it was currently pooled, making smoke literally come off my body.

He laughed again. "Hey, speaking of food, I've been watching the Pioneer Woman a lot on Food Network. She's from Osage County too, right? Have you ever seen her?"

Food. I could talk about food. And I loved Ree Drummond. "I've seen her a few times at her Mercantile store. She's really nice. I met Ladd and Paige once too."

"That's so cool. When I visit, you have to take me there. And to their pizza shop."

He said "when." Not "if." I closed my eyes, imagining a bare-chested Matt here in bed with me. My breath quickened again and I swear, I could orgasm right now without even touching myself.

"Yes, oh, yes."

Matt's laughter had my eyes popping open and I realized I'd just said that out loud. "You must be really hungry." He dropped his voice. "Or else you're thinking about something . . . naughty?"

"Oh, god, yes." I couldn't help myself. The combination of the image of Matt in my mind combined with his husky voice . . . and I was going to combust if I didn't get off the phone with him. "I have to go." That came out in a breathless rush.

"Hmm . . ." he murmured, as if he was having fantasies himself. Hopefully about me.

When we hung up, I took a very cold shower. And took care of some business.

TWELVE

Instagram Post

1,423 likes

mycraftybaokim I've always wanted to go to New York City, but for various reasons it hasn't happened. But lately, things in my life are pushing me toward NYC. Do you believe in signs? I have a confession: I'm scared to leave Oklahoma. So what should I do? Fake it until I make it! I tell myself I can and will make the right choice when the time comes. And because I don't feel confident if I don't at least look the part, I came up with designs that make me feel good. When I feel good, I'm more confident and that is part of the battle.

That's why I designed this new shoulder bag. I'm imagining myself confidently walking down the streets of NYC with my cute bag slung over my shoulder, but held snugly against my side. A confident Kim, taking the subway or shopping for groceries. (How do people in cities carry their groceries home without cars? If you're a New Yorker, drop a comment below and let me know!)

That's the beauty of finding your own confidence, of

faking it until you make it. Because if you believe in you, no one can tear you down. So be you. Pick a bag that says you. And if someone doesn't like it, that's on them. Not you.

Be daring, be bold, be you.

xo, Kim

VIEW all 182 comments

leahinthecity43 OMG. It's like you've picked my brain and just wrote exactly what I was feeling. How do you do that? You're a mind reader—LOL.

gretchenbanks33 I needed to hear this today. Thank you. And I just bought one of your shoulder bags with the hedgehogs on them. Hedgehogs are my jam!

melissafoster Damn, now I need that shoulder bag. I'm spending all my allowance and babysitting money on your Etsy shop. But seriously love it!

totallymikec I live in NYC, and hello, ever heard of delivery? That's how we get our groceries.

matte194nyc You amaze me, Kim. You're smart and compassionate!

ambersmalley8 I don't get it. Those shoulder bags are so ugly. Who'd buy them?

melissafoster (in response to ambersmalley8) You're obviously a bitter person. Go hate on someone else. Kim is great and her products are amazing!

dancermilayang I loved this message and love the shoulder bags!

Matt

I stood at the stove in the firehouse kitchen, stirring the pot of chili I'd made. It was my turn to make dinner and I'd pulled from my pathetically small arsenal of recipes. Before I'd started working for the FDNY, I didn't know how to cook. I could flip a burger when my family was at our Hamptons house in the summer, but beyond that, boiling water for ramen noodles was about as fancy as I got. But being a probie had forced me to learn.

I'd started watching cooking shows, my favorite being the Pioneer Woman, because her recipes were usually good for feeding a large group of people. They were pretty easy, and what cowboys eat was pretty much what firefighters would eat. I sprinkled a little more salt and pepper into the chili and checked to see if the rice was done.

The other junior guys who were helping me started pulling out bowls and dishing up the rice into them. Dave ladled the chili over it and sprinkled each bowl with shredded cheese and sour cream and handed them off to Joe, who put them on the table. I let them finish getting the bowls ready and walked out of the kitchen toward Hector, who was on house watch.

"Dinner's ready. Call it out?"

Hector nodded and got on the intercom to let the rest of the guys know it was time to eat. I went back into the kitchen as guys started coming in from all over the firehouse. A bunch of them had just sat down when a shout went up behind me. I turned to see them jumping up. Chairs scraped along the floor as they hooted and fanned the air with their hands.

"Frank. What the fuck? You couldn't have done that somewhere else?" Bill had been the closest to Frank and now ran to open a window.

"My God, what did you eat for lunch?" Jack moved away from Frank.

The captain walked into the kitchen, got a whiff, and immediately walked out again. And when I finally got wind of what they were all yelling about, I threw up a little in my mouth. Jeezus, that was disgusting.

"Sorry." Frank held up his hand, a sheepish look on his face. "My stomach's a bit funny."

"Don't let him eat any of that chili tonight. Or else he's going to have to sleep on the apparatus floor. No way I'm sleeping in the bunk room with him tonight," said Bill.

"You've watched that Let Her Rip video too many times, Frankie boy," Jack said, still fanning the air in front of his nose. "Try and control yourself, will ya?"

Everyone sat down again and the captain walked back in a minute later. I sat at the table next to Jack.

"She can really dance though," Bill said as he ate. He was watching that viral video again. "I think Frankie's in love with her."

The others started poking fun at Frank, whose face

turned red. He looked down at the rice and bread on his plate. For once, I felt sorry for him. Maybe he gave me so much shit because he'd had to take a lot when he was a probie.

"Pass that over here. I wanna see," said Jack. "You see this yet?" he asked me.

"Some." I glanced at the phone. It was too far from me to make out details, but I could tell the woman was a great dancer. But man, did I feel bad for her, going viral like that. If that happened to me, I'd have wanted to move to another planet.

As I was finishing my meal, my phone lit up with a text. I always had my phone on silent at the firehouse. As a probie, I wasn't supposed to spend too much time on it. I put the phone in my lap and smiled when I saw it was Kim.

K: *How was dinner tonight?*

I had told her it was my turn to cook and was hoping not to poison the guys.

M: *Good. Everyone's still alive.*

K: *Oh, good.*

M: *What did you have for dinner?*

K: *Haven't eaten yet. Hana is making zhajiangmian.*

M: *What's that?*

K: *It's a Chinese noodle dish. With this fried bean sauce. So good. There's a Korean version too. Hana is combining the two versions.*

M: *Wow. That sounds really good. Can I get that in NY?*

K: *I'm sure. It's a popular dish.*

M: *Okay, I'll have to try it.*

K: *I love that you love to eat as much as I do.*

M: *And I love that you're introducing me to new foods. I just had a great idea.*

K: *What?*

M: *I'll call you when I'm done with cleanup.*

After everyone had finished and the other junior guys and I had scrubbed the pots, taken care of the dishes, and swept the floor, I went up to the locker room on the top floor to get some privacy. I couldn't stay on the phone long, but I wanted to hear her voice.

"Hi, Matt." She sounded breathless.

"Am I interrupting anything?" I couldn't help thinking this would be what she sounded like when she was close to coming. The thought had my blood heating up.

"Nope. Just exercising. I found this great YouTube channel—Workout with Lyn. Have to stay active if I'm going to eat all the food, right?" Her laugh brought a smile to my face. Man, I loved her laugh. I could listen to it all night.

"Want me to call back?" I was already picturing her, clad in something tight, moving with the same kind of grace as the woman from the viral video.

"I'm done. I can talk." She paused. "Sorry, needed some water. Okay, I'm all yours." And she laughed that musical sound again, which shot right to my crotch.

My pants grew uncomfortable and I wondered how a laugh could turn me on like this.

"Hello? Matt?"

I cleared my throat, shifting on the bench. "Sorry. Um, so, yeah. My idea. Let's do a food challenge together. We'll take turns giving each other some new food to try and document it with pictures."

"You mean, like, we'd eat our way through each of our towns, or city in your case, together, but separate?"

"Exactly. What do you think?" I could hear the guys downstairs and knew I had to get off the phone soon.

"Sounds great. You know I'm always open to new foods.

What are you going to introduce me to? Vegemite? Bangers and mash? Fish and chips?"

I'd told her in one of our conversations that my father's family was originally from England.

"Yes. But others things too. What about you? Where's your family from?" I was curious, after what Jason had asked me the other day about her heritage.

"I'm Ch . . ." She cut herself off and coughed.

"Cheeky? Ha!" I laughed. She was so cute.

"No." Now it was her turn to clear her throat. "Sorry, something went down the wrong pipe. Um, my father is—" A loud crash came over the phone.

"Kim? Everything okay?" I called.

There was a lot of rustling, some more crashes, and then she came back on the line. "Sorry, a pot fell off the counter. I have to help Hana. Can I text you later? The food challenge sounds good!"

"Oh, okay, sure."

But she'd already hung up. I stared at my phone and then shrugged. That was a loud crash. I hoped everything was okay.

I sat there because I couldn't stop thinking about Kim, and ended up on her TikTok. I scrolled through her videos, stopping on the "fake it until you make it" one. She looked good, her long hair flying behind her as she turned, eyes sparkling. I tried to picture the images before me with the laugh that turned me on so much and I couldn't. Her pictures looked more like how my ex-girlfriend Melanie looked. Always perfectly made up, knowing how to play up the camera to catch her best angles. But the image of Kim I'd imagined in my mind was of a more down-to-earth woman, someone who didn't care about always looking perfect, who was raw and real. Although she wouldn't Face-Time with me the other day because of how she looked, so what did I know?

I stood, ready to go back downstairs, but my phone lit up with a text. It was my father.

Matt. Please call me. I need you.

Fuck. I let out a frustrated growl and scrubbed a hand over my face. He wasn't going to let this go. And I wasn't going to quit the FDNY. The fact was, I loved the job. I respected the guys I worked with, even Frank, because though he was an asshole, he was a great firefighter. He was always in the right position at a fire, willing to go in first and looking out for everyone else.

How was I going to get my father off my back? I looked at my phone, which was still on Kim's TikTok. And suddenly, I knew. Kim's brand was all about positivity. Her signature sign-off, "be daring, be bold, be you. xo, Kim," was exactly the message that Endless projected. My father had created an empire of retail stores built around the image of wholesome goodness, a return to the past, when women didn't need to go viral to attract attention. Endless was all about the "organic experience" and being uniquely you, targeted for all ages, from millennials all the way to the golden agers. And that was exactly the brand Kim was building.

My heart raced as I started down the stairs. I had a lot of free time as a firefighter, since technically, our schedule was "twenty-four hours on, three days off." It never worked out that way because guys were always swapping tours or we were short on guys and had to do overtime. But regardless, the fact was I had some downtime. Many of the other guys had a second job. I couldn't right now, since I was a probie, but soon I'd be able to. Maybe I could work a few hours a week for my father.

I had a feeling about Kim's brand. I thought my father would get it too. My mind was suddenly buzzing with ideas.

FOURTEEN

Kimmie

I got off the phone with Matt and stared at the mess I'd made. I'd purposely knocked over the steel bowl that Hana had put the cut vegetables in because I knew it would make a loud noise as it crashed to the tile floor.

"Kimmie. Why'd you do that?" Hana stared at me, incredulous. I'd come downstairs while I was on the phone with Matt to see if she needed help with dinner. She'd watched me swipe the bowl off the counter and then kick it a few times to make extra noise.

"I'm sorry." I'd been desperate. I couldn't lie to Matt and tell him my father was half white and half Mexican and that my mother was Japanese. Because *my* parents were Korean. It was *Alicia* who had those parents.

"Now I have to chop the vegetables all over again." Hana made an exasperated noise and leaned down to clean up the mess. "What's gotten into you?"

"I'm sorry," I said again. "I'll clean it up. And chop the vegetables. I just . . . I had to get off the phone and . . . I'm sorry." I got some paper towels and cleaner and bent down, swiping at the spilled onions, garlic, and ginger that was all over the floor.

Hana stood and I knew she was staring at me. I couldn't meet her eyes.

"Okay. What's going on?" Her eyes were practically burning a hole through me.

I blew out a breath. "It's my social media. I was glad when everyone thought Alicia was me. Because of the meme. But now I've met this guy and I really like him. He's amazing. He listens to me, he gets me, he's so kind and smart and sweet and..." I bit my lip as I gathered a handful of the vegetables and stood to put them in the garbage. "And he thinks I look like Alicia."

"Oh." Her tone made me look up. "You still haven't told everyone that the pictures are of Alicia?"

"No." My mouth pulled down at the corners.

"How'd you meet him?" Hana's voice softened.

I told her all about Matt while I took out the vegetables to chop again. "I tried to tell him the other day but I looked seriously awful and I didn't want to scare him." I washed my hands and then started chopping the onions, garlic, and ginger. "What am I going to do?"

"Kimmie. If you really like this guy, you can't start off a relationship with a lie like that."

"I know." I sighed. "But he lives in New York and I didn't think it would even get to this point."

Hana took a package of fresh Korean noodles, Korean black bean paste, and ground pork out of the fridge. She'd made a trip to Tulsa the other day. I watched her line them up on the counter, remembering the times when my parents and I would go to Tulsa or Oklahoma City so we could eat food we couldn't get here and stock up on Asian groceries.

Staples like instant Korean ramen and soups, frozen rice

cakes with fish cake (tteokbokki), mandu (dumplings), and seafood pancakes. Also, fresh banchans, little side dishes of prepared food like fish cakes, pickled cucumbers, seasoned soybean sprouts, and spinach, and mung bean jelly with a spicy sauce. My mouth watered now just thinking about them. My dad and I also used to sneak a small container of kimchi and hide it from my mom because we loved it. My mom was still traumatized from the teasing she got when she was younger about the kimchi smell in her house and refused to buy it. She wanted to erase that part of her and be as un-Korean as possible, especially given the kind of community we lived in.

My aunt tapped me on the arm before she put a pan on the stove. "You need to tell him the truth."

I knew she was right. It had been an honest misunderstanding that I hadn't corrected because I hadn't wanted anyone to know I was Let Her Rip. But now with the way I felt about Matt, I knew it wasn't right.

I handed Hana the cutting board with the vegetables I'd just chopped. She slid them into the pan and stirred them around. Then the ground pork went in and the fragrance made my stomach rumble. It'd been a long time since I'd had Hana's version of this dish, and I could already taste the chewy noodles bathed in the black bean sauce, served with cabbage, onions, and cucumbers.

I sat at the counter to watch her cook. My dad and I used to cook together on Sundays, trying new recipes or making old favorites. But we never made Korean food. Which was why it was so nice when Hana moved in and she made me Korean and Chinese meals.

"Mom didn't like to cook," I said out loud.

"Yeah." Hana laughed and scooped shredded cabbage into the pan. "Min hated it. She didn't have the patience to chop vegetables and measure things. She just wanted the food to be ready when she was hungry."

"Do you think Mom was drawn to Ruby because she'd wanted to be a ballet dancer like Ruby?" Hana had told me about my mom's dreams of being a ballet dancer. But her parents, my grandparents, hadn't thought it was an appropriate career. They wanted her to focus on academics. Dancing was a hobby and my mom had let go of her dreams by high school.

"I think so?" Hana turned to flash me a smile.

"And my grandparents weren't happy about the adoption." Hana had told me that Koreans were weird about adoption. It was a taboo subject, because the importance of bloodlines was deep-rooted and ancient.

"No, they weren't. But Min and Ben had made up their minds. Min had had so many miscarriages and it took such a toll on her, physically and emotionally." Hana started frying the black bean sauce in a separate pan.

My mom and Hana had been born in California where my grandparents had moved from Korea when they were in their twenties. My dad's family had been in the States for generations so weren't as traditionally Korean as my mom's family. I was brought up more American than Korean. I never learned to speak Korean and they rarely spoke it to each other.

"Your parents loved you very much," Hana said. "They were heartbroken at my parents' attitude. You know Min tried to appease my mom by naming you Kim."

I smiled, because Kim had been my grandmother's maiden name.

"I wish I knew them better." My grandparents had moved back to Korea soon after I was born. My mom had gone to Korea to visit them a few times, but my dad and I had always stayed here. I'd only met them twice, once when they came to visit us years ago, and again for my parents' funerals.

"I wish you did too." Hana gave me a sympathetic look before she combined all the elements of the noodle dish together.

Once it was ready, I helped her plate it, still thinking of my family. We sat down to eat. I wasn't sure where Alicia was. But there would be plenty left over if she wanted some later.

"This is so good." I slurped up a long piece of noodle. The black bean sauce was perfect. I'd rather be slightly overweight and be able to eat all the food I loved, than starve myself for the sake of looking "good." Food made life worth it, in my opinion.

We ate in silence, my thoughts still on my parents and Ruby. And then I put my chopsticks down.

"I'm going to reach out to Ruby." I picked up my phone. "Now." I had no idea where the sudden urge came from, but it felt right. I was ready.

Hana's eyes widened, but other than that, she didn't react. "Okay."

"Right now." My hand hovered over my phone, but it didn't do anything.

"Okay," Hana said again.

"Okay." I took a deep breath. Ruby was in my contacts and I pulled it up. "What should I say?"

Hana gave me an encouraging look. "Just tell her you'd like to talk to her."

I nodded. "That's good. I can do that." And I did, typing the words in and hitting Send before I could change my mind.

"Okay." I looked up, my eyes wide. I'd finally reached

out to my birth mother for the first time in my life. And even though I knew she wanted to get to know me, I was suddenly worried. What if she didn't respond? What if my silence had made her upset, and now she didn't want to hear from me? What if I'd texted the wrong number and someone somewhere was right now wondering who this Kimmie person was who said she wanted to talk?

This was a big mistake. What was I thinking? How did I take back a text? I looked at my phone, ready to search Google, but then my text alert dinged. I sucked in a breath and there it was, a reply from Ruby Chen. My birth mother had responded to me.

FIFTEEN

Matt

My father and I were having dinner at a restaurant by his place on the Upper West Side. He still lived alone in the enormous three-bedroom apartment that I'd grown up in. I thought he should sell it, but he'd cut me off the one time I'd brought it up. Just like he cut me off every time I brought up my mother.

"Matthew." He sat back and studied me after saying my name. A dirty martini sat in front of each of us. I reached out and took a big gulp of mine. I needed fortification to deal with him.

"Yes." He'd asked me to join him for dinner and I'd only agreed because I wanted to tell him about my idea for Kim's Etsy shop. I really didn't want to argue with him, but I knew it was inevitable. I tapped my fingers on the table, looking around the restaurant. It was new, not somewhere we'd ever been with my mother, which I was glad about. I took another sip, feeling the liquor warming my throat as it slid down smoothly.

He let out a breath. "I don't know what to say to you."

I gave him a look. "I don't know what to say to you either."

"You can't just throw away all your years of business school. What about our plans for you taking over the business someday?"

"Those were your plans. And things changed when Mom died." I saw the way his mouth tightened.

He looked away and I let out a frustrated grunt. I was sick of the way he avoided all mention of her.

"Why can't we ever talk about her?" My voice rose and I saw the couple at the next table glance in our direction. I lowered my voice. "I miss her every day but you act like she never existed."

His jaw clenched and I saw the way his entire body stiffened. I was breaking a code between us but I suddenly didn't care.

"Why, Dad? I want to talk to you about her. She's gone, but that doesn't mean we have to never mention her again." I put my glass down before I broke it because I was gripping it so hard. "I'm sick of walking on eggshells around you whenever I bring up Mom. Tell me why we can't talk about her."

He looked away and I saw the way his entire face tightened. For a moment, I thought he wasn't going to answer me. That he was going to ignore me and pretend I hadn't spoken. But then with a fierce look, he turned back to me and put his hands on the table.

"We will not talk about her." He said it in a whisper, but I heard every word loud and clear, even in the din of the restaurant. My mother was off-limits as a topic.

Before I could respond, the waiter came up with our appetizers.

"Grilled octopus for you," he said as he put it on the table in front of me, "and the pâté for you."

"Thanks," I managed to murmur, but my father just sat there, staring down at his dish.

Once the waiter left, my father looked at me but didn't say anything. I didn't want to be here. We had nothing to say to each other and I knew we were going to end up arguing again. My appetite fled, when just minutes before, I was looking forward to the food. I'd ordered the octopus because that was the challenge Kim had given me, when she found out I'd never had grilled octopus.

We didn't say anything, only sat in silence as the restaurant buzzed around us. My father finally picked up his fork and started eating. I did the same, cutting a piece of the octopus. It was delicious. Tender and not chewy like I'd imagined, seasoned just right with a smoky char. I took a selfie of myself eating a bite to send to Kim later.

"What're you doing?" My father stared at me.

I put my phone down. "Nothing." I wasn't about to explain my relationship with Kim to him. But now was a good time to mention her shop. "There's something I wanted to run by you. First, I'm not quitting the FDNY."

He shook his head but didn't speak.

"I recently came across an Etsy shop, and the owner and her brand are exactly what Endless is all about. I think we should partner with her to mass-produce some of her more popular items, maybe have her pick out exclusive items that would be carried only at Endless. That way, she can keep her Etsy shop if she wants." I scrolled through my phone and pulled up My Crafty Bao on Etsy. "Plus, her social media has been growing organically, which is in line with the culture at Endless." My father knew social media was inevitable in this day and age, especially for a business, but he hated people who would do anything for attention.

I held my phone out to him, and with a lift of an eyebrow, he took it from me. I watched him scroll through the shop as I cut another bite of the octopus. He nodded to himself every once in a while.

"Click on her social media sites at the bottom of the page so you get an idea of her brand." I pointed to show him.

He did and I watched his face. At first it was passive, but as he scrolled through her posts and watched the videos, a gleam came into his eyes. He nodded to himself again and stroked his chin, something he always did when he was deep in thought. When he finally looked at me, there was a faint smile on his face.

"I'm intrigued," he said. "This young woman is impressive. She's got quite a following and it's not all selfies and attention-getting stunts like so many do these days."

"Exactly. She's the timeless image that Endless is all about, and her products fit right in line." A spark of excitement lit inside me.

"How do you know her?"

"I bought a tote for Nana, and Kim and I started messaging. We're online friends now." I didn't add that I thought we were much more, that I wanted us to be much more despite our distance. I knew most people would tell me to play it cool, not let her know that I was really into her. But what my mother's death had taught me was that you never knew when your life would end. Why play games if you knew what you wanted? There was something about Kim, something that really got to me. We'd never even met, and I'd only known her for just over two weeks, yet I felt like I *knew* her. The chemistry between us was insane, and we'd never even seen each other in person.

"I'm impressed. Have you seen her profit and loss? What are her goals? Would she even want to partner with Endless or does she want to keep her business on Etsy?"

"I haven't talked to her about any of this yet. I wanted to run it by you first." I sat back, satisfied that I'd piqued his interest. Maybe there was a way for me to do some work for Endless without losing myself in the company. I didn't want to go back to the long hours at the office that I used to put in.

"I'd like to see numbers. Also hear what her projected goals are. Any new ideas she's working on, and if she'd be willing to come up with some exclusive designs just for Endless." My father looked at me and for the first time since I'd told him I quit, there was no judgment or disapproval in his eyes.

"I'll talk to her tonight, see if this is something she'd be interested in." I smiled, thinking of talking to Kim.

"And if she is, set up a video conference so I can meet her." He dabbed at his mouth with his napkin.

I nodded. "Got it."

"Where's she located?" My father directed his gaze at me.

"Oklahoma." I put the last bite of the octopus in my mouth, my mood considerably lighter than it had been when we first sat down.

"If she's interested, I'll fly her in for a face-to-face meeting so we can discuss the details." My father looked off into space and I knew he was already envisioning ideas for incorporating Kim's line into Endless.

"I put together some ideas and possible projections for what I was thinking about. Maybe we could develop a stuffed bao in various sizes. People would go crazy for them.

We could give away mini baos for the first orders from Kim's line." I took a sip of my martini. "I'll forward you what I've done when I get home tonight."

My father pointed at me. "This is why you shouldn't have left the company. You're good at your job. You know what's going to trend and be big. For the love of God, please come back to work. What do I have to do?"

I shook my head. "I'm not quitting the FDNY. But I've been thinking." I paused when the waiter came to clear our plates.

Once he'd gone, I said, "What if I helped out on a project-by-project basis, kind of like this one with Kim? Technically, as a probie, I shouldn't be working another job, but once I'm no longer on probation, I can."

My father sat up straight, but I put up a hand before he could say anything.

"No guarantees. We could give it a try, see how it works. The FDNY will be my number one priority. If they need guys, I'm going to go in. This would have to work around my schedule, which, as you know, can change at the last minute." I looked my father in the eyes. "Which also means my time will be flexible. I don't want to be tied to a desk job anymore."

My father studied me without a word.

"And if we try and it doesn't work for you or me, then I want you to be fine with the fact that I'm no longer an employee of Endless."

He stared at me for another long moment. I finished my drink and sat back, waiting for him to speak. I knew he wouldn't until he knew exactly what he wanted to say.

When the waiter had placed our main entrees on our table and left to get us another round of drinks, my father finally spoke. "Fine. I'd rather have some of you than not at all. Let's talk to Kim first and go from there."

I nodded and then turned my attention to the fish I'd ordered. We didn't say any more as we ate, but the air was lighter. The tension that had been between us since my mom died eased somewhat. And I couldn't wait to get home, call Kim with the news, and hear what she thought of a potential collaboration with Endless.

I TEXTED Kim as soon as I got home.

M: *Can you talk?*

K: *Sure. Another exciting Friday night in Oklahoma —ha ha.*

M: *What're you doing?*

K: *Self-care.*

M: *What does that mean?* 😏

K: *You've got a dirty mind.*

M: *Yes, I do. And I like what I'm picturing.*

K: *LOL. Oh, and I texted Ruby. She answered right back!*

M: *No way. What'd she say?*

K: *Wants to talk to me. We're going to FaceTime on Sunday.*

M: *That's great. How do you feel?*

K: *Nervous, but excited.*

M: *So you'll FaceTime with her but not with me? I'm starting to think it's me.*

K: *. . .*

M: *It is me, isn't it?! Oh, Kim, you're breaking my heart.*

K: *Ha ha very funny.*

M: *I have something to tell you.*

K: *Uh-oh. That never ends well.*

M: *No it's good. Can we FaceTime? I want to see your reaction when I tell you.*

K: *. . .*

Those three dots stayed on the phone for a while. Just when I'd decided she really was never going to FaceTime with me, she replied.

K: *Ok. But remember what you said before, that you like me no matter what I look like?*

M: *Yes.*

K: *You still mean it?*

M: *Of course.*

K: *Okay. Just wanted to put that out there and remind you of it once you see me.*

I grinned. I couldn't imagine why she thought I'd have to be reminded that I said that. I really didn't care what she looked like.

M: *Calling you now.*

I went to my FaceTime app and dialed Kim's number. After two rings, she picked up. And when I finally saw her face, I took one look and burst out laughing.

SIXTEEN

MyCraftyBao

Handmade Purses and Accessories
* Star Seller Osage County, OK
1,002 Sales
Contact Shop Owner: Kim

Kimmie

I watched Matt's face go from surprised to collapsing in laughter. I stared at him, absorbing every detail of his face. He was even hotter in person. Those eyes—oh my goodness, I could drown in them, even though they were squinted in laughter. That face—chiseled jawline, a straight nose, and those smoldering eyes. I felt my entire body ignite at the sight of him. His biceps strained against the sleeves of his gray T-shirt and his forearms just begged for me to wrap my hands around them. I could see them because he brought a hand up to his face as he laughed. Holy hell, he was beyond scrumptious. I was heating up like an electric blanket.

"You promised you would still like me no matter what I

looked like." I gave him an injured look. "And now you're laughing at me? How rude."

"Oh my god. I'm sorry." Matt held up a hand. "I was not expecting this. I thought maybe you didn't have makeup on or—what was it you said the other day?—you didn't brush your hair. But this . . ." He pointed to his screen. "This I did not see coming at all."

"You still like me?" I fluttered my eyelashes, angling my head so he could get a good look. I'd just put on a face mask and had my hair wrapped in a shower cap to keep it out of the way. And the face mask was blue. I was essentially a Smurf wearing a shower cap.

"I still like you a lot." Matt gave me a mock leer. "I just wasn't expecting you to be quite so . . . blue."

I realized when he wanted to FaceTime that this was the perfect opportunity to tell him the truth. I'd scare him with my blue face and then ease into letting him know I was Kim. The mask would inject humor, and hopefully he wouldn't be too mad when I explained the misunderstanding.

I snorted. "What did you have to tell me? You said it's not bad, right?"

"It's good. At least I hope you'll think it's good." He paused. "Have you ever heard of Endless?"

"Have I ever heard of Endless?" I scoffed. "Where do you think I live, under a rock? Of course I've heard of Endless." They were only the biggest retail stores aimed at women from millennials all the way to the golden agers. Everyone I knew shopped there because they had the cutest clothing and accessories.

"Oh, good. Well, my father is the CEO."

My eyes flew to Matt's and my mouth dropped open, which was a feat in and of itself given the constraints of the face mask. His father was the CEO of Endless? How had Matt never mentioned that in any of our chats?

"What? Why did you never tell me this?" I stared at him in shock, the mask tightening even more.

Matt shrugged. "It just never came up. I didn't know if you even knew what it is."

"Hello." I looked at him, incredulous. "You know I love designing and making things. Endless carries accessories too, kind of like what I make." A thought suddenly came to me. "Wait. You said you used to work for your father's company. Are you telling me you worked for Endless?" My voice rose.

"Yes. I've worked there for a long time. First as an intern in high school, and then eventually a part-time job until I finished business school and worked full-time." He pushed a hand through his hair and my eyes followed it, turned on even through the shock.

"Wow. Just wow." I closed my eyes for a second. Now I was embarrassed that Matt had bought something from me. My shop must seem so homemade to him, coming from the big retail world like he was.

"That's why I appreciate your shop so much. You make quality products and your designs are beautiful and would appeal to all ages." Matt's face was animated and I couldn't help the sigh that escaped from my lips. "Plus, your brand is very much what Endless is all about."

I grimaced. "You didn't think my products were . . . well, hokey, not professional?"

"Of course not. I would never have bought from you if I thought that." He shook his head. "I showed my father your Etsy shop and your social media platforms and he was as blown away as I was."

My eyes widened. "No. You showed the CEO of Endless my shop."

"Yes." Matt's eyes danced and his smile got bigger. "He loves your products and brand. I told him we should partner with you and potentially carry an exclusive line of yours at Endless."

"No way." Okay, I was dead. Like, my soul had left my body. Matt's father was the CEO of Endless. He liked my products and wanted to partner with me. Was this for real?

"What do you think?" Matt waited for a reply.

I couldn't speak. I was freaking out big-time. While the outer Kimmie sat there calmly looking at Matt with her blue face and striking shower cap, inner Kimmie was running around the room shrieking at the top of her lungs and jumping up and down. I was so elated it felt like I'd just taken flight and was hovering in the air.

What did I do? What did I say? This was everything I'd ever dreamt of. But then reality crashed in and I landed with a thump back on planet Earth. Everyone thought I looked like Alicia. My whole public image was based on her physical appearance. I might be the brains, but Matt's father most likely wanted to partner with me because he thought I looked like Alicia. WHAT WAS I GOING TO DO?

"Hello? Are you okay?" Matt's eyes crinkled in concern.

Meanwhile, I was literally hyperventilating. I had been ready to tell him the truth, but now this was dropped in my lap. Things were getting way too complicated.

"What do you think? If you're interested, I'd need to see a profit and loss statement, go over your financials, get a better idea of your projected growth, how your products are selling . . ." Matt kept talking but I tuned him out.

"Um . . ." What could I say? I mean, this was big-time.

This wasn't some brand that I'd never heard of reaching out, wanting me to showcase their products in my social media posts. This wasn't a boutique like Let Her Rip in the middle of nowhere. This was Endless. Endless! They were huge! Excitement bubbled up in me, waiting to be released like the bubbles in a champagne bottle. Of course I had to say yes. But first I had to tell him who I really was.

Just tell him now. Stop lying to him. It was an honest mistake. He'll understand. But the words refused to leave my mouth. I didn't know how to tell him. Just blurt it out, get it over with, like plunging into a cold pool? But I'd always hated that, being more of a toe-testing-the-water kind of person.

"What do you think, Kim?" Matt asked again.

I finally found my voice. "I'd love to. But listen, I'm not who you think I am." I blurted it out and then my shoulders slumped in relief. There, I'd said it.

"That's great. And I know." Matt laughed. "You're not really a blue person."

"That's not what I mean—" I started to say, but he cut me off in his enthusiasm.

"I'll email you a list of the stuff I need, and just send them to me when you can." His eyes seared into mine and my mind emptied. He looked so hot, with his arms crossed in front of his chest, that I wanted nothing more than to lick those forearms.

I clapped a hand to my cheek, forgetting about the mask. I couldn't control my thoughts. Looking at Matt was like looking at my wildest sex dream come to life. When I coupled that with what he'd just told me, I felt like I was going to explode right then and there.

I nodded as if in a trance. "My best friend, Alicia, has

taken over the financials for me. She's really organized, so I should be able to send them to you by tomorrow morning."

"Perfect." Matt nodded. "I'm really excited about this, Kim."

"Me too, but about what I said, I'm not—" I tried to bring the conversation back to my confession.

"I forgot to ask how things are with Ruby." Matt cut in before I could finish.

"Oh, my, uh, Russian birth mom. She's great. We've texted a few times." My mind was going in a million directions at once and I didn't realize what I'd said out loud until Matt's next words.

"She *is* Russian! That's great. I'm a quarter Russian on my mother's side." Matt looked pleased. "What part of Russia is she from?"

Oh, fuck. What had I done? My brain could not keep up with this conversation.

"Um, the cold part?" *Right. Smart answer, Kimmie.*

Matt laughed, and my insides curled with pleasure at the sound, even though I was beyond flustered and my cheeks warmed with embarrassment.

"You're so funny," he said.

"Right. Ha ha, so funny."

I winced, because I was so not funny. I needed to get off the phone. Stat. I needed to regroup and figure out how this had all gone wrong. I was so flustered that I was afraid of what else was going to come out of my mouth. I realized it was probably best that he didn't understand when I told him I wasn't really me. I needed to think. I didn't want to jeopardize this opportunity when my brain wasn't functioning.

"Listen, I have to go. My face is cracking." I had to get off the phone so that I could wash this mask off and then really run around screaming and jumping up and down. "I'll talk to you tomorrow?"

"Sure. I have a great feeling about this." He gazed at me and I literally melted into a puddle of longing and want. Did he have any idea the effect he was having on me? "My father wants to talk to you and then maybe fly you to NYC for a meeting if everything goes well. I can't wait to meet you in person."

No fucking way. I had to get off the phone before I expired. "Okay. Thanks so much. Bye."

"Bye."

We hung up and I booked it into the bathroom. I had to get this mask off so that I could properly freak out without my face cracking into a million pieces.

SEVENTEEN

Kimmie

Two days later, I was on yet another FaceTime call, this time with Ruby. I'd never been a fan of video calls and now I was really beginning to hate them. I was so stressed-out that hives had broken out all over my body and I was about to meet my birth mother looking like I'd been stung by rabid mosquitoes.

My FaceTime rang with a request and I stared at it, at the 917 area code number from New York. My fingers shaking, I accepted the call.

"Hello?"

"Kimmie? It's Ruby, Ruby Chen."

I swallowed and stared at her. She looked so young. "Hi."

"Hi." She gave a soft laugh. "I'm really nervous."

"Oh, me too." I expelled a big breath and sank back into my desk chair in my sewing room. We were quiet for a moment as we took each other in.

She looked exactly like the pictures she'd posted on her Instagram account. She was in her late forties but easily looked early thirties. Her hair was still long and I could see a hint of myself in the shape of her face and in the nose.

"This is weird, right?" I finally blurted out. "I mean, I'm not calling you weird. You're not weird, it's just weird that we're talking. You know?" *Shut up, Kimmie. Stop saying "weird."*

"I know what you mean. And it is weird." She paused. "I'm glad you agreed to talk to me."

Her hesitant voice made me feel bad. I didn't know what to say.

"I respect your decision not to reach out before." Ruby spoke up before I could find words. "I hadn't wanted to interfere in your life unless you wanted me in it. I kept hoping you'd reach out. And I always said to myself that if you hadn't by the time you were thirty, I would try once. I thought of you every day." Her smile was sad.

"You did?" My voice trembled.

"Yes. I knew I couldn't take care of you at that point in my life and I wanted you to have a stable life. I thought it would be too confusing if I was a constant presence. That's why I told your parents I wouldn't interfere. They knew how to find me if you ever wanted to." Ruby took a breath.

"I'm sorry I haven't done so before." Ruby looked so sad it made me sorry that I'd never thought to reach out to her. I never thought about what she was thinking and feeling. She'd had me when she was younger than I was now.

"Don't be sorry. Your mother Min told me they weren't going to tell you that you were adopted unless anything happened to them." Ruby's eyes gazed at me. "When they passed away, the lawyer reached out to let me know. That's why I sent you those cards for your eighteenth and twenty-first birthdays. I wanted you to know I was here if you needed me."

I let out a breath. "I was glad to get them." When I said that, I realized it was true. I'd kept them in a drawer in my desk. "And to be honest, I wasn't ready to meet you before. It felt like a betrayal to my parents . . ."

"I understand." She smiled, and I couldn't believe this was my birth mother. That she'd carried me in her tiny stomach and given birth to me. The thought suddenly brought tears to my eyes and I blinked to keep them back.

We looked at each other for a few more moments before she spoke again.

"I'm getting married. For the first time." She gave a quick laugh. "It took me this long to find a man I wanted to spend my life with. When I told him about you soon after we met, he could tell how sad I was." She gave a little shrug. "He was the one who said that maybe you were waiting for me to reach out. And what did I have to lose? If you didn't want anything to do with me, then at least I'd know and could stop wishing every day that I could talk to you."

I'd never thought about it from her point of view. She wasn't a part of my life and I'd had no idea she'd even thought about me at all. Now I saw how wrong I was. While I'd been floundering after Hana and then Alicia left Oklahoma, I could have had another person who was connected to me somehow in my life. But I'd chosen to keep her away.

"I'm sorry. I just—"

"Were you angry at me when you found out I gave you up for adoption?" She rushed in. "I mean, I totally understand if you're mad. You must have so many questions."

"I wasn't mad." And that was the truth. I was confused and maybe a bit hurt, but I wasn't angry. "It was more of a shock than anything. Here I thought I was Korean all my life, and turns out I'm not. I'm Taiwanese. At least part Taiwanese?"

"You're actually full Taiwanese. I think."

I sucked in a breath. "What do you mean?"

"The boy I was with, Sean, he was Taiwanese. As far as I know. We met at a Taiwanese party. We hit it off and I ended up going home with him. I'd never done that before, had a one-night stand." She stopped and cleared her throat. "Is this weird? Me telling you that?"

"No. I want to know anything about my . . . birth father."

"I'm sorry I don't have more to tell you. We had a great time, but I never saw him again. There was no expectation on either end. It was just a fun drunken night. I didn't know anything about him." She paused again. "I hope that doesn't make you think less of me."

"No, of course not." If she hadn't had that one-night stand, I wouldn't be here. "I'm glad you did. I mean, not glad it was a one-night stand but that it made me."

"I told your parents all this. We only met a few times. I chose them because even though it was an open adoption, none of us wanted to confuse you by having me in your life. I knew they would be good parents to you. I'm sorry they're no longer with you."

"Thank you." I got up and started pacing around my room. "They were great."

Ruby's eyes roamed over my face, as if trying to memorize every feature. "I knew as soon as I met them that they'd be the perfect parents for my baby."

My baby. She had just called me her baby. "I'm glad you sent that letter. I don't think I'd ever have reached out if you hadn't."

"I'm glad I did too. Can we . . ." She hesitated, her eyes searching my face again. "Can we stay in touch?"

I nodded. "I'd like that." And I realized that was true. I hadn't been sure if I wanted anything to do with her when I got her letter. It had sent me into a tailspin, the result being that viral video when I quit my job. But now that I'd met her, I suddenly craved to know everything about her. Seeing her in the flesh in front of me, I berated myself for not having done this sooner.

"What should I call you? Ruby?" I couldn't call her "Mom" or anything like that. It would be too weird.

"Yes. That would be nice."

I sat back down and relaxed, as Ruby started to tell me about her dancing and life in New York and her fiancé. My heart rate slowed to normal, and I no longer felt like I was trying to impress someone without knowing what would impress them. I was just a woman, getting to know the woman who'd given birth to her. And it felt right.

WHEN I GOT off the call with Ruby, I sat there for a few minutes, absorbing it all. But the quiet of the house was disturbing. Where were Alicia and Hana? They'd both been disappearing a lot. I walked into my bedroom and flopped on the bed. I realized the person I wanted to talk to right now was Matt.

K: *Hey, are you busy?*

He answered right away.

M: *At the firehouse. But I'm free right now. How'd it go?*

He remembered that I was talking to Ruby today.

K: *I talked to her. It was so much better than I expected.*

M: *That's great. I want to hear all about it. Also have good news about Endless. Can you talk?*

K: *Yes.*

A few seconds later, my cell rang.

"Hey."

"Hi." I was suddenly shy. I liked this man. A lot. He'd become someone I talked to every day, even from over a thousand miles away. He was the first person I turned to when something happened to me. He got me, made me laugh, and every time we talked, the chemistry was through the roof and threatened to set us on fire. We'd spent hours talking long into the night. I'd never known a man this well and we hadn't kissed or seen each other in real life.

"Tell me about Ruby."

I put two pillows behind me and leaned back. "She's really nice. It was weird at first, but once we got over that, it felt right." I told him all about Ruby; her apartment in Chelsea, a one-bedroom that she'd bought ten years ago, her mother and her younger sister (I had an aunt and a grandmother! her father had died years ago), her fiancé, Eric, whom she'd known for three years, the ballet company she used to dance for, the yoga classes she taught at a large yoga studio, and her cool life in New York City.

"That's amazing, Kim," Matt said when I finally stopped talking. "Well, you might be meeting her sooner than you think."

"What?" What was he talking about?

"I have to get off soon, but I wanted to let you know my father is really impressed by the paperwork you sent over. He wants to schedule a call with you for this week." Matt's voice vibrated with energy.

"No way." I'd forgotten all about Endless. Well, not

really, but I'd been so focused on the call with Ruby that Endless had gotten pushed to the side.

"Yes. We're both really excited about the prospect of working with you." I heard rustling and the sound of people talking in the background. "Are you free Wednesday morning, around nine your time?"

"Um, yeah." Was this happening? I was going to talk to the CEO of Endless?

"Okay. I'll text you later. I've got to go before one of the senior guys finds me on the phone and makes me scrub the floors with a toothbrush or something."

I laughed with him. He'd been telling me about all the shit he had to take as a probie. "Okay, thanks, Matt. Be sure to clean that grout nicely."

"Funny, Kim." He chuckled and then we said good-bye and hung up.

I couldn't wipe the smile off my face. Every time I talked to him, my mood lifted and my life no longer felt like a disaster. And now I had Endless and Ruby to think about too. Things had definitely improved in my life.

EIGHTEEN

Matt

"How's that lovely young woman of yours?" Nana gave me a cheeky smile over her bagel. We were having breakfast at a coffee shop in my neighborhood since Nana had a doctor's appointment nearby.

I gave her a mock glare. "She's not my young woman. But she's great." I couldn't help the way my lips curved when I thought about Kim.

"I bought some of those double-frame purses from her shop to give as gifts and my friends absolutely adored them." She took a sip of her coffee.

My lips twitched. "I saw the picture you posted." It was of Nana and three of her friends, each holding up a My Crafty Bao double-frame purse, making faces at the camera.

"It's getting serious, then?" Nana cocked an eyebrow at me.

I laughed. "About as serious as something can get when I'm here and she's in Oklahoma." But then my voice sobered. "But it's strange. I've known her for three weeks now, and the only time I've seen her face was when it was blue." I'd told Nana about that and she'd cackled.

Nana narrowed her eyes. "Do you think she has something to hide?" She put her coffee down and picked up her phone.

"I don't know." I peered over at her. "What are you doing?"

"Texting Kim." She didn't look up.

"What do you mean, texting her?" As far as I knew, they only knew each other from Instagram.

"I asked for her cell since I don't check my DMs all the time." She finished tapping on her phone and beamed at me.

"What?" My mouth dropped open. Nana had been texting with Kim?

She picked up her bagel and took a bite, her eyes trained on mine. "You didn't think I was not going to check up on her, seeing as how taken you are with her?"

I snapped my mouth shut. I couldn't believe they'd been texting and neither told me. But then my urge to find out if my grandmother approved got the best of me. "And?"

"She's a real sweetheart. Just like Lily." Nana's eyes were still on mine.

"Wow." I sat back against my chair. That was high praise coming from Nana. "What did you just text her?"

She flashed me a grin. "I asked her why she doesn't like to FaceTime with you."

"Huh." I nodded. Trust Nana to get to the heart of the truth.

She picked up her phone. "She just replied. She says she just doesn't like video calls."

We looked at each other for a moment and then both shrugged. I guessed there were people who didn't like them.

"But you'll finally get to talk to her face-to-face today?" Nana finished her bagel, dabbing at her mouth with her napkin.

I'd told her all about my idea for bringing Kim's shop to Endless, and about the video call my father and I had scheduled with Kim today.

"Yes." I looked at the time on my phone. "I should probably start heading down to Dad's office."

"And I've got to get this spry old butt to my doctor's appointment." Nana shot me a mischievous look.

"You look great, Nana." I knew it was just her annual physical, so I wasn't too worried. But just the same, I added, "Let me know how it goes, okay?"

She gathered her garbage and we stood to put it in the trash bin. "I'm fine. I have no intention of going anywhere yet." We walked outside, where she enveloped me in a hug. "At least not before meeting your young woman."

And with a kiss on my cheek, she strode down the sidewalk in her high-heeled boots. Yes, my eighty-three-year-old grandma still wore heels. And she looked damn good in them.

I CAUGHT the subway downtown and got out at the Fifty-First Street stop, then walked a few blocks west to my father's office building. We had a ten-o'clock call scheduled with Kim and I couldn't wait for my father to meet her. I hadn't told him I had feelings for her. I wanted to keep this meeting professional.

When I got off the elevator on my father's floor, the receptionist, Sarah, looked up with a smile. She'd been working for my father for as long as I could remember. She'd always brought me cookies and other homemade baked goods when I worked here.

"Matt! So great to see you." She stood up and gave me a hug. "You coming back to work?"

I laughed and hugged her back. "Nope. Just meeting with my father. Maybe help him out with a new product line."

"Darn. We miss your handsome face around here." She sat back down as the phone rang. Answering the call, she pointed down the hall, indicating that my father was in his office.

I waved to her and made my way back, calling out greetings to the people I knew and smiling at the new ones I didn't. My father's office was at the end of the hall and I could see that his door was partly open. He saw me coming and stood up behind his desk.

"You're right on time. Good to have you back." He didn't hug me like Sarah had. We weren't a hugging kind of family. Well, my mom had been when she was alive.

"Nice to be back." And I meant it. Just because I no longer wanted to work here didn't mean that I didn't miss some aspects of it. I'd been good at my job. I just hadn't wanted to do it full-time.

"Let's use the conference room. It will be easier." He gestured down the hall and I followed him into the room. I pulled my laptop out of my bag as my father settled at the large table, sifting through the printout of the financials that Kim had sent over.

I sat next to him and pulled up the FaceTime app. "Ready?" I couldn't wait to see Kim again. And this time, hopefully her face wasn't blue.

He nodded and I put the call through. Kim picked up after a few rings, and at first, we could only see the side of her face as she gasped. Then the phone tilted and everything went black. My father and I both peered at my computer screen.

"You have Wi-Fi on that thing?" My father pointed to my laptop.

"Of course." I moved my finger around on the mouse pad, but nothing happened.

Then the screen came back in focus, but we could only see a ceiling.

"Hi, sorry, sorry, I'm having trouble with my screen for some reason," Kim's voice said, but we couldn't see her.

"No worries. Hi, Kim," I said. "I'm here with my father, Robert West."

"So good to meet you, Mr. West." Suddenly, the screen blurred and a thump came from her end. "Oh, no, sorry, I dropped my phone. Hang on. So sorry." She sounded really flustered and I wondered if she was okay.

My father turned to me and raised an eyebrow. I shrugged, just as the FaceTime call disconnected.

"Hm." That was all my father said, but he had to be wondering what was going on. I was too.

My phone rang. Digging my cell out of my pocket, I saw it was Kim.

"Hi, Kim." I put it on speaker so that my father could hear.

"I'm so sorry about that. Something's wrong with my phone screen. Is it okay if we just meet on a regular call?" She sounded calmer. "I apologize for my first impression, Mr. West. I'm not usually that klutzy, well, maybe I am, but I'm usually more poised." She gave a little laugh. "But I'm here now, and it's a pleasure to meet you."

"It's a pleasure to meet you too." My father gave me another look before focusing on the phone. "I'm very impressed by what you've done, Kim." He spoke for a few moments, praising her products and designs and the image she was projecting for her brand.

I sat back and let them get acquainted, glad that Kim seemed to have recovered her composure. I listened to them talk, and while I was focused on the conversation, a part of my mind wondered what was going on with Kim. Why did she seem so averse to having a video chat with me? Was she hiding something? I didn't believe that there was something wrong with her phone at all.

When my father turned to me, I jolted out of my thoughts. I could tell by the way his mouth turned up and the relaxed expression on his face that he was impressed with Kim. "Matt came up with an idea how to launch you at Endless if we decide to collaborate."

I took over the conversation. "What if we took the bao from your logo and make stuffed bao toys? We would make them in different sizes. We could give the smaller ones away to launch the opening of your line and sell the bigger ones. It would really tie into your brand, and who wouldn't want a stuffed bao?"

I had planned on showing her prototypes of other stuffed toys we'd had made to go along with a line, but now that we weren't on a video call, I guessed I'd just have to email them to her.

Kim squealed. "What a great idea. A stuffed bao. I love it."

"How did you come up with the idea to use 'bao' in your shop name?" my father asked.

"Actually, from my father. We all love baos and they're hard to find where we live. He drew the bao that I use as my logo."

"A personal connection. Even better." My father

nodded in satisfaction. "And the fact your father drew that is a great tie-in to your brand."

"I love the eyes and mouth he drew," I put in. "People are going to go crazy for these stuffed baos. We could even have a whole line of home décor, like towels, blankets, and hooded towels for kids with the bao on them."

"And T-shirts," Kim supplied.

My father and I exchanged a look. I could tell he was excited. Kim was just what Endless was all about.

"Kim, I think your brand will fit in at Endless perfectly. We'd love to collaborate with you. I assume you'll want to keep your Etsy shop and continue handmaking items?" My father was getting down to business.

"Um, I guess?" She sounded unsure.

"What my father is saying is that we're not asking you to give up your Etsy shop. We can decide together which products we want to carry at Endless, and those would become exclusive to the company, but under your brand. Whatever else you want to keep producing on your own will be yours." I wished I could see her face right now. I wanted to reassure her that Endless wasn't going to come in and swoop over her shop.

"Oh, okay." Kim's voice was stronger now.

My father leaned closer to the phone. "I'd like to fly you to Manhattan soon so that we can discuss and also see your products in person. If you're interested, that is?"

A clatter came from the phone and both my father and I drew back. There was a series of thumps before Kim came back on the line.

"Sorry. This darn phone keeps slipping out of my hands." She gave a laugh and my father and I exchanged another a look. "I'm sorry I'm so nervous. This is all unbelievable. I can't believe I'm talking to the CEO of Endless." And she gave a little shriek.

My father chuckled, which surprised me. He usually didn't have much of a sense of humor. "That is so refreshing, Kim. In this day and age, the young people are so full of themselves, thinking they deserve everything and trying to grab attention on social media. That's what's so appealing about your brand. You didn't do anything outrageous to gain attention. Your reach has grown organically because you're being yourself. It's truly refreshing."

"Oh." Kim hesitated and I knew she was at a loss for words. Then she said, "Thank you."

"I know it's short notice, but do you think you can come to New York next week?" my father asked.

"Um, yes. I work for myself, so no need to ask for time off." The laugh she gave this time had a tinge of hysteria. I knew her well enough to know that she was freaking out. "But, um, can my friend Alicia come too? She's the financial brains behind the shop, the one who put those numbers together for you."

"Yes, of course. I'll get both of your full names from Matt and have my assistant, Tina, get in touch with you about booking tickets and hotel." My father clasped his hands in front of him. "I look forward to meeting you both."

"Thank you, Mr. West. I look forward to meeting you too." Kim's voice was really high-pitched.

"Call me Robert."

"Thanks, Robert. And you too, Matt."

"I'll call you later, Kim," I said. "Bye."

When I hung up, I found my father staring at me.

"How well do you know Kim?" he asked.

"Pretty well." I stared back at him.

He gave me a look. "You interested?"

I shrugged. "Maybe."

"And you've never met her in person."

"No." That was all I said, and we sat there in silence for a few seconds before he stood up.

"Okay, well, if you need me to get you into a restaurant or tickets for a show when she's here, let me know." And he winked at me.

My mouth dropped open. My father did not usually joke around with me.

"Good seeing you, Matt. I think you're onto something here." He laid a hand on my arm and then walked out of the conference room.

With a shake of my head, I put my laptop back in my bag and slung it over my shoulder. Kim was coming to New York. We would finally meet in person. The thought had a smile spreading over my face but also made me nervous. I hadn't felt like this about anyone in a long time. Whatever this was between us, it was different from any of my past relationships. I felt different. But why was she acting so weird about showing me her face when I already knew what she looked like?

NINETEEN

Kimmie

I was literally drenched in sweat by the time I got off the phone with Matt and his father. My heart was racing, my palms were damp, and I couldn't slow the thoughts in my mind. There was so much going on that it couldn't decide what to focus on.

Endless wanted to partner with me! They were flying me to New York! I'd almost outed myself by picking up the FaceTime call! I'd thought it was a voice call meeting, not a video call! The CEO of Endless liked my brand! I'd thought it was going to be a voice call! *They must think I'm an idiot! I'm going to New York! OMG!*

Around and around my thoughts circled. I was so hyped-up that I couldn't stay still. I popped off the chair and walked into my bathroom to throw cold water on my face. As I dabbed it with a towel, I peered at myself. What would Matt think when he finally laid eyes on me? Would he be disappointed I wasn't Alicia? Would he care? How had we gotten to this point and he *still* didn't know what I really looked like? I'd never really cared about my looks. I wasn't like Alicia, who knew how to apply makeup expertly. She was always dressed nicely, hair done, makeup on.

I let out a moan. I was so, so excited about going to New York and working with Endless. I literally died inside of happiness when they mentioned the stuffed bao. How cute was that? It was my wildest dreams come true. And the fact that they were going to make a toy based on my dad's drawing for me, well, that was just more than my poor heart could take.

Walking back to my room, I got on the bed, needing to lie down. How I wished my dad could be here to see his drawing come to life. It was just one more thing that my parents would never get to see. We'd all loved baos so much. Knowing I was adopted, it made sense. At the time, though, I'd thought it was strange that one of their favorite foods was bao, a Chinese food, and not something Korean.

The last time we'd gone to Oklahoma City for dim sum, a month or so before they'd died, I'd devoured an entire serving of baos stuffed with pork and vegetables by myself, making my dad laugh.

"I'm so glad you love food, Kimmie," he'd said.

And that night, when we were home from our all-day trip to Oklahoma City, he'd pulled out his sketch pad and drawn me a bao, complete with eyes and mouth. He tore it out of the pad and handed it to me and I'd put it away in a desk drawer. I'd forgotten about until after they'd passed away. When Hana had encouraged me to open an Etsy shop, I knew right away I was going to name my shop after the bao, and use my dad's drawing as the logo.

My mind went back to the problems I was facing. What would Matt think when he found out that I wasn't the model-thin, gorgeous creature that Alicia was? My last boyfriend, Andrew, the one I'd met in college, had loved my body. I wasn't unhealthy at all, since I liked to do exercise videos at home and take long walks. But I was definitely not skinny. I just had extra meat on my bones, which was one of the things Andrew had loved about me. But he'd moved to California for work after we graduated from college. We'd tried the long-distance thing for two years, but the relationship had eventually petered out because he wasn't moving back to Oklahoma and I wasn't interested in moving to California.

My stomach growled, interrupting my frenetic thoughts, reminding me it was almost lunchtime. Where was Hana? For someone who'd come back because she was worried about me, she hadn't been around much lately. I got up and went downstairs, grabbing my purse from the living room and then putting on my shoes. I knew Alicia was working at the diner and decided to have lunch there and tell her we were going to New York. Next week. I knew she would be as psyched as I was.

"OH, HELL NO." Alicia threw me a look as she walked away from where I was sitting at the counter. The diner was crowded, and since I was by myself, I had taken one of the stools.

"Wait, Alicia. Come back. This is Endless. Do you not understand?" I called after her, but she didn't turn around. She headed to a table and whipped out her order pad, writing down their orders.

Okay, that had not gone as I planned. I was certain she would be ecstatic. We'd have so much fun together. If I had her with me, I knew I'd finally get rid of my fear of leaving

Oklahoma. I *needed* her. Plus, this was Endless we were talking about!

When she walked past me again on her way to put in the order, I touched her arm. "Alicia, I thought you wanted to go back to New York. We'd be going together. And it's Endless. Don't you get how big this is?"

"It is amazing, but they think I'm you." Alicia put her hands on her hips. "Or you're me. Whatever. Unless you told them the truth?"

I winced. "No. I've tried to tell Matt a few times but something always happened."

"So how can we possibly go to New York when they don't know who Kim really is? Plus, from everything you've told me, Matt really likes you. But he thinks you look like me. What am I supposed to do when he tries to kiss me, thinking he's kissing Kim? You also can't start a business relationship with a company like Endless with a lie."

"I know." I moaned and buried my face in my hands. "What am I going to do?"

"Alicia! Order up!" someone from the kitchen yelled, and she turned away.

"I'll be right back." Alicia walked behind the counter to the window at the kitchen to pick up the order.

I dropped my hands and took a bite of my burger. But I had lost my appetite. I'd ordered the mushroom Swiss burger, which I usually inhaled in a few bites, it was that good. But now I couldn't eat, since butterflies had taken over my stomach. What was I going to do? This was an opportunity I'd never even dreamed was possible. And I'd finally get to meet the man I'd been falling for these past few weeks. I shouldn't have let things get this far. But I hadn't known they were going to get this far. And now I was stuck.

"Hi, Kimmie," a young voice said.

I looked up at and saw the teenage daughter of the owners of the diner. "Violet. You got so tall."

She blushed. "Yeah. The girls make fun of me about it."

"What?" My face screwed up in indignation. "That's stupid. It's good to be tall."

She shrugged and looked down, and I could see that she was upset. I used to babysit her sometimes, when she was younger. She was a junior in high school now.

"Is everything okay?" I looked at her in concern.

"My best friend won't talk to me anymore. I have no friends." She traced a circle on the counter in front of her.

"Violet. I know how brutal high school is. But it'll get better, I promise."

She didn't look like she believed me. "I hate high school."

"I did too." I reached out and touched her lightly on the arm.

Alicia walked by just then and I called out to her. "Alicia, help me. I don't know what to do." She'd always been better with men and relationships than me. And as much as I hated to admit it, I was hoping my best friend would somehow fix this mess that I'd gotten myself into.

Alicia stopped in front of us, her arms laden with plates of burgers, meat loaf, and a salad. "You know what you have to do."

My chin wobbled and to my shame I realized I was about to cry. Ever since my parents died, Alicia and Aunt Hana hated it when I cried. It made them sad. But I couldn't help it. The thought of losing this opportunity and Matt made the tears fall.

Violet shot me a worried look and then disappeared into the kitchen.

"Oh, no. Don't cry, Kimmie." Alicia's voice changed, softening when she saw the tears. "I'll be right back. Let me just deliver these plates." She rushed off to deposit the food.

I took a shuddering breath, telling myself to stop it, stop using tears to get to Alicia. But I couldn't. The more I thought about the mess I'd gotten myself into, the harder I cried, dabbing my eyes with my napkin while the man sitting next to me pretended it was normal for someone to be sobbing into their burger. By the time Alicia came back to me, I knew my eyes were red and my cheeks puffy.

I turned away from her, not wanting her to see my face.

"Kimmie." Alicia touched me on the shoulder. "We'll figure this out together." She gave my shoulder a squeeze before letting go.

"Alicia!" The manager called out from behind the cash register. "Table 6 needs you."

Alicia nodded at him and then turned to me. "I gotta go. But when I get off, we'll talk it out, okay?"

I nodded. "Thanks."

She left with a worried smile and I sat there on my stool, my untouched burger in front of me. I couldn't eat. Because how was I going to get out of this complicated mess without losing Matt or the opportunity at Endless?

LATER THAT NIGHT, both Hana and Alicia were finally home. Hana had gone to Oklahoma City and come home with pho and banh mi sandwiches from our favorite Vietnamese restaurant and bakery there. Over bowls of chicken pho for me and the brisket noodle soups for Hana and Alicia, I told them about the opportunity with Endless.

"Kimmie, that's amazing." Hana cut one of the

barbecue pork banh mi sandwiches in half so we could share it. She handed me a piece. "Why don't you look more excited?"

Alicia and I exchanged a look. I was still ashamed that I'd cried in front of her.

"Kimmie?" Hana was waiting for an answer.

"Because Matt still thinks I look like Alicia." I looked down at my bowl and used my chopsticks to pick up rice noodles along with bean sprouts and a piece of chicken. I popped it into my mouth before looking up to check my aunt's reaction.

"You never told him the truth?" Hana's forehead was wrinkled. "I thought you were going to."

I looked at her imploringly. "I did try to tell him. But one time I looked hideous and another he thought I was talking about my blue face. We keep getting sidetracked and now it's gotten out of hand. I don't know what to do."

I dropped my gaze and picked up the piece of sandwich and took a bite. Heaven. The pork was perfectly cooked and the pickled daikons and carrots were the perfect complement to the marinated pork. Why couldn't I just drown in food and not have to face reality?

"What blue face?" Hana's face was scrunched in concern. "And you have to tell them the truth."

"I know. I've tried so many times." I frowned. "I like him so much. It was supposed to be just a flirtation, something fun. It didn't matter what he thought I really looked like since we were never supposed to meet in person. And now . . . I don't want to just text him a picture and be like, surprise! I want to see his reaction when I finally tell him."

"Maybe it'd be better to tell him in person as soon as we get there?" Alicia put a spoonful of soup in her mouth.

My eyes widened and I turned to her. "You're going with me?"

"Yes. I'll go with you and tell Matt. If he sees us together, it might make it easier to explain the misunderstanding to him. That you hadn't meant to mislead him or anyone." Alicia's lips curved. "And you're right. It would be great to see Manhattan with you."

I jumped up and wrapped my arms around her. "Thank you, thank you." With her by my side, I was sure I wouldn't have a panic attack at the airport. And I could face Matt and tell him the truth.

Alicia hugged me back but then shrugged out of my embrace so she could keep eating.

Then I had a thought. "But what if we tell him and they get mad and don't want to collaborate with us anymore? And we went there for no reason? I should just tell him now."

Hana nodded at me. "You know what I think."

I made a face. Yes, honesty was usually the best policy, but honesty had never gotten itself in a mess like this. I blew out a breath. "Fine, I'm going to tell him right now." I put my chopsticks down and picked up my phone.

I called Matt, putting the phone on speaker so Alicia and Hana could hear. I was hoping they would give me courage.

"Kim!" Matt sounded happy to hear from me. We'd see how long that lasted after I dropped my bomb.

"Matt, I have to tell you something. I'm not who you think I am." I got right to the point.

"Kim, I know. It's fine. I told you, I don't care what you look like." There was laughter in his voice.

"No, that's not what I meant. I mean, those pictures on Instagram, they're not me—"

BE-BONG

A loud alarm sounded and scared me so much I dropped the phone. By the time I picked it up again, Matt was saying, "We got a call. I've got to go. I'll call you back later."

And then he was gone.

"See?" I pointed to my phone. "This happens every time I try to tell him. He either doesn't believe me or something happens before I can finish telling him. It's like the universe doesn't want me to tell him the truth!"

Alicia and Hana looked at each other and then at me.

"I still think you should just wait until we get there. When he sees you and hears your voice, he'll know the truth." Alicia pointed between us. "Our voices sound nothing alike and he's been talking with you enough to know."

I sighed and Hana reached out to stroke my hair. "Everything will work out."

I played with my phone. "I should email Robert's assistant and tell her we're both coming." Tina, the assistant, had called me earlier to confirm our names. She'd said to email her, no matter the time, and she'd take care of the plane tickets and hotel reservation. It was already Wednesday night and Robert wanted us to meet with them next Tuesday morning, which meant we would have to fly in on Monday.

"You know, I need to meet with my publishing team. I think I'm going to go too. I can show you two around, be there to support you." Hana tipped her head to the side. I knew she was thinking about the panic attack I'd had the last time I tried to go to New York.

I looked up from my phone, my heart full. "That would be amazing." I didn't say out loud that under my excitement was also terror. I'd never flown in a plane as an adult. I'd have to leave Oklahoma, something I hadn't done since my parents died. But if Alicia and Hana were with me, I knew I could do it. And somehow, I would finally tell Matt what I really looked like.

TWENTY

Instagram Post

3,134 likes

mycraftybaokim You don't have to look like everyone else. For me, living in the middle of nowhere, the desire to conform and be like everyone else is so real. I didn't want to stick out and bring attention to my otherness. Tonight, on the eve of my first trip to New York City ever (eek!), I realize I am still hiding the true me, the real Kim. There's something I have to do there, and confess to you all, something I'm afraid to do. But I know I have to be true to me, to finally let what's inside show to the outside.

In a way, I'm like these double-frame coin purses. From the outside, it's just a coin purse. But then you open it and there's a coin purse inside the coin purse. How clever is that? You can sort your items easily: bills in one pocket, coins in another, and cards in the third. Or get the bigger one and it'll fit your phone too. And with the wristlet strap I attached, you can just dangle it from your wrist, freeing up your hands. Just like these double-frame purses, there's more to me than what you see on the outside.

Be your own brand. Find something that says you and just do you. Find what makes you happy and just own it. I need to take my own advice—ha. That's what I'm going to do in New York. Wish me luck!

Be daring, be bold, be you.

xo, Kim

VIEW all 75 comments

iammichaelag I love cute T-shirts with sayings! My favorite is "I'm sorry. Did I roll my eyes out loud?"

gretchenbanks33 LOL. That is so me! And can't wait to hear what you have to confess! • •

brenda549y But I like name brands. My mom has always told me that name brands make better quality clothes. That anything else is too cheap and not worth the money. So, what do I do?

melissafoster You are such a role model.

stevenpatrick Just bought the double frame purse with the yellow flowers because they make me feel good!

matte194nyc Sliding in to say you nailed it, as always.

ambersmalley8 Ugh. Who are you? Why does anyone care about you?

melissafoster (in response to ambersmalley8) Who are *you*? Obviously, you're just as taken by Kim since you keep showing up here so don't try to pretend you don't love her too.

leahknowsbest: Yeah! What Melissa said.

dancermilayang You're really killing it, Kim. I'm in NYC—I'd love to meet you!

mycraftybaokim (in response to dancermilayang) I'll DM you!

everlovingclothes We DMed you yesterday because we'd love to partner with you. You are sending the exact message we want to send. We hope you will work with us!

TWENTY-ONE

Matt

"So, you're finally going to meet your future wife?" Jason grinned at me from where he was manning the grill on his back deck.

I took a swig from my beer bottle, shooting him a dirty look. "Shut up, wiseass." But I had to bite back a smile. "And yeah, we're finally going to see each other in real life."

I couldn't believe I'd be meeting Kim tomorrow. She was flying in with her aunt and Alicia and had asked to meet with me as soon as they got to the hotel. She said she had to tell me something important.

"The one in Oklahoma?" Mandy sat at the table on their deck, bouncing Ollie on her lap. It was unseasonably warm for late October and I'd taken the train out to Connecticut for lunch.

"Yes." I turned to Mandy. "She gets in tomorrow." I wondered what Kim had to tell me. She'd sounded nervous and worried the last time we'd spoken.

"He's a goner," Jason called out to his wife. "Just look at him."

They both turned to me and my cheeks heated. I couldn't stop thinking about Kim. I was sure it was all over my face. Jason knew me too well and Mandy and Jason had been together since college, so she knew me pretty well too.

"Stop teasing him, Jason." Mandy gave me a sympathetic look. "I've never seen you like this though, Matt. Not even with Melanie."

Melanie and I had spent a lot of time with Jason and Mandy. They'd liked her well enough but hadn't ever really taken to her. Jason had told me once that Melanie was a bit fake—too well put together, always with her makeup on. I'd asked Jason when we first started dating if Melanie was good people. He'd never answered me.

Now I shook my head. "This feels different. Which is weird since I've never even met Kim in person. We might not connect in real life."

"From what Jason has said about you two, I don't think you have to worry about that." Ollie smacked his mother in the face right then with the toy truck in his hand. "Ow. Ollie, that hurt." The truck got tangled in Mandy's long red hair as she pulled away.

I put my beer bottle down and walked over to them, taking Ollie out of Mandy's arms. She shot me a grateful look as she rubbed her forehead, which was already starting to turn red.

"No smacking your mama, Ollie," I said as I bounced him up and down. He gave a gurgle and waved the truck dangerously close to my face. I ducked. "You are a menace."

"You look good with a baby." Mandy was watching us, her eyes twinkling. "Thinking of having one of your own?"

I flushed again. My mind couldn't help jumping to Kim, and if she wanted children. I shook my head. I was getting *way* ahead of myself. "In the future, yeah. If whoever I end up with wants them."

Mandy gave me a knowing look as Jason hooted. "Someone is already thinking marriage and babies." He flipped the sausages on the grill and I flipped him the bird.

I addressed Ollie, staring into his big brown eyes. "Your daddy thinks he's so funny. I hope when you get older, you can put him in his place." Ollie chortled and reached out a chubby hand, grabbing my nose. "Ouch." I winced as his nails dug into my face. "You have some sharp nails, little man."

"Sorry," Mandy called out. "I hate cutting his nails. I always feel like I'm going to hurt him and he squirms so much."

"See, these are the things that I'm not ready to handle yet. I don't even think I could feed a baby, let alone have to cut his nails." I turned back to Ollie. "No offense, but as cute as you are, if you started crying right now, I'd be very happy to hand you right back to your mama."

"That's because he's not your son." Jason pointed at me with the spatula. "Just you wait, when you have your own children. You won't ever want to let them out of your sight." He made faces at Ollie, who laughed again.

"What a happy baby." Ollie grabbed at my face again, but this time I was quick enough to pull away.

"Lunch is almost ready," Jason said. "Babe, can you get some plates?"

Mandy stood and went inside, coming back out a minute later with the plates. As Jason took the sausages, chicken, and corn off the grill, I walked Ollie to the sliding doors.

"Let's get you inside." I bounced him and he shrieked, grabbing on to my hair. "Ow, that's some grip you've got."

Mandy laughed as she came inside after me, carrying my beer. "You have no idea. I've got so many bruises and scratches from him." She reached over and took Ollie from me. "Let's get you into your high chair so I can eat in peace."

I headed for the fridge. "I'll get the pasta salad I made."

She nodded at me. "Thanks. Some woman is going to be very lucky to snag you."

I flashed her a smile. I'd put together a pasta salad I'd gotten from the Pioneer Woman and brought it with me, along with a six-pack of Kona Longboard.

Jason came in with the plates of food and set them on the table. "I still can't believe you're cooking. I guess that's one thing you can thank the FDNY for."

"Yeah." I rolled my eyes. "I'm also great at cleaning toilets."

"I bet Kim will appreciate that." He opened the fridge. "Want another one?"

"Thanks." I drained my bottle and put it by the sink, then went to sit down, glad to be with my friends. I couldn't stop thinking about what Kim had to tell me, and it was making me anxious in a way I rarely was. Something was going on, something related to her aversion to FaceTime.

I'd been working a lot the last few days so that I could be freer while she was in New York. We hadn't had time to talk much and had mostly texted the last few days. I had to work in the morning, but the plan was for me to meet them at their hotel in Midtown as soon as I got off work tomorrow night. And then I'd finally see her in person and find out what was going on.

Kimmie

I took a deep breath outside of Let Her Rip. Blowing it out, I pushed the door open, walking into the store for the first time in a month. It was a Sunday and the store was crowded, as I'd known it would be. That's why I'd decided to come today to finally pick up my last paycheck. I cursed the fact that Rip hadn't caught up to the times yet and still paid us by check instead of direct deposit.

Was it too much to hope that Rip wouldn't be here today? I hadn't seen or heard from him since that video went viral a month ago. I was hoping to grab my check and slip out without any fanfare, but the minute I walked in, people turned in my direction. I heard a buzz running through the crowd and then someone yelled out, "It's her. It's Let Her Rip!"

"Oh, no." My eyes opened wide in panic as people starting closing in on me, calling out greetings, asking for autographs, and someone even asked me to dance. This was a bad idea. A *very* bad idea.

I turned to run out of the store, but there were people behind me too. I was literally surrounded as the crowd began to chant, "Let Her Rip! Let Her Rip!"

Oh. My. God. A roomful of people chanting for me to let her rip, just fart. Right here. Now. Just as I was ready to die of humiliation, a loud voice called above the din, "Everyone, give her room. Let her breathe, will ya?"

The crowd parted and Rip stood there, smiling at me. I could literally feel everyone holding their collective breath, as people glanced back and forth between me and Rip.

"Kimmie. It's good to see you." I couldn't believe Rip was actually smiling. At me.

"Hi, Rip. I, um . . . just came to get my paycheck." My cheeks heated; I was unused to having so many eyes on me.

Why were they staring? Why weren't they minding their own business?

"I'm glad you finally came in. I've been wanting to thank you." He walked to me. The people closest to us practically had their ears pressed against us. "I didn't realize what an asshole I was until you called me out on it. I've realized the error of my ways and have made strides to improve myself. Isn't that right?" He looked around, catching the eyes of his employees, who all nodded. He turned back to me. "And it's all thanks to you. Sure, I was hopping mad when it first happened, but my wife made me realize you did me a favor. So, thank you."

He held out his hand and I stared at it.

The crowd studied me, and with no choice, I reached out and shook his hand. Everyone burst into applause and then people finally started shopping again. I let out a sigh of relief.

"Come on. Let's get your paycheck." Rip turned and I followed him back to the counter, where Hallie was ringing people up.

"Hi, Kimmie," she said. "So good to see you." She handed the customer the bag after she put the receipt in it. "Thank you and come again." She beamed a smile at me. She'd texted to thank me when the video went viral, and I was glad she looked more confident now.

"Everything good?" I asked her.

She glanced at Rip, who was flipping through the envelopes looking for mine, and then back at me with a nod.

Rip finally found my envelope and handed it to me. "Hey, let's have Hallie take a picture of us together. I want to post it on social media."

"No!" I practically shouted. I did *not* want more media

exposure for Let Her Rip. Me, not the store. "Sorry, I'm, uh, not camera ready today."

Rip looked disappointed but let it go. "I meant what I said. Thank you for all the attention you brought to my store. I had no idea people were laughing about the name. In my mind, it was a reference to racing, but people told me it brought to mind farting." He shook his head. "Who would have thought, right?"

I gave a weak laugh, eyeing the door.

"I'm going to change the name. We've been brainstorming." He leaned a hip against the counter. "What do you think of 'Rip Roaring Trunk'? Kind of a play on 'rip-roaring drunk'?" He threw back his head and laughed. "Or how about 'Rip-ped Bodice'?"

My face must have shown my horror because he asked, "Too spicy, that one? My wife thought so too. I also came up with 'Rip Van Wrinkles,' 'The Big Rip,' and 'Rip It Right.' Which one is your favorite?"

"Um." These names. I forced myself not to laugh in his face. I bit my lower lip, trying really hard to pretend like I was contemplating the names. Hallie made crazy eyes at me, which almost made me lose it. "They're all great, Rip. Really. Can't go wrong with any of them."

"Great, great. Glad to get your opinion." He was lost in thought, running over the names in his head. Gone was the mean-spirited, grumpy man I knew. In his place was a much more laid-back Rip, someone I'd rarely seen. Had he really changed this much, all because of that video?

Just then, one of Rip's teenage employees dropped a box, causing a loud bang. Everyone's heads swiveled in that direction, including Rip's. I saw the look of irritation cross his face and the way his mouth tightened. But he quickly blew out a breath and clamped his lips together. For just a second, I saw the old Rip.

"I gotta go. I'm going to New York tomorrow." I couldn't help throwing that out there. Rip knew how much I'd wanted to go to school in New York and become a designer.

"Oh, wonderful. I'm happy for you." He smiled at me, suddenly the new, sunny Rip again.

"Thanks. Good seeing you." And with a wave and a smile at Hallie, I turned and practically ran out of there.

I fast-walked until I was a few stores away, and then slowed my pace. I was glad I no longer worked for Rip. It would be like working for Dr. Jekyll and Mr. Hyde now. I had contemplated never picking up my last paycheck. But I needed the money for my trip to Manhattan. Even though Endless was paying for our airfare and hotel, I wanted to be able to eat out, go shopping, and do all the things in New York that I'd heard about. I'd reached out to Mila Yang, who had been following @mycraftybaokim on Instagram without realizing it was me. She was so surprised when I DMed her, and we were going to try to get together. I couldn't wait to tell her I was Taiwanese like her. She understood when I told her I didn't want anyone to know who I really was.

So much was riding on this trip. I really hoped things worked out with Endless. Because even though my Etsy shop was doing so well, there was no way I could make enough money to support myself in comfort. Handmade meant it took much more time to make than mass-produced. In the long run, unless I had employees and was able to produce at a much faster rate, which defeated the whole purpose of the handmade aspect of Etsy, I'd need to find a job again soon.

As I walked back to my car, random people called out to

me, "Let Her Rip!" I smiled each time, but inside, I was dying of humiliation. This was exactly why I hadn't wanted to associate the meme with my Etsy shop. Why I hadn't wanted Matt to know who I really was. But the time had come. And I could only hope the spark between us wouldn't die and the opportunity with Endless wouldn't come crashing down before it even started.

TWENTY-TWO

MyCraftyBao

    Handmade Purses and Accessories
    * Star Seller Osage County, OK
    1,115 Sales
    Contact Shop Owner: Kim

MY SHOP WILL BE on a temporary break because I'm going to New York City! I will be back on October 26.

If you placed an order before the shop went on vacation, don't worry, you will still get your package in a timely manner. I will be checking my messages, so if you have any questions, please feel free to contact me!

Be bold, be daring, be you.

xo, Kim

Matt

I headed upstairs to get my phone to text Kim that I was almost done. As soon as someone came in to relieve me, I would take a shower and then head to Manhattan to meet Kim and Alicia. In about an hour, I'd see her in real life. It was finally happening. My heart rate picked up and I drummed my fingers against my thighs as I ran up the stairs. I couldn't believe how nervous I was. If Jason saw me now, he'd definitely be busting my balls. But I didn't care. I was about to meet Kim.

Just as I got to my locker in the locker room upstairs, the alarm bells sounded.

BE-BONG

I groaned and dropped my head into my hands.

"No." I was so close to leaving. "Fuck." Now I had to go back downstairs, get my bunker gear on, and go on a run.

The house watchman on right now, Bill, called the location over the intercom. "Everybody goes, first due for a phone alarm fire at 1032 Southern Park Boulevard, cross street Winchester Avenue and Alden. Fire on the second floor."

I cursed again. The address wasn't close to the firehouse. Even if it was a false alarm, it would be at least twenty minutes before we got back here. "Fuck, fuck, fuck." I ran for the stairs.

When I got to the apparatus floor, I jumped into my boots and pulled up my bunker pants. Shrugging on the suspenders, I grabbed my bunker jacket, putting it on as I ran for the engine and jumped on the rig. I went to my seat, where my helmet was hanging on a hook. Once I was seated, I pulled on my hood, and began strapping on my breathing mask. The engine chauffeur—Tom tonight— turned on the lights and pulled out of the firehouse. Once we were on the way, the lieutenant, who was up front with Tom, turned on the alarm and we were off.

As we drove, I finished strapping on my mask and then

made sure all my equipment and gear were on properly, checking and double-checking everything, before putting on my gloves. I was still new enough that the thrill of being on a fire truck hadn't worn off, but I had to make sure everything was on right. It could mean the difference between life and death if we really had a fire.

The other guys talked among themselves, and after a minute, when there wasn't another call from a second source, everyone relaxed a bit.

"Probably a false alarm," Hector said.

"I wish we were going on a real job," Dave said.

Hector hit him over the head. "Never wish for a real fire."

Dave ducked his head and fiddled with the strap of his mask.

I stayed quiet, still checking my equipment. Now that the urgency was gone, my mind went to Kim again. I hoped we'd get back in a reasonable time. If it really was a false alarm, I wouldn't be too late getting into Manhattan.

My left leg jiggled up and down and I put a hand on it to stop it. I couldn't believe how nervous I was. The anticipation of meeting Kim coupled with this run was making my blood pump hard as the adrenaline flowed. My leg jiggled again and I had to laugh at myself. I was acting like a high school boy, taking a girl out for the first time.

"You okay?" Hector asked me.

I nodded and forced my leg to still. "Fine."

When we got to the site, we all jumped off the rig, equipment ready. We were on the lookout for the source of the fire and I scanned the building to see if I could spot smoke. The lights still flashed on the rigs and the radios went off intermittently.

It turned out to be a false alarm. Someone had thought

they'd seen smoke and called it in. We had to wait until the inside team on the truck checked everything to make sure there was no fire anywhere. When they came out to say nothing was going on, the chief asked the dispatcher to call back the caller. There was a lot of waiting around before we got the all clear to head back to quarters.

We jumped back on the rig and I took off my helmet and hood and unbuttoned my jacket. The others did the same and the talk was now on what they were having for dinner. Hopefully, I'd be long gone by the time dinner was served.

"You're off, right?" Dave asked me.

I nodded. "Should be. Hope whoever is relieving me is already at the house."

Dave grinned at me. "Hot date tonight?"

I gave a small smile. "Something like that."

Dave hooted right as we got back to the firehouse. We got off the engine to stop traffic so that the rig could back into the quarters. Just a little while more and then I'd be on my way. As soon as the rig was parked, I walked inside, already shedding my bunker jacket. Taking off the rest of my gear, I left it by the rig since I couldn't put it away until I was relieved. Just when I was thinking about Kim again, Bill, who was still on house watch, called out to me.

"Hey, probie, we just went down a guy. We don't have anyone to relieve you. You have to wait until someone can come in."

"Fuck, man," I muttered under my breath.

"Sorry." Bill shrugged. "You're the junior guy leaving, so you're stuck. They messed up the manpower. We're looking for someone now, but so far, we haven't been able to find anyone."

"Fuck!" I let out a sigh. To Bill, I said, "Keep me posted."

Nothing was going as planned today. I had to call Kim and tell her I would be even later than I already was. I took the stairs two at a time, and once I got to the locker room, I took my phone out of my locker. I sat on the bench and dialed her number.

"Hello?"

Just the sound of her voice calmed the storm brewing inside me but raised my body temperature. "Kim." I paused. "I'm stuck here for a bit longer. We're short guys, and as the probie, I have to be the one to wait. Hopefully someone comes in soon."

She gasped. "Oh, no."

"I'm sorry. I wish I could leave." I scrubbed a hand through my hair. This sucked. It really did. She was in Manhattan already, so close. But I knew this was the life of a firefighter. In emergencies, or when things happened, I had to step up, do the job.

She didn't say anything, but I could hear her breathing on the phone. I knew she was disappointed. I was too.

"I'm sorry," I said again. "I'll get there as soon as I can. Hopefully someone will come in within the hour."

"Okay. I understand. We might go out, then, maybe to Times Square. Let me know when you're out and I'll meet you back at the hotel?"

"Sounds good. Enjoy Manhattan."

"I already am." Her voice got lighter. "I can't believe I'm here. I've wanted to come here since I thought I would apply to FIT."

I smiled to hear the excitement in her voice. "And? What do you think?"

"It's so big, and noisy, and smelly." She laughed. "But I love it."

That laugh. It simultaneously lifted my mood and turned me on. "Have fun. I'll text you as soon as I'm done."

We hung up and I went downstairs to wait for someone to relieve me. An hour later, I was still waiting. Kim had been sending me pictures from around Times Square and I was itching to get into Manhattan. I was hanging around the apparatus floor when Bill poked his head out of the house watch.

"It's not looking good, man. We can't find anyone. I think you might be stuck here for the night." He sent me a sympathetic look.

"No." I stared at him in disbelief. Of all the nights to get stuck on an extra tour. Usually, I didn't mind because I didn't have to be anywhere. But *tonight*—tonight was different. I *needed* to get out of here.

"Sorry." Bill went back into the watch room and my entire body slumped.

This sucked big-time. I let out a grunt of frustration. When I got up this morning, I'd turned on the shower to find that there wasn't any hot water. That should have clued me in that today was not going to be a good day.

I went back up to the locker room so I could call Kim. With all this running up and down the stairs today, I was really getting a workout.

When I told her the bad news, Kim sucked in a breath. "I really need to talk to you." Her voice trembled. "I feel awful and I need to tell you . . ."

"What is it?" A fissure of concern went through me. What did she feel bad about?

"I don't want you to be mad at me. I didn't do it to

deceive you or anyone. It was a misunderstanding and it all just got out of control." It sounded like she was trying not to cry.

"Kim, it's okay, whatever it is. I'm sure I won't be mad at you." I couldn't imagine what it was that she was so worried about.

She took a breath. "I've been lying to you. Not everything you think you know about me is true."

"Okay." What could she have possibly lied about? I leaned forward, resting an elbow on my knee.

"Well, first of all, everyone calls me Kimmie. No one calls me Kim."

"Kimmie." I liked it. It suited her, the woman I pictured in my head. Which still didn't jibe with the pictures from her social media. "I can call you Kimmie. I like it." A loud roar of laughter came from downstairs and I knew I had to get down there soon.

"Oh, Matt. I wanted to tell you in person. Those pictures on my Instagram aren't—"

BE-BONG

The alarm sounded, and even though I should be used to it by now, I jumped. I'd been so engrossed with what Kim, or Kimmie, was saying that I'd forgotten for a moment that I was at the firehouse.

"I'm so sorry. I have to go. Hold that thought. I'll try to call you when I get back, okay?" I was already up and moving, a déjà vu of this exact scene just over an hour ago.

We said good-bye and I hung up, running back downstairs. This was going to be a busy night. I could feel it. Some nights were like this, nonstop calls, jumping in and out of our bunker gear. And other nights were quieter, but here in the South Bronx, we tended to see more activity than some firehouses in Manhattan. I usually loved all the activity. But tonight, my mind was on Kim. I couldn't stop thinking about what she needed to tell me and why she sounded so sad. But I had to put that aside and focus. I couldn't get distracted when we were on a run.

TWENTY-THREE

Kimmie

"Why is this happening to me?" I moaned into the pillow.

"Yeah, this is weird." Alicia stood next to my bed. Hana had gotten a room in the same hotel, but she was on another floor.

It was our first night in New York City and Hana had taken us to Times Square. Alicia and I had gawked at all the lights and buildings and the Broadway shows. Mila had met up with us since she lived close by in Hell's Kitchen.

She'd given me a big hug when she saw me. "I had no idea My Crafty Bao is your shop. I love it."

"Thanks for keeping our secret." I'd told her why we were in Manhattan. She didn't know Alicia, since Alicia hadn't gone to our school and didn't live in town.

"You two will crush it at the meeting tomorrow." Mila looked back and forth between me and Alicia. "And if you do work with Endless, I'll show you around New York City whenever you're here."

"Thanks." I was surprised by how much fun I'd had

with Mila tonight. Maybe I should have given her more of a chance back in high school. When she hugged me good-bye, I'd asked her, "Are you okay? You don't look good."

I wasn't trying to be rude, but Mila looked really tired and had dark circles under her eyes. She'd sighed and said, "I'm just down these days. I haven't gotten a part lately even with all the auditions I've been going on. I love to dance, but I hate the cattle calls and the backstabbing in the dance world." She'd waved a hand in the air. "But it's fine!"

I'd made a note to talk to Mila more. Alicia and I were now back in our hotel room. We should have met Matt by now and he should have known who I really was. But the universe seemed hell-bent on keeping the truth from him.

"Why can't I just tell him already?" I said. "What's going on?" My face was still buried in my pillow so my voice came out muffled.

Alicia sat on my bed and leaned over to wrap an arm around me. "It's going to be okay. I feel it. Everything will be out tomorrow and it'll be fine."

I turned to look at her. "How do you know? I have this bad feeling in my stomach, like everything's about to blow up in my face. Matt, Endless, New York."

Alicia stared at me and then pulled me up by the hand. "You are not going to stay here and wallow on your first night in New York City. We're going to go down and have a drink at the hotel bar and pretend we're sophisticated New Yorkers. And celebrate the fact that you finally left Oklahoma after all these years."

I smiled, a burst of pride going off in my chest. I'd been a champ at the airport and on the flight, no panic attack at all. It'd been easy with Alicia and Hana at my side. "Yeah. That sounds nice."

"Text Hana and tell her to meet us downstairs." Alicia went into the bathroom to touch up her makeup.

I didn't know how she had the energy to always be working on her makeup. I barely wore any and couldn't be bothered to reapply once it was on. But she'd always cared about how she looked more than me. As long as my hair wasn't sticking up and I didn't have hives on my face, I really didn't care.

Once the two of us were seated at a table in the hotel bar with drinks in front of us, I lifted my cosmopolitan for a toast. Hana had decided to go to bed since she had an eight-o'clock breakfast meeting with her editor tomorrow.

"Cheers to finally being in New York, and to you for coming with me and holding my hand at the airport."

We clinked glasses and I took a sip of my first cosmo. It was good. No wonder the women from *Sex and the City* liked it so much. It was pink and pretty and went down smoothly. Suddenly, I was excited again that I was actually here. I'd seen Times Square. No matter what happened tomorrow, I had this to hold on to. I'd left Oklahoma without having a panic attack, and to be honest, I don't know why I hadn't left earlier. It had all been in my head, the fear of leaving home. Nothing bad had happened and I was finally in the city I'd dreamed about since junior year of high school. Mom and Dad would have been so happy for me.

My phone dinged and I looked down.

"Is that Matt?" Alicia said, squinting at my phone.

"Yes." I opened his message. "Looks like he's going to be there until tomorrow morning." My bottom lip stuck out, even though I'd known this was most likely what was going to happen. I'd held out hope that someone would come in and he could have met us late.

"Shit." Alicia scrunched up her nose.

"When am I ever going to tell him the truth? I wanted him to know before we went into the meeting." I took a big gulp of my drink. I needed to slow down. The last thing I needed was a hangover tomorrow.

"Maybe you can see him before the meeting with his father?" Alicia put her drink down on the table. "What time does he get out of the firehouse?"

"It depends on when someone comes in to relieve him. But our meeting isn't until ten, so maybe that could work." I sent off a text to Matt, asking if this was possible.

He replied right away.

M: *That sounds good. There's a coffeeshop in the lobby of my father's building. Want to meet there at nine thirty?*

K: *Ok, yes. That works.*

M: *I'm so sorry again about tonight. I can't wait to see you tomorrow.*

K: *No worries. It's not your fault you have to work.*

M: *See you soon, Kimmie.*

My breath caught when he called me that. I'd tried to tell him the truth. At least he knew me as Kimmie now.

I looked up to see Alicia watching me.

"We're going to meet him at nine thirty tomorrow. That okay with you?"

She nodded. "Of course. I can't wait until everything is out in the open." She took a sip of her drink.

"Me too!"

Alicia's text alert sounded and she looked at her phone. A smile crept over her face as she texted back.

"What?" I asked. "Who is it?" I knew my best friend well enough to know that it wasn't her parents who had sent that message.

She smirked at me. "Just this guy . . ." She took another sip of her drink, looking at me from the side of her eye.

"What? You're seeing someone?" I knew that look.

"Maybe."

"Stop. Where did you meet him? Definitely not in Oklahoma since you said you didn't want to end up with a cowboy." I narrowed my eyes at her.

Alicia pursed her lips and tilted her head. "I knew you wouldn't approve."

My eyes widened as I took that in. Why wouldn't I approve? "I've never been judgmental of you. Have I?"

"No, I just meant . . ." Alicia stopped, and I could have sworn she blushed. But she never got embarrassed.

"What? Tell me." My hands stilled on my martini glass.

"Well, his name is Todd. And he's . . ." She stopped again and bit her bottom lip.

What? Why was she having such a hard time telling me? I thought we could tell each other everything.

When she didn't go on, I said, "What? He's into kinky sex? He only eats meat and no vegetables so he never poops? What?"

Alicia laughed, breaking some of her tension. "No! Kimmie, you're so gross."

"We live in cattle country. I bet a lot of cowboys don't eat anything but meat. Can you imagine? How do they get their poop out without veggies or fruit to move things along?"

"Kimmie, stop!" Alicia put up her hands as if to shield herself from me.

"Well, then, what is it?"

"He is a cowboy. But he eats veggies." She pulled her bottom lip into her mouth and looked at me, waiting for my reaction.

"Oh." *That's* why she didn't want to tell me. She'd always told me that she didn't want to end up like her mom, the wife of a cowboy, living in the middle of nowhere and always smelling like cow manure.

"It's nothing serious." Alicia turned her big eyes on me.

I held up my hands. "Hey, I'm not judging here. I have nothing against the cowboy lifestyle." I never understood why she hated it. It didn't seem so bad to me. But then again, I lived in town, not on a ranch at least twenty minutes from the nearest town.

"No, I mean, it's really not serious. He came into the diner three weeks ago, the first day I started working there again." She wrinkled her nose. "He asked me out. I said no, since I knew he was a cowboy. He came back every day for a week and finally wore me down. I like him, physically. His body is smoking." She pretended to fan herself. "But there's nothing there besides that."

I nodded at her. "Okay, if you're both just having fun . . ."

She picked up her drink, taking a sip. "I've made it very clear to him that it wasn't going anywhere beyond the physical."

"Then I'm glad you have someone to spend time with. And take care of your needs." I tried to elbow her in the side but almost knocked over my martini glass in the process.

Alicia looked at me from under her lashes. "Oh, he definitely takes care of my needs." And we burst out laughing.

We finished our drinks as we talked about all the things we wanted to see in our short, three-day trip. I was supposed to have lunch with Matt tomorrow and dinner with Ruby. My stomach knotted just thinking about Matt. I prayed that after I told him the truth, he'd still want to take me out. And that his father wasn't going to be too mad.

With a sigh, I drained the last drop of the delicious cosmo. Just one more sleep and then I could finally come clean and hope that my world wasn't about to blow up again.

TWENTY-FOUR

Matt

I got to the coffee shop early the next day. The guys leaving this morning had taken pity on me when I said I had an important meeting. After a lot of ball breaking, they'd let me leave first. Nothing was going to keep me from finally meeting Kim.

I found a table and carried the coffees over to it. Kim had texted that they were a few minutes away and I'd told them I would get the coffees. Too nervous to sit, I hovered next to the table, tapping a foot on the floor. My eyes roamed over each person who walked in, disappointment setting in every time it wasn't her.

When I finally spotted her, my breath hitched. She was even more gorgeous in person. Taller than I expected too. She was with an Asian woman, who I assumed was Alicia. They hadn't seen me yet. My eyes jumped over to Alicia when she let out a laugh, and for a second, my heart leaped, recognizing that musical sound. Alicia was shorter than Kim and had a fuller figure. And her face—wow, there was something I recognized about her. If I hadn't known what

Kim looked like, I would have thought that *this* was Kim. Because she looked exactly how I would have pictured her; cute, down-to-earth, with an expressive face that caught my attention right away.

And then I wondered why Alicia's laugh was so familiar when it was Kim whose laugh I should have recognized. Before I could work it out, the two of them spotted me and Kim waved. Alicia hung back, staring at me with wide eyes. I walked up to them.

"Kimmie." I headed straight for her, taking her hands and staring at her, guilt over finding her friend attractive making me focus more on Kim. "I can't believe we finally meet in person."

"Um, Matt." Kim tugged her hands out of mine. "I'm not . . ."

Alicia walked forward just then and said, "I'm Kimmie."

I did a double take and turned to look at Alicia. "What?"

The Asian woman took another step closer to me. "I'm Kimmie." She pointed at the woman I thought was Kim. "That's my best friend, Alicia."

My mouth dropped open and my mind went blank. The Asian woman continued. "I'm so sorry. It was all a misunderstanding. I didn't think people were going to think that Alicia was me when I had her pose with some of my merchandise. And then that stupid viral video was still going around and I was horrified. I didn't want anyone to know that was me."

As she spoke, understanding dawned on me and I studied her. I knew this voice. This was Kim, whom I'd been talking to on the phone every day. That was why I recognized her laugh. I'd listened to it every day for the past month, sometimes while we were already in bed, and I wasn't ashamed to admit I'd had more than one sexual fantasy about her. *This* woman was Kim. Not the one whose face I recognized. And my first thought was one of relief. And my second thought was, *What the fuck is going on?*

"Matt." Kimmie's eyes widened with alarm. "Say something. I'm so, so, sorry. I tried to tell you a few times but you misunderstood or something would happen like the fire alarm. We thought it would be easier to tell you in person."

I finally snapped out of my stupor. "Let's sit down. I got us a table." I gestured behind me, and with another anxious glance at me, Kimmie pulled out a chair, with Alicia following.

Once we were seated, I looked back and forth between the two of them. "I'm . . . I don't know what to say . . ." It was rare for me to be at a loss for words, but I was blown away right now. Kim was not who I thought she was.

Alicia held up a hand. "Let me just say something, and then I'm going to leave the two of you to talk." She flashed a look at her friend. "It was honestly a misunderstanding. And then because of that viral video, Kimmie didn't want anyone to know who she is." Alicia shook her head. "Anyways, it was all just a big mess and we're really sorry but please don't be mad at Kimmie. She really likes you . . ."

Kimmie hit Alicia on the arm.

"Anyways, I'll let you two talk . . ." Alicia started to stand up, but I held up a hand.

"Wait. Can you just back up and tell me what happened? And what video?" My mind was still trying to reconcile that the woman I'd been talking to, whom I'd been falling for, didn't look the way I thought she did. That she'd lied by omission.

Alicia sat back down and turned to Kimmie, reaching out to give Kimmie's arm a squeeze.

Kimmie took a deep breath and the whole story came out. I sipped my coffee as I listened, watching her face as the voice I knew so well told me what happened. And as she spoke, something happened. I recognized the way her eyes rounded when she was anxious, the way her lips twisted when she was saying something hard, and the way her hands fluttered around her face to emphasize her point. This was how I'd envisioned her when we'd talked on the phone. I remembered thinking that I had a hard time putting Alicia's face to the voice and now I knew why. It was because Alicia wasn't the one I'd formed a connection with.

Kimmie's voice petered out and she stared at me anxiously. And I realized I wasn't angry. It sounded like a series of misunderstandings that kept building, and she had tried to tell me the truth a few times.

"We're going to tell your father today. I don't want to start off a professional relationship on a lie." Kimmie's hands twisted together on the table. "And I totally understand if he no longer wants to work with me." She lowered her eyes to the table. "And if you don't want anything to do with me either, now that you know what I really look like."

"I'm not mad," I said, because I wanted her to know that. "But I don't understand what video you're talking about and why you didn't want me to know who you really are."

"You don't recognize me?" Kimmie's voice rose in surprise.

I shook my head as I wracked my brains. She did look vaguely familiar, but I wasn't sure if it was just because I knew her voice so well by now.

They exchanged a look and then Alicia stood up. "I'm just going to step outside and let you two talk."

She picked up her coffee cup and was about to turn away when we all heard a voice calling out, "Matt."

I looked up to see my father walking toward us. I stood, and Kimmie did too. "Dad."

My father's glance went to Alicia and then he stopped in front of her, holding out a hand. "You must be Kim. So nice to meet you. Robert West."

Alicia shook his hand, shifting from one foot to the other. "Um, nice to meet you too." She threw a desperate look at Kimmie.

"And you are Alicia?" My father walked over to Kimmie and shook her hand. She didn't say anything, only smiled weakly at him. "I'm glad you're here early. Let me grab a coffee and then we can go up together." He nodded at me and then turned to get on line.

I looked after him. Of all the days for him to get his own coffee. I needed to talk to the women before meeting with my father.

"Well, that was awkward," Kimmie said. "We need to tell him as soon as we get upstairs."

"So awkward." Alicia took a gulp of her latte. "I almost peed my pants when he came up to me."

I turned to Kimmie. "Why did you think I would recognize you? What video are you talking about?" I studied her face. She was really cute, with dark hair just past her shoulders and a full figure. And she had a great butt. Wait, was I allowed to think that? I was still confused over which woman I had been falling for.

Alicia leaned toward me and whispered, "She's Let Her Rip."

At first, that didn't make any sense, and I stared at

Alicia blankly. But then I remembered the video Frank had been so obsessed with at the firehouse. Something about a woman dancing and telling her boss off. I remembered thinking the woman could really dance. I turned to Kimmie, and as the realization that that was Kimmie dawned, my mouth dropped open a second time this morning.

"You're the girl who twerked in that video? The one that went viral?" Holy shit. I remembered feeling sorry for the woman when I saw parts of the video. Now I understood why Kimmie hadn't wanted anyone, including me, to know who she really was. I would have died of embarrassment if that had happened to me. And knowing Kimmie as well as I did from the hours we'd spent on the phone, I knew she hated the spotlight.

"Yeah." Kimmie's voice was defeated. "That was me. I lost my shit on my boss and one of my co-workers recorded it. She didn't mean for it to go viral. It was only just supposed to be for people who knew our boss. But some YouTube star saw it and shared it and . . ." She broke off, shaking her head. "I didn't want to connect that meme to my Etsy shop. It has nothing to do with my products. So when people assumed Alicia was me, I let them because it wasn't hurting anything. But then I met you. And I didn't know what to do."

She looked at me, her dark eyes worried, biting her lower lip. This was the woman I'd been thinking about nonstop. The one I had really strong feelings for. And now it all made sense why she hadn't wanted anyone to know the truth. Before I could reassure her that I understood, my father gestured to us.

"I'm ready." With one last look at each other, the two women walked toward my father as I took up the rear and we headed to the elevator.

Sarah greeted us, and after introductions were made, we followed my father to the conference room. There was a moment of awkwardness as we shuffled around, trying to figure out where to sit. But we finally settled on Kimmie and Alicia on one side of the conference table and my father and me across from them. As soon as we were seated, Kimmie cleared her voice.

"Mr. West . . ." she started.

"Please. Call me Robert." My father smiled at her.

"Oh, okay." She glanced at me out of the corner of her eyes. "Robert." She cleared her throat again. "There's something we need to tell you." She looked over at Alicia, who gave her a slight nod.

My brain had been processing everything they told me in the coffee shop, but now my head snapped up when I realized that Kimmie was about to tell my father the truth. And with a sickening sense of dread, I knew she couldn't. Not until we had a chance to talk things out.

Because Endless was all about that throwback era before reality shows and before people started doing anything they could to go viral. Endless was about organic growth and being your true self, not pretending to be something you weren't. That Let Her Rip meme was everything my father despised. He would see it as a ploy to get attention, which went against the entire Endless culture. Kimmie had been smart to keep it away from her brand. But now she was about to jeopardize everything by telling the truth.

I jumped up so suddenly my chair tipped over backward with a loud bang. My father gave me a disapproving look.

"Sorry. But yes, Dad. Kimmie—I mean Kim—has some exciting news."

Both Kimmie's and Alicia's heads swiveled my way, confusion on their faces.

"Yes." I nodded at them, trying to telegraph with my eyes for them to stay quiet. "She has, um." *Oh, fuck. What was her exciting news?*

"Yes?" My father was looking at me with that look he always got whenever he knew I'd done something wrong. Knocking over a chair during a meeting was not something I usually did.

"Um." My arms flailed at my sides as my brain scrambled to come up with something. Any news but the truth. And then I said the first thing that popped into my head. "She has decided to move to New York."

Kimmie's mouth dropped open and her forehead crinkled in confusion. Or maybe it was shock. I didn't know. We stared at each other as my mind spun. I hadn't realized it was something I hoped would happen, since I couldn't leave New York and Kimmie had told me she'd always wanted to live here. I hadn't wanted to get ahead of myself, but the way I'd felt whenever I talked to her, I knew I needed to be in the same city as her. But she wasn't who I thought she was. I didn't know what was going to happen, with Kimmie or this Endless venture.

I righted my chair and then collapsed into it, closing my eyes for a brief moment. This meeting was not off to a good start.

TWENTY-FIVE

Kimmie

I stared at Matt, my mouth open in shock. Why had he just told his father I was moving to New York? What did it mean? Had he forgiven me for lying to him? My heart gave a hopeful thump. Did this mean that he wasn't disappointed that I didn't look like Alicia? Could he possibly like me? *Calm down, Kimmie. Him lying to his father does not mean he's about to drop to one knee and propose to you.*

When I'd finally seen him for the first time down in the coffee shop, it was as if everything had stopped. He was the only thing I could see. Matt was standing in the flesh in front of me and he looked even better in real life, dressed in a light blue button-down shirt. And his eyes. Oh, my, his eyes. They were lit up, shining with kindness and so much of what I'd come to know of as Matt, that it was a shock to finally see them in real life. All the conversations we'd had, all the times he'd laughed at my stupid jokes, all the ways we'd connected mentally and emotionally swirled in the air between us.

Our eyes had met for a brief moment, and I swear, there

was a jolt there. As if he recognized me. But then he'd turned to Alicia.

"Well, that is great news." Robert's voice brought me back to the conference room, where silence had reigned for the last few moments. I knew everyone in here was in shock for different reasons. Robert's eyebrows were raised as his eyes shifted between Matt and Alicia. Alicia, whom he still thought was Kim. Because Matt had interrupted me as I was about to tell his father the truth.

Why had he done that? Alicia and I exchanged another confused look. My nerves were shot. This was a thousand times more stressful than I'd imagined. When we'd been in the elevator on the way up here, my stomach had dropped, not only because of how fast it rose to the thirty-seventh floor, but also because of everything I had to tell them today. Before I could collect myself, the elevator doors had opened. We were in an impressive entryway, all glass and modern furnishings in muted colors and a crisp, professional air. A perfectly made-up woman in her fifties with shiny hair wearing a cream silky blouse sat behind the desk. She made me feel like a schoolgirl in the handmade black jersey tunic I was wearing over colorful leggings. She stood to greet us and Matt introduced her as Sarah. I could see the affection she had for Matt in the way she beamed at him.

Robert was talking now, but I couldn't focus. I knew I should be paying attention, but there were too many questions running through my mind. What was going on? How did Matt really feel about me? Why had he cut me off when I'd tried to tell his father the truth? I put my hands on the large conference table, which was bigger than my bed and took up most of the room. I stared at Matt and watched him run a hand through his hair and then steeple his fingers together on the table in front of him. I noticed the way his shirt sleeves were rolled up on his forearms, and I swear, my blood got a little hotter and my face a little redder. I looked at his face, my glance lingering on his lips, wondering what it would be like to kiss him. But all my daydreaming came to a halt when Alicia stepped down hard on my foot.

"Ow." I couldn't help the exclamation. I looked over at Alicia, and she was staring daggers at me, gesturing with her head toward Robert.

"Are you okay, Alicia?" Robert asked.

"I'm fine—" Alicia started to say, but I quickly cut her off.

"Yes, I'm fine," I said really loudly, to drown out Alicia. I gave her a look. "Sorry, what did I miss?"

"My dad was just talking about the bao." Matt gave me a reassuring look and I wished we had had the chance for me to explain more and clear the air.

"We did a test run and found out that Endless customers would love merchandise with the bao on it. I'm envisioning not only the bao stuffed toys, but like you and Matt had suggested before, plush blankets printed with the cartoon bao, shirts, pillows, even key chains and notebooks."

"That's great," Alicia and I said at the same time. I bit my tongue. I'd forgotten I wasn't supposed to be Kim. I was Alicia.

"The entire concept of your logo is also a selling point. It's very personal and would appeal to many because of the human-interest angle. Losing your parents, and then honoring them with the bao your father drew. I like it. I like it." He looked over at Alicia. "I'm glad you didn't grab that image off the internet so we don't have to deal with copyright issues."

Alicia nodded back at him.

"This is what I'm thinking. We introduce your line by

offering a stuffed bao as an incentive, maybe for the first few days of the launch." Robert picked up a remote and clicked on it, and a big white screen came down at the front of the room. He clicked something else and an image appeared on the screen. "This is the prototype we came up with. We can make it in three sizes. Stuffed animals and objects are big right now and I have a feeling these baos will fly off the shelves."

He continued talking, clicking through his presentation, showing us the different products, all featuring the bao that my father had drawn. I stared at that logo enlarged on the screen and felt a lump form in my throat. I wished so badly my dad could be here to see his little bao up there on the big screen. I was so deep in memories that I didn't realize Mr. West had asked a question about our sales numbers.

Before I could react, Alicia spoke up and took Mr. West through a summary of my shop's progress over the last year. As I listened to her, my eyes widened and my mouth dropped open. What? How had I not known my shop had grown so much just in the past month? I mean, I knew we were doing well, but seeing the numbers laid out in front of me, I was shocked by how well we were doing. No wonder the bank account I had opened for my Etsy shop was so healthy. I'd thought it was because I hadn't been spending money lately. Apparently, it was because Alicia had been doing such a good job at keeping our costs down, while our sales had increased.

I stared at Alicia in admiration as she spoke. I mean, I knew she'd helped me crunch numbers and deal with sales tax, which I had no idea about, but she'd done way more than that. She had projection charts, and predicted sales based on what was selling in my store. She had graphs of things about which I had no idea what she was saying. I'd emailed all this to Matt, but I had to admit I hadn't looked at it. Because numbers always made my eyes cross.

As I watched her, so confident, I realized we were a great team. Her number smarts and my creative smarts, her face in social media posts and my ideas for posts and videos—we were great together. She should be getting credit as part of my shop. I'd been using her and it wasn't right.

As she wound down, I looked at Matt and my heart lightened at the warm look he sent my way. Robert asked more questions, and as I answered, I kept sneaking looks at Matt. My hands itched to touch him, my body yearned to be held by him, and my lips wanted to be pressed against his. He was every fantasy I'd ever had brought to life and he was right here in the flesh. When everyone turned to me, my face flushed and I looked in panic at Alicia. I had no idea what had just transpired. She pointed to my roller suitcase.

I jumped up and took out the merchandise to show Robert and Matt. Alicia explained what each one was, which was good, since I couldn't speak. I could only gaze at Matt like a lovestruck school girl, sighing whenever his forearms flexed when he reached for a product.

The other three suddenly stood and I realized the meeting was over. Robert was smiling widely, and Alicia was beaming. I hoped that meant he'd liked the merchandise. The Wests walked around the large table toward us.

"My son tells me he's taking you on a date?" Robert asked Alicia.

"Um . . . no . . ." Alicia looked from Robert to Matt and then to me.

"Dad." Matt shot his father a look, making Robert laugh.

"What, son? I'm glad you're interested in someone." Robert turned to us. "Matt is so picky. He's always had so many women texting him, or whatever it is you all do on those social media apps. But he hasn't had a girlfriend in a while." Robert gestured to Alicia. "It's nice to see him interested in an accomplished young lady like yourself."

"Dad, really?" Matt's face was red, and he glared at his father.

Robert ignored Matt and focused on Alicia. "I'm so impressed by you that I'm going to call in a favor and reserve a table for the two of you at Nobu for dinner." He pulled out his cell. "How does that sound?"

"Amazing." Alicia breathed out the word. Her eyes lit up. Nobu was on her list of places she wanted to go. But then her smile dropped and she turned to me with a worried look. "But no, I'm, um, that is, she . . . I mean me, I'm meeting my birth mother tonight?" She shot me another desperate look.

"Dad, it's fine." Matt jumped in. "I'm taking Kim out for lunch today." There was irritation in his voice, which I understood, even as my heart wondered if he was still taking *me* out for lunch.

Robert ignored him and said, "I'll call it in for tomorrow night, then." He made a quick call as the three of us stood there, looking helplessly at one another. When Robert hung up, he clapped his hands. "Okay, you're all set." He tucked his phone back in his jacket pocket. "Kim, can you stay for a few more minutes? I want you to meet Tara, who's the head of marketing, and see if we can set up a photo shoot for tomorrow. Since you're here, I'd like to get some shots."

"Um . . ." Alicia looked at me. I could clearly hear her cry for help, and I felt like crying too.

Matt saw our exchange and said, "I'll take her down, Dad." He walked up to Alicia, and it looked like he was trying to tell her something with his eyes. I suddenly felt like a pathetic loser. I'd just watched Robert plan a dream date for Matt and Alicia, and now it looked like Matt wanted to be alone with Alicia. I needed to get out of there, to get some air.

"If you don't need me, I have to make a phone call," I mumbled, and then with a thank-you tossed to Robert, I rushed out of the conference room, forgetting about the suitcase full of my merchandise, and headed for the elevator.

I heard Matt call out, but when I looked back, no one had followed me. Blinking back tears, I stabbed the elevator button and, thank goodness, it came right away. I could see Sarah shooting me curious looks while she was on the phone, and I waved right as the doors closed.

I slumped in a corner, willing the elevator to hurry up as more people came on. When it finally got to the ground floor, I rushed out with everyone else and burst out onto the sidewalk, gulping in a big lungful of air. It felt like all my hopes and dreams were literally about to explode right before my eyes. Did Matt like Alicia more than me? Would he rather get to know her, the woman he thought he knew, than me, the one behind the voice? Were they going to go to Nobu together tomorrow night?

And my dreams for Endless seemed on a rocky path too. Robert was enamored with Alicia; anyone could see it. He thought she was not only smart, but also beautiful, just right for his company. She was the whole package. They didn't need me.

I looked around, trying to remember which direction I'd come from. Our hotel was only a few blocks away, and when I finally recognized a building, I took off in that direction, my tears starting to blind me. Someone came up to me, so close they were invading my personal space. I waited for them to go around me but they didn't go away, and I finally looked up.

"I was right! You're Let Her Rip! OMG—I loved your video." The woman standing in front of me was in her twenties and had long curly dark hair. "Can I have your autograph?" She rummaged around in her purse.

"No, that's not me." I backed away from her as I noticed more people pointing at me. "Sorry." And I turned and ran in the direction of the hotel, not waiting for a reply.

Hold it together until you get to the hotel. I clenched my teeth and tried not to feel sorry for myself. I was in New York, and I'd finally made it out of Oklahoma and . . . And what? People recognized me from that damn video, Matt might like Alicia better than me, and I might lose my one chance to make it big-time doing something I loved. And to make matters worse, right as I got to the hotel and was about to go in, a pigeon flew overhead and pooped on my head. I automatically reached a hand up and came away with a mess of goo. Great. Just great. *Welcome to New York fucking City, Kimmie.*

TWENTY-SIX

Matt

I watched Kimmie run out of the room and I wanted to chase after her, but now that I'd told my father I'd take Alicia to meet Tara, I had to follow through. I had wanted Kimmie to come with us so I could explain why I'd cut her off when she was about to tell my father the truth. But she'd taken off and I realized my heart had gone with her.

Once my father left, Alicia turned to me, her eyes worried. "We need to go after Kimmie."

"I'll go. Let me take you to Tara and you two can make a plan for tomorrow." I grabbed the suitcase Kimmie had left behind and followed Alicia to the elevator.

"Why did you stop us from telling your father the truth?" Alicia turned curious eyes on me as we waited for the elevator.

"Because he would hate that video. It represents every-thing he hates about this era. The three of us need to meet and talk about this and decide what to say to him." The elevator came and we got on it. I pressed the button for Tara's floor and turned back to Alicia. "I didn't want him to shoot you guys down before we could figure out what to tell him."

"Oh, no." Alicia looked dismayed.

"I know." The elevator opened and I followed her out. "Listen, can you tell me what your hotel room number is? We need to talk."

"You do." Alicia stared at me hard, her eyes narrowed. "Are you going to hurt her?" She stopped just outside the elevator and crossed her arms over her chest.

I studied her, looking from her expertly applied makeup to her styled hair and killer body, and felt nothing. Only a fondness, as one does for a sister or friend. It was Kimmie, the person I'd been talking to all this time, who had been driving me mad the past few weeks.

"No offense, but when I first saw the two of you, my eyes went right to Kimmie. She was exactly how I'd envisioned her when we spoke. I always had a hard time putting your face to her voice." I lifted a brow at her. "So, no. I have no intention of hurting her." I lifted my chin, meeting her challenge.

She studied me for another moment and then laughed. "I'm glad you weren't attracted to me. Kimmie is really . . . special. To me and to Hana. She likes you. A lot."

"I like her. A lot." My tone matched hers and I didn't break eye contact.

"Okay." She nodded. "We're in room 1207."

I touched her on the shoulder. "Thanks, Alicia. Let's get you to Tara."

FIFTEEN MINUTES LATER, I stood in front of room 1207. I should have texted first. I wasn't even sure if

Kimmie had returned to the hotel or had gone somewhere else. I raised my hand and knocked, hoping she was inside.

I heard a noise and then Kimmie's voice calling through the door, "Did you lose your key?"

She pulled the door open and then stared at me. "What are you doing here?"

I looked at the side of her hair, where something whitish green was streaked through it. "What's that?"

She made a face of disgust. "Bird poop. As if my day couldn't get any worse."

I stifled a smile. "It's supposed to be good luck when a bird poops on your head."

She leaned against the door frame with her arms crossed over her chest. "They only say that to people to make them feel better."

"But it could be true." I gave her a slow smile. "Can I come in? You forgot your suitcase."

She swiped a hand over an eye and nodded, then went back in without another word.

I followed her and put the suitcase by the door. Then I walked to where she sat on the edge of one of the two queen beds. She was looking down so I could only see the top of her head. I waited to see if she'd look at me, and when she didn't, I touched her on the arm.

"Kimmie."

She finally looked up and met my eyes. They were wide and a dark chocolate brown, so expressive that I knew what she was thinking without her having to say a word. She pressed her lips together but didn't look away.

"I'm sorry about what happened back there. I had to stop you from telling my father who you really are." I rubbed a hand along my jawline.

"Is it because you're disappointed that I don't look like Alicia?" Kimmie looked away when she asked that.

"No." I gestured to the spot next to her on the bed. "May I?"

She nodded, sneaking a peek at me.

"I was shocked when you told me that you're Kim. I mean, you can't blame me, right?"

Her mouth quirked up but she didn't say anything.

"But you want to know what was the most shocking to me?" She turned and met my gaze. "All those times we talked on the phone, I could never quite picture you as looking like Alicia. I had this image in my head of what you were like based on our conversations, and they never looked like Alicia." I held up a hand. "Don't get me wrong. Alicia is gorgeous and her picture was the reason why I first DMed you. But it was you I had a connection with, when we started talking. And when I first saw *you*, I was attracted and then immediately felt awful."

Kimmie's expression softened as she looked at me. "Really?"

"I'm not disappointed that you're Kim. Because you're exactly who I think Kim is." And I meant that. I reached out to touch her hand, and after a moment of hesitancy, she slipped hers into mine. I wasn't prepared for the jolt that went through me when our fingers interlaced.

"You pictured me as Asian?" Her fingers fluttered over the back of my hand.

"No." I gave her a smile. "It was more who I thought you were."

"Do you mind that I am?" Her fingers tightened in mine for a second. "I mean, have you ever dated anyone who was Asian?"

"I've been on a date with someone who was Japanese.

But no one serious." I used the hand that wasn't linked with hers to touch her gently on the cheek. "Why?"

She turned and gave me a sunny smile. "I just wanted to make sure you didn't have yellow fever."

I laughed. I had enough Asian friends to know she was referring to men who only like Asian women because they're Asian. "I promised you before that I didn't care what you look like. And I really don't. I recognized your voice and laugh before you told me who you were."

We stared at each other and my heart literally stopped before it started pumping again. Because Kim, Kimmie, the woman who had filled my thoughts and heated up my dreams, was sitting here in front of me.

"I'm so sorry I lied to you. I tried so many times to tell you who I really was but . . ." She squeezed my hand. "I'm glad you're not mad."

"I'm not. It was an impossible situation to be in. But now we have to figure out what to do about my father." I explained about the meme and what my father's reaction to it would be.

She groaned and pulled her hand away, and I immediately missed it. "What are we going to do? We can't start a business relationship on such a big lie." Those expressive eyes trained on my face.

"My father dislikes people who would do anything for attention, like going viral intentionally and angling for fame. You didn't do that. Someone took that video without your knowledge. She put up that video, also without your consent. And then it went viral, against your wishes. I know he'll understand once we explain it to him, but I didn't have time to warn you, so I made up that 'moving to New York' thing." I gave her a half smile. "Sorry about that, by the way. I couldn't think that fast."

She gave me an amused glance. "Can't say it was all a lie. I *wish* I could live here."

"You're everything that Endless believes in. You, not Let Her Rip."

She blew out a breath. "Even if he gets that, there's still the fact that I lied about what I look like. I saw the way he admired Alicia. He thinks she's the whole package, and she is. He doesn't need me."

"Kimmie. You are the one who created the products. You're the one who put up those posts. Alicia may be the face, but the entire brand is you." She shot me a look and I backtracked. "Okay, maybe not the entire brand."

"If your father will still have us, I want to make Alicia an equal partner. She's been integral to the shop's growth." Kimmie tilted her head. "I realized while we were in the meeting that I haven't been fair to her."

"Okay." I nodded and then smiled at her. "Let's go to lunch like we planned. Get to know each other in real life, not think about any of this for now. But we'll figure it out. Okay?"

"Yes." The worry left her eyes and my lips curved to see how her face lit up.

This woman was so fucking beautiful to me. I wanted to touch her, feel her soft skin, feel her lips on mine and her arms around me, but I didn't want to move too fast. My glance went to her hair and my nose crinkled.

"You might want to take a shower first though, and wash that out."

A laugh escaped from her. "What, you don't like the bird-poop look?"

I made a face. "I mean, I did say I didn't care what you look like, but that poop might start to smell after a while."

She laughed out loud, the full belly laugh that made my

cock harden hearing it so close to me. I shifted and stood up. I needed to leave this room.

"I'll wait in the lobby?" I turned toward the door, hoping she didn't notice the bulge in my pants. I didn't want her to think I was a perv.

She nodded. "I won't be long."

"Great." I practically ran for the door. I walked out of the hotel room, every nerve in my body jangling. She was even better than I'd imagined.

TWENTY-SEVEN

Matt

I took Kimmie to a Thai restaurant because she said she wanted food she couldn't get easily in ranch country. We walked east, to a little restaurant I liked that had great food and wasn't pretentious. I was very aware of her presence next to me. She took my hand as we walked and I was glad. Whenever I glanced down, she met my eyes and smiled.

Right before we got to the restaurant, a teenage boy came running up to us. "Hey, you're Let Her Rip, right? I loved that video!"

Kimmie ducked her head. "No, you've got the wrong person."

"No, it's you. I recognize you." The boy was literally hopping around the sidewalk in glee. "Can you dance with me? I want to take a video. My friends will die."

Kimmie turned to me, a desperate look on her face. I stepped in front of her and said, "You've got the wrong person, pal." I tugged her hand and we literally ran away.

We could hear the boy shouting after us in disappointment, but we didn't slow down until we were in front of the restaurant.

Kimmie panted slightly. "That's bad, isn't it? That's the second time today that someone has recognized me."

I winced, because it was bad. If people were recognizing her, then that video really had global reach, which my father was *not* going to like. But I knew we could make him understand.

"It is." I wasn't going to sugarcoat it for her. "But that's why I wanted to talk with you and Alicia first, get the facts straight so we can present it to my father."

We walked in and the hostess showed us to a small table in the back. We sat across from each other and I realized this was the first time we were face-to-face and alone. We both took a breath and let it out at the same time. Her mouth quirked.

"Finally," she said. "I feel like I've been running on adrenaline the past few days."

I nodded. "I can't stop looking at you. To be able to see your expressions when I hear your voice."

She blushed. "I'm glad you weren't disappointed that I'm not gorgeous like Alicia." She slanted me a look. "I'm not putting myself down."

"Beautiful." That was all I said as I took in her face, trying to put her expressions to every conversation we'd had. This was the woman I'd been dreaming of and she was beautiful to me.

Her cheeks grew red again and her eyes roamed my face, as hungrily as mine were taking her in. Needing contact, I reached my hands across the table and she took them in hers. I saw the way her eyes fluttered and the soft gasp that escaped. Her skin was so soft and I rubbed my thumbs up and down the sides of her hands. We were so busy drinking each other in that we didn't even look up when someone placed glasses of ice water on the table.

When we were alone again, she said, "Hi."

"Hi yourself," I said back with a smile.

"This is . . . amazing."

I nodded in agreement and then we finally broke contact to look at the menu.

"Let's do our food challenge together." We'd been texting each other foods to try and it'd been fun. But it was going to be even better to be able to do it in person. "I'll order for you and you order for me."

"Deal," she said. Our eyes met again before we both perused the menu. Neither of us was allergic to anything and both of us were willing to try everything. It was the ideal relationship to me. I couldn't be with someone who was a picky eater. Food was just too damn good.

Once the waiter took our order, I leaned my forearms against the table. "We should talk about what to do."

"Your father." Her tone sobered. "I feel so bad. This is why I didn't want that stupid meme associated with my brand at all. Because it's so not me. I'm not like that in real life."

"I know." I thought for a moment, drumming my fingers on the table as Kimmie took a sip of her water.

"What should we tell him?" Her eyes were anxiously scanning my face.

I thought a bit more, my forehead scrunched in a frown. And then I realized something and a smile came over my face. "With my father, you have to present him with facts, cold, hard data. He doesn't care about sentiments at all." I looked her in the eyes. "To play devil's advocate for a moment—to him, the facts show that a video of you dancing and telling off your boss has made you infamous enough that people in Manhattan are recognizing you on the streets. And then you lied and let everyone think Alicia is you."

Kimmie gasped, one hand flying to her face. "That sounds so awful." Her shoulders slumped.

"But the fact that you did lie and let everyone think Alicia is you is actually a point in our favor." I stopped when she gave me a puzzled look. "If you're the kind of attention-seeking person who craves going viral and fame, you would have linked that meme to your brand. You would have done everything you could to drive traffic to your store and capitalized on that fame, hashtagging all your posts with #letherrip. But you did the exact opposite. Which points to the fact that you are not an attention-seeking millennial intent on achieving fame."

I sat back in satisfaction as the waiter placed our food in front of us. Once he was gone, she gave me a delighted smile. "You're right."

"I just needed time to think it through." I looked down at my plate. "What is this again?"

"Tofu rama." She peered at my dish. "Yum. Is that some sort of peanut sauce?"

I dabbed my fork in the sauce and tasted it. "Yes, it's good." I pushed my plate toward her. "Want to try it?"

She nodded eagerly and used her fork to spear a square of fried tofu and ran it through the peanut sauce. I watched her take a bite, her eyes widening. "It's really good. I've never had it before."

I pointed at her plate. "And that's the drunken noodles." She'd told me she always ordered pad thai whenever she had Thai, and I wanted her to try my favorite, the fresh flat noodles with shrimp, made with Thai basil and chili paste.

My phone dinged and I looked at it. It was from Nana.

Well? was all it said.

I looked up to meet Kimmie's eyes. "It's Nana. She wants to know how our meeting went."

"Oh, no. She's going to hate me when she finds out I lied to you," Kimmie moaned, which distracted me for a moment.

"No, she won't. I'll tell her the story later." I got up and went to her side. "But let's send her a selfie now."

"No!" Kimmie practically shrieked. "She's going to be so shocked that I'm Kimmie."

I snapped the picture and laughed to see the look on Kimmie's face, her mouth open. I sat back down while Kimmie covered her face with her hands.

"Matt. Don't send that."

"Too late." I grinned at her. "Don't worry, Nana has a sense of humor. I told her I was very happy that you turned out to look like this."

My phone dinged again, making Kimmie open her eyes. I read Nana's message and then laughed. "She wants to know what's going on." I texted that I'd call her later, and then went back to my food, ignoring the glare Kimmie was shooting my way.

As we ate, my eyes met Kimmie's from time to time, the chemistry between us sizzling. I was relaxed for the first time in two days. She was finally here, sharing a meal with me. And she was everything I'd been imagining, and more, since the real Kim finally fit the Kim I'd been envisioning.

"What's it like being a hot stud of a fireman?" she teased me, winding a long piece of noodle with her fork.

"You think I'm a hot stud, huh?" I wiggled my eyebrows at her.

"I mean, if the shoe fits . . ." She broke off and giggled.

I needed to bottle her laugh. It was like an elixir, intoxicating and able to set every nerve ending in my body on fire.

I gave an exaggerated sigh. "It's hard work being such a stud, but someone's got to do it."

"So, do girls really throw their underwear at you?"

I had just taken a sip of my water and almost sprayed it all over the table. When I could speak, I said, "What? Where did you get that ridiculous notion?"

She shrugged, her eyes dancing. "I don't know. I just pictured women throwing their underwear up to you all as you ride down the street on your truck without a shirt on and one suspender falling over a bulging biceps . . ." She let out a soft sigh and I stopped breathing. I had never been so turned on so fast, and while sitting in a restaurant.

I shook my head, unable to speak.

"You mean to burst my bubble and tell me that doesn't happen?" Her voice was wistful.

I shook my head. "I mean, yeah, it's been a slow week. Usually, I get dozens of them. Clean ones, dirty too . . ."

"Ew!" Kimmie shrieked, drawing the attention of the other diners and the hostess. She covered her mouth with a hand and shook with silent laughter. "That's gross, Matt," she whispered.

"Hey, you're the one with the perverted mind thinking we get underwear thrown at us as we're just doing our job. You know, it's hard to fight a fire with underwear hanging off our heads but . . ." I smirked at her before reaching across and taking a shrimp off her plate.

She watched me and then said, "I like that we're sharing our food."

"Me too."

"Well, I'm disappointed for you. You deserve to have underwear thrown at you." She gave me an impish look.

"I think I'll survive without it." I leered at her. "Now, if you want to throw your underwear at me, I certainly won't object."

"Matt!" She swatted her napkin at my face and I grinned. I couldn't help it. I always had so much fun with Kim on the phone, and now in person, it was even better. This woman made something light up inside me, as if I was a house overdecorated for Christmas.

"But seriously, our job is not that glamorous. The bunker gear is heavy and hot. We do a lot of grunt work when waiting for a call. Or, I do, as a probie." I gave her a wry look and she laughed. "And believe it or not, we actually keep all our clothes on when on a run."

"You must know though that every woman has daydreamed about a hot fireman wearing only his bunker pants, bare chested, his chiseled abs and broad chest all tanned and smooth, maybe a thumb hooked into his pants, pulling one part down low . . ." She gave a dreamy sigh, propping an elbow on the table.

I snorted. "Really? You want me to dress up for you?"

Her eyes lit up. "Yes. I can't wait to see you without a . . . I mean . . ." She blushed and looked away.

I couldn't help it. My heart literally stopped when she did that. She was so adorable, and that shyness—she was the real deal. This was the real Kim. This was the woman my father needed to see, the woman behind My Crafty Bao.

"Hey, you want to see the firehouse? I can take you after lunch."

She turned to me, her eyes wide. "Yes! I'd love to see a real FDNY firehouse."

"As opposed to a fake one?" I teased her and she pretended to glare at me.

The waiter and busboy cleared off our table, and after I'd paid, we left the restaurant. "Want to take the subway?"

"Really?" Her eyes lit up. She'd told me she wanted to take the subway while here. "But didn't you say you'd never let your grandmother take the subway up to the firehouse?"

"You'll be fine with me." I smiled down at her.

"You do know how sexist that sounds, right?" She glared at me. "I mean, I'm fine with it since I'm chickenshit, so I need you to take me, but also, I don't really *need* you, if you get what I mean."

"I'm not trying to be sexist. It's just a reality. A lone, attractive female by herself in that neighborhood is a target. Me, not so much." I threw up my hands. "I mean, yes, I potentially could be a target also, but they're familiar with my face from the firehouse so the likelihood of someone attacking me is less than with you."

"Okay, big, strong, scary fireman," she teased me. "Take me to the Bronx. I trust you."

Those three little words shook me. She trusted me.

She let out a laugh and grabbed my hand. Every nerve ending in my hand jumped to attention and I felt like I'd been hit with a jolt of electricity. Giving her hand a squeeze, I led her to the subway so I could show her the place that had come to mean so much to me.

TWENTY-EIGHT

Kimmie

Matt held my hand tightly when we got off the subway in the Bronx and walked the few blocks to the firehouse. I looked around and didn't think it looked as bad as Matt had described. It was mostly tall brown rectangular buildings, kind of ugly but completely nondescript, to be honest. I didn't see any drug dealers or prostitutes like he'd told me about. We passed a man walking a beautiful gray pit bull and I started toward the dog, but Matt pulled me back.

"What?" I turned to him. "Pit bulls aren't as dangerous as people think."

"I know." He looked back at the man. "But he's a known drug dealer around here."

"The dog?" I turned to stare after the pit bull.

"No, the man." He gave me a look, his lips twitching.

"Oh. I hope he treats his dog right. As long as he does, I don't care what he does." I looked back again. The dog seemed healthy and happy.

"You love dogs, right?" Matt's question had me turning back to him. I had told him how I thought dogs were better than people and how I'd always wanted one but my dad was allergic and we never had any.

"Yes. I don't know why I never adopted one." I shrugged. Maybe I should. The thought of returning to an empty house once Alicia and Hana left made me sad. I didn't want to be lonely anymore.

"If I could have one right now, I'd adopt a pit bull," Matt said. "I told you about Cleo. She was all white and so sweet, with the biggest head and heart. She was really my mom's dog." He fell silent and I squeezed his hand. He gave me a squeeze back.

"Did you know that was what first attracted me to you?" I shot him a look from under my eyelashes. "It was the way you were with Cleo in your Instagram pictures. Dogs are the best judges of character."

"Really?" Matt drawled, raising his eyebrows at me. "So it was my dog that drew your attention? I mean, she was the sweetest dog. Wouldn't hurt a fly. My mom loved her so much."

"Yes." I was about to say more, but we had turned a corner and suddenly the firehouse was in front of us. All brick with giant arched windows on the top floor and an American flag flying, the building rose in front of us. It had two giant car doors, one for the engine and the other for the ladder. Matt had told me he was with the engine.

"Here it is." He smiled at me. "Ready?"

I nodded as we walked up to one of the closed garage doors. It was then that I noticed a normal door carved into the apparatus door. Matt punched in a combination and then opened it and held it for me. I walked into what I knew was the apparatus floor. The engine stood before me, majestic and as red as I'd pictured, and the smell of diesel fuel hit my nose. This was where Matt had talked to me from so many times. I looked around, wanting to capture everything, at the same time remembering our conversations when he'd told me he was standing here.

A tall man with sandy hair sprinkled with silver appeared from behind the engine. "Hi, Matt." He looked from our linked hands up to my face and smiled at me.

"Hey, Tom. This is Kimmie. She's visiting from Oklahoma."

Tom gave me a salute. "Nice to meet you." He turned a questioning look to Matt. "Girlfriend?"

Matt smiled down at me, raising his eyebrows. "Kind of."

Tom cocked his head. "A kind-of girlfriend?"

"Yes," I said. Because it was true. We'd never defined what was going on between us, especially because I'd been uncomfortable that he didn't know what I really looked like. But right now, I was more than happy for him to be my kind-of boyfriend.

"I'm going to give her a tour." Matt gestured with a hand.

Tom nodded and walked into what Matt told me was the house watch.

"I can only show you around the first floor, basically the kitchen, apparatus floor, our bunker lockers, and the house watch." Matt gestured above us. "I'm not supposed to take you upstairs."

"Okay."

We headed to the doorway at the end of the apparatus room. As we walked through, I realized we were in the kitchen. There were a few guys in there and Matt introduced me as I took in the room. It wasn't fancy, but I could picture Matt over there by the stove cooking. I beamed up at him, trying to take in every detail so that I could envision it in my mind when I was back in Oklahoma talking to him on the phone.

The men asked me some questions, all friendly and respectful but poking fun at Matt. I saw what Matt meant when he told me about the camaraderie among the men.

"Want to see my bunker gear?" he asked me. When I nodded eagerly, he took me to his locker. "Here, try this on." He pulled out his bunker jacket with his last name on the back.

I held out an arm and he slipped the jacket on me. And I almost collapsed. It was *heavy*. Much heavier than I'd thought. "How do you wear this and run around in it?" I pretended to collapse.

Matt laughed, putting his helmet on my head, which slipped down and basically covered my eyes. "Between the bunker gear and our equipment, we basically have about a hundred pounds on us."

I peered out from under the helmet. "I don't think I can move, even just with the jacket on."

"Don't move."

"What?" What was he doing? And seriously, I couldn't have moved even if I wanted to. How the heck did they run into burning buildings with this weight on them?

"Here, look." His cell phone appeared in my line of vision and I saw he'd taken a picture of me with the gear on. I looked like a little girl playing dress-up.

I shoved the helmet up so I could see him. "I look so funny."

"You look hot." He took the helmet off my head and put it back in his locker.

The look he gave me made my knees weak, and I would have fallen over if he hadn't reached out to steady me. And then all I was aware of was the heat emanating from his body. I looked at his lips and I swear, if he didn't kiss me now, I was going to self-destruct.

He leaned in, a question in his eyes. We could hear the guys talking elsewhere, but right now, I could only see him. My breath caught as I nodded.

And finally, his lips were on mine, softly at first, and then he deepened the pressure and I was lost. My eyes closed and I relaxed against him as I kissed him back. It didn't last very long, but when we pulled apart and stared at each other, I could see it had affected him as much as it had me. His eyes were hooded and the look he gave me made my heart thunder even louder. I was screaming inside. This beautiful, incredible man had kissed me.

"Kim." His forehead rested against mine.

"Can you take this off before I collapse?" I was starting to sweat in this thing. I had a whole new respect for fire-fighters.

He burst out in laughter and gave me a quick kiss on the lips. "You never cease to amuse me." He took the jacket off me and hung it back in his locker.

"Sorry." I gave a sheepish shrug. Here he was, being all romantic, and all I could think of was that the jacket was going to kill me.

"Want to go on the rig?" He closed his locker.

"We can?" I looked back at the apparatus floor.

"Sure." He led me to the engine, pointing to the door in the middle. "This is where we sit when we're on a run."

"What's back there?" I pointed to the end of the engine.

"That's the hose bed. Want to see it?"

I arched an eyebrow at him. "Hose bed, huh?" Without my permission, my eyes dropped to his crotch and he sniggered.

"Yeah. Hoses are *very* important. We firefighters need

to know how to handle our hoses." He gave me a searing look and then turned to walk to the back of the rig.

"I bet you're really good with your hose." I followed him, keeping a straight face.

"I am," he drawled, and I suddenly envisioned throwing him down on that hose bed and checking out his, um, hose.

The step to get up was really high and Matt had to give me a shove from behind. On my ass. I turned around, a mock frown on my face.

He gave me an innocent look. "Just helping you up like a gentleman."

We stared at each other and his look shot straight to my center. I quickly turned and stepped into the hose bed. I felt so tall up here. Matt came up behind me and I turned to him.

"This is where you catch all that underwear thrown at you?" I waggled my eyebrows.

"Of course." He pretended to brush himself on the shoulder. "I don't like to brag, but I get way more underwear thrown at me than the other guys."

"I'm sure." I looked him up and down. "I mean, look at you."

He suddenly looked shy and blushed. "I'm just kidding."

"I'm not." Did the guy not know how appealing he was? Easy on the eyes, but also the most generous heart, who got me in a way few people did. He'd wakened something inside me and I was wondering how I'd gone so long without sex. I wanted to run my hands over his chest, down to his hard abs. I wanted to wrap my hands around his forearms and rub my face against his biceps.

He must have sensed my thoughts because his eyes darkened and smoldered. The smolderest eyes I had ever seen. We stared at each other again and I swear, the air between us crackled. But then a loud voice jolted us out of our trance.

"Hey, probie! I hear you brought a girl to the house. Gonna introduce me?"

Matt's head turned toward the voice with surprising speed and I could see the scowl on his face. "Yes, Frank. Try to be civilized, okay? There's a lady present." He gave me a look before jumping off the rig. I followed him.

He caught me as I jumped off and we paused for a moment, his arms around me, my chest against him. My breath hitched. He smelled so good, clean soap and his own unique masculine scent. I wanted to bury my nose in his neck.

A burly guy walked over to us. Matt pulled away and addressed him. "Frank, this is Kimmie. Kimmie, Frank."

Oh. I recognized the name. Matt had told me how much shit Frank gave him. I sized him up with my eyes. Okay, so he was huge, tall, and wide, but I'd take him if he insulted Matt in any way in front of me.

"Nice to meet you, Kimmie." Frank reached out an enormous paw, and after hesitating a beat, I shook his hand. My own hand disappeared in his grasp.

Before I could speak, Frank's eyes widened and he studied me closely. "Wait, I know you. You're Let Her Rip!" His entire face lit up, and I swear, he looked like a little boy on Christmas morning. "I'm a huge fan. Huge. What're you doing here?"

Beside me, I felt Matt stiffen and I glanced at him.

"Kimmie doesn't like to be associated with that meme," Matt said.

I turned to Frank. "He's right, I really don't. In fact, I hate that video and I wish it would disappear."

"But you looked so good. The way you dance. Man. I can't believe Let Her Rip is standing in front of me." Frank shook his head, his gaze on me. Something close to adoration, as if he really was a big fan, shone from his face. Really?

"Ugh." I shook my head, wanting to hide. "That video has been the bane of my existence."

"I can't believe Let Her Rip is standing in front of me," Frank said again. He couldn't take his eyes off me and I squirmed in embarrassment. "Hey, can I get a photo with you?"

Matt made a noise. "Frank, I don't think she . . ."

"Please. Matt. You have no idea." Frank looked at Matt and I was taken aback at the pleading in his eyes. This wasn't the wisecracking ball buster that Matt had told me about. I didn't feel any animosity toward Matt from Frank.

"It's okay." I put a hand on Matt's arm. "I don't mind." I turned to Frank. "As long as you don't post it publicly."

His face fell, but then he nodded. "Thank you." He handed his cell to Matt. "Take it in front of the truck, will you?"

Matt gave me a questioning look and I nodded at him. Frank's tone and demeanor bordered on reverence, which made me want to giggle. I moved to Frank's side and he put an arm around my shoulders after giving me a questioning look first.

"Smile, Frankie." Matt snapped off a few pictures and then handed the phone back to Frank.

Frank studied them and then looked at me. "I can't believe you're here. How did you two meet?" He turned to Matt. "And why didn't you tell me you're going out with Let Her Rip?"

"Um, could you not call me that? My name is Kimmie." I hated that nickname. Just hated it.

"I'm sorry." Frank sounded so apologetic I expected him to drop his knees to beg for forgiveness. "Kimmie. Of course. So, how did you two meet?" He was staring at me as if I was Jennifer Lopez.

"Um, we knew each other from my um . . ." I floundered around.

"We met online." Matt jumped in.

"Oh, cool. I should try that." Frank's face turned pink. "Um, Kimmie. You have a sister or something? Cousin?"

"No, sorry. Only child, and I do have cousins on my father's side but they're all married."

Frank's face fell and I felt bad for letting him down. "I guess I'll try the online thing." He looked at Matt with something like new respect, and I wanted to laugh. Maybe this would elevate Matt in Frank's eyes and he'd ease off on Matt.

"You should," Matt said kindly.

"Do the rest of the guys know who's here? Who she really is?" Frank turned and headed back into the kitchen before we could stop him.

"Frank, no . . ." I called after him.

But he didn't hear, or else he ignored me. "Wait 'til they hear!" And then he was gone.

I turned to Matt. "He's going to tell everyone."

"I know. We need to tell my father before word gets around that Kimmie Park is Let Her Rip." He put an arm around my shoulders, drawing me close. "You've made quite the impression at the firehouse, young lady." I realized he was imitating his father's tone and I laughed.

"Well, this young lady has a whole new respect for firefighters."

"I'm glad." He took my hand. "Want to head back to Manhattan? You said Hana wanted to take you and Alicia shopping before your dinner with Ruby?"

I blew out a breath at the mention of Ruby. I'd forgotten I was meeting her tonight.

"Shouldn't we say good-bye to the guys? And Frank?" Even though I knew he'd been an asshole to Matt, his obvious reverence for Let Her Rip endeared him to me.

Matt grinned at me. "Frank has a fan club too, it looks like."

"Not really. But he wasn't as bad as you said." I pursed my lips.

"Oh, he's obsessed with you. I remember the way he used to stare at that video, watching it over and over again. The guys used to poke at him that he was in love with Let Her Rip."

"How . . . embarrassing." I didn't know that.

"Maybe he'll ease off on me now that he knows Let Her Rip is my kind-of girlfriend." We grinned at each other. "Thanks, Kimmie."

"Anytime, Matt." I gave him a flippant smile but inside, my heart swelled with pride that my meme had helped Matt in some way.

TWENTY-NINE

Kimmie

That night, Hana and Alicia took me down to China-town on the subway. I clutched the shoulder bag I had designed close to me, remembering the Instagram post I'd written about walking confidently down the streets of Manhattan. Except right now, I was more huddled protectively at Hana's side, hanging on to a pole and darting my eyes nervously, studying all the people crammed into the subway car. I could see Alicia a little ways down, squashed between a really tall woman and a really round man, as she hung on to the pole above her.

"Is it always so crowded?" I shouted to Hana over the din of conversation and the roar of the subway. When I'd been on the subway with Matt earlier, it hadn't been this packed. And I'd felt safer with him. So much for my feminist side.

"It's rush hour." She spoke into my ear so I could hear her.

"It smells." I wrinkled my nose. Maybe the subway

earlier had smelled just as bad but being in Matt's presence had made me immune to everything around me.

Hana laughed. "Welcome to the city."

We bounced along and I looked around, taking in all the different nationalities of people. I was so used to mostly white people in Oklahoma that this wide mix from all over the world was a welcome sight. I didn't stick out here. In fact, I counted at least ten Asian faces just in our car. What would it be like to live here? To not be seen as a minority? Or were Asians still treated as less, even in New York?

Once the subway got past Fourteenth Street, Union Square, the crowd thinned and we were able to find three seats in a row. I sat squashed between Alicia and Hana, but I hadn't felt so alive in so long. The afternoon with Matt had energized me. I hadn't realized I'd been slowly dying inside my safe world in Oklahoma. Now all the possibilities that had once been available when I was sixteen suddenly stretched in front of me again. As dirty, crowded, and odorous as the subway was, I realized I loved it. I could picture myself as a seasoned New Yorker, confidently hopping off one subway to connect to another one, knowing which cars to sit in for every stop.

Alicia leaned toward me. "Are you nervous about meeting Ruby?"

I nodded. "I think I'm going to throw up."

Hana put her hand over mine. "You'll be fine."

"Enjoy it," Alicia said. "And your date with Matt later." I'd told her a bit about my afternoon with Matt. She leaned in to whisper in my ear. "If you need the hotel room, just say the word. I'll sleep with Hana."

I smacked her on the arm. "I'm not sleeping with him on the first date."

"It's technically the second, since you had your first this afternoon." She smirked at me.

I smacked her again, this time harder, making her yelp. Hana made a face at us.

Alicia and I looked at each other and giggled, knowing we were acting like teenagers. I looked from her to my aunt, so glad they'd come on this trip with me. Whatever happened tomorrow in our meeting with Robert, I'd face it.

The subway jolted to a stop, and I would have pitched forward, if not for being squashed against Hana and Alicia. The lurch didn't help the queasiness in my stomach either. We were at Canal Street. I swallowed hard.

Hana got up and Alicia and I followed her as we went through the turnstiles and up the stairs to the street. I knew immediately we were in Chinatown from all the Chinese characters on the signs. Hana led us confidently down the street, weaving in and out between people, sometimes stepping off the curb into the street to get around the crowds. We went down a side street away from Canal Street and then down another alley-like street, getting deeper into Chinatown. After one more turn, I saw the Taiwan Pork Chop House up ahead.

And there, standing to the side of the front door, was Ruby. I stopped in the middle of the narrow street and stared at her. She was so much smaller than I'd imagined from our FaceTime talks. She was about my height, but much slimmer than me. Her long hair was unbound and floated down her back, and she had on a light fitted black jacket that was perfect for the cool late October night. She turned her head and caught sight of us, and her face broke into a big smile. Moving forward, she closed the space between us.

"Kimmie." She reached out her hands and I was finally

able to move. I walked to her and hesitated, but she embraced me. I stiffened for a second, and then relaxed and hugged her back. The noise of Chinatown and the people walking around us faded away, and I breathed in the slight citrusy scent of her hair, the clean soap smell from her skin, and the firm pressure of her arms around me.

When I finally pulled away, I looked up to see Alicia and Hana watching us, both with tears in their eyes. I turned back to Ruby, my nose stinging. "I don't know why I'm getting so emotional." I hadn't realized I spoke out loud until Ruby answered.

"Me too." She smiled and reached out to swipe away the tear that fell down her cheek. She turned to Hana and Alicia and they introduced themselves.

I couldn't stop staring at Ruby, to see all the ways we were the same and all the ways we were different. I was suddenly very glad she had reached out and that I was here. This woman had given birth to me. I had been in her stomach. How I ever fit in that tiny stomach I'll never know.

"Just text us when you're ready to go back to the hotel," Hana said. She and Alicia were going to have dinner in Little Italy and then walk around Soho.

"Have fun!" Alicia waved to me as she linked arms with Hana and they walked away.

"Let's go in." Ruby held open the door for me and I walked into the tiny restaurant.

We were led to a small table for two. As we settled in, I inhaled the delicious aromas wafting throughout the room, a mixture of fried pork chops and chicken, aromatic soups and other smells that weren't familiar to me. I was eager to eat Taiwanese food for the first time. "It smells so good."

Ruby smiled at me. "I hope you're hungry. I know it's

not much to look at, but they have the best pork chop rice. Do you want me to order for us?"

I nodded, since I had no idea what to choose.

I listened to Ruby ordering in Taiwanese. I still had a hard time remembering that I was really Taiwanese. I'd been Korean for all my life until I thought I was Chinese. If circumstances were different, I wondered if I too would be able to speak Taiwanese.

Ruby turned to me after the waitress walked away. "You're really here."

"I am." My shoulders rose and then fell. This was a momentous occasion.

Before Ruby could speak, a waitress started putting down small plates in front of us. Ruby pointed each dish out to me. "These are Taiwanese pickled cucumbers with jelly-fish, and this is marinated seaweed and dried bean curd with soy sauce paste on top. And these are wontons in a spicy oil. I grew up on stuff like this."

I reached out eagerly and spooned some of everything onto my plate. The garlic and spice of the cucumber and jellyfish were so good, and Ruby put a scoop of the restaurant's homemade hot sauce on my plate. I dipped a bean curd in it and my taste buds practically burst out into dance from the salty goodness. I couldn't get enough. I'd never tasted anything like this, such strong spicy flavors, nothing bland about the Taiwanese food. I loved it.

I looked up to see Ruby smiling at me. "You like it, huh?"

I swallowed, not wanting to talk with my mouth full. "I love it. This is exactly what has been missing in my life. Now I wish I'd known I was Taiwanese earlier." I nearly bit my tongue as I said that. It was my own fault that I hadn't known. Ruby had first reached out to me when I was eighteen.

Ruby gave a soft smile. "It's okay, Kimmie. I understand that you weren't ready before."

"Thanks." We exchanged a look before I continued eating.

"There's more to come. I got a lot of food so you could try everything."

We talked as we ate, and because I was so distracted by the delicious food, I forgot to be nervous. She asked about my childhood, my parents, and my Etsy shop. She asked me about Endless and about Matt. My heart gave a skip when I thought about tomorrow. It would either be the end of my dreams or the start of something new and exciting.

When the waitress put the bowl of pork chop rice with pickled mustard greens and napa cabbage in front of me, I leaned down and inhaled the tantalizing smell.

"What is this heavenly goodness?" I tried a bite of everything in my bowl and sighed in contentment.

"Taiwanese food. The food of our people." Her smile lit up her face and I stopped in mid-chew.

Our people. As I stared at Ruby, it became even more real that I was a part of her, that her people were mine too. And I realized I wanted to know more about my heritage. But before I could ask, Ruby spoke up.

"Tell me more about Matt." She used her chopsticks to pick up a piece of rice cake with mushrooms and vegetables from the plate in front of us.

"He's . . . so . . . I mean . . ." I laughed. I didn't know how to describe him. He was hot, dreamy, everything physically that made me swoon. On top of that, he was kind and thoughtful and so respectful. Another guy might have been disappointed or upset that I didn't turn out to look like

Alicia. But Matt had told me on the phone he didn't care what I looked like, and he'd stuck by his words. I told Ruby all about him.

Then I asked about her mother, who she'd told me lived in Taiwan, but who wanted to fly to New York to meet me next time I was here. I also asked about her fiancé, and as she told me about Eric, I continued to savor our meal. The rich saltiness and spice from the pork chop, mixed with the slightly sour but delicious pickled greens followed by the blandness of the white rice and crunch of the cabbage, were just perfect.

"You met Eric when he played in the band for a production you were in?" I asked her. She'd told me he was a musician.

"Yes. That was over ten years ago. We knew the same people and would often see each other through the years. But for some reason, we never got together until two years ago, when I ran into him at a gala." Ruby looked up as the waitress approached our table.

My eyes bugged out of my head when the waitress put a bowl with a smaller empty bowl in front of us. "More?" I looked at our tiny table, every inch covered with this new food that I was just discovering.

"You can't be Taiwanese and not have niu rou mien, beef noodle soup. It's one of our best-known dishes." She laughed at my expression. "Don't worry, I'll take home any leftovers."

As I ate, I wondered what it would have been like if Ruby had kept me, if I'd known I was Taiwanese from birth. Would food like this be a fact of life to me, something I took for granted? There was so much I didn't know about my background, about Taiwanese history, and about Ruby's family. The questions fought for space in my head, and I knew I wanted to get to know Ruby better so she could answer them.

When we were finally done and I was so stuffed I literally wanted to unbutton my pants (okay, I did unbutton my pants), I watched the waitress box up the leftovers. I was sure we were done, but then Ruby said, "A bowl of shaved ice with just the tapioca and taro balls, please."

"What?" I gaped at her. "I couldn't possibly eat any more."

"You can't finish a meal here without the shaved ice. We'll share it." Ruby smiled at me. She'd told me earlier that Taiwanese people were very serious about food, and I could see this was true.

"How do you stay so skinny?" I'd watched her eat, and she'd matched me bite for bite.

"I exercise a lot. But I don't usually eat so much in one sitting." She reached across the table and squeezed my hand briefly. "This is a special occasion."

"It is." I was surprised at how comfortable I felt around her, given my reluctance to meet her. But food had a way of bringing people together. "I'm so glad I'm here."

"Me too," Ruby said.

The waitress placed a bowl of shaved ice mounded with tapioca and taro balls and drizzled with a syrupy liquid in front of us. I had sworn I couldn't eat any more, but the bowl looked so refreshing that I picked up a spoon and dug in. And as the ice melted in my mouth in a sweet burst of coldness and my teeth bit into the chewy tapioca and taro balls, my eyes widened. While Ruby laughed, I closed my eyes, letting the contradiction of flavors and textures meld in my mouth, and I knew I was tasting the flavors of my heritage.

THIRTY

Matt

I was waiting in the hotel lobby when Kimmie, Alicia, and Hana walked in.

"Matt." Kimmie waved at me and ran to my side.

I leaned in to give her a kiss on the cheek, the smell of her shampoo tickling my nose. "I take it dinner went well."

She nodded, her cheeks rosy. She looked so cute and I wanted more than anything to take her in my arms. "This is my aunt Hana."

I went to shake Hana's hand but she squeezed me in a hug instead. "So nice to meet you, Matt," she said.

"Hi, Matt." Alicia waved at me. "Take care of her tonight, okay? Don't let her loose in the city." She leaned in and said in a loud whisper, "And remember. If you need the hotel room, just say the word. I'll sleep in Hana's."

I watched with amusement as Kimmie swatted her best friend on the arm so hard that Alicia hit her back. Kimmie's face was now bright red. Hana laughed, which didn't help any, because Kimmie turned to glare at her aunt.

"I think we'll be fine." Kimmie literally pushed Alicia toward the elevators. "Bye."

Alicia threw us a kiss before veering off course and heading for the bar. "I'm having a drink. Hana?"

Hana followed her after waving to us. When Kimmie turned to face me, I couldn't suppress the grin on my face. "Good to know we have an option for tonight."

"Matt." She planted her hands on her hips. "I don't sleep with people on the first date." She stopped and thought for a moment. "At least, I never have."

I held up my hands. "I respect that, but this is technically our second date."

"OMG, do you and Alicia share a brain?" She scowled at me, but it was so cute I couldn't help laughing.

"Did you just say OMG?"

"Again, you and Alicia with the same brain." She muttered something under her breath that sounded like "I must attract wiseasses."

I offered her my arm. "I apologize for being a wiseass. Ready for our second date?"

She slipped an arm through mine and we left the hotel lobby. "Where're we going?" she asked, once we were outside.

"I'm taking you to a rooftop bar. You can see the entire Manhattan skyline."

"Oh!" Her eyes lit up. "I've always wanted to see the city at night." She gave a little hop and then landed in a crack in the sidewalk and would have stumbled if I hadn't been holding her up. "Oops."

"You really are awkward, aren't you?" She'd told me that on the phone many times and I'd never believed her. But she was right. And I loved it.

"I told you." She looked at me quickly before resuming

her hop. "I'm just so excited I'm actually in New York City. It's everything I've ever thought it was and more." She threw out the arm that wasn't attached to me and almost smacked a man who was hurrying by. "The energy makes me feel so alive." She was oblivious to the man now giving her a dirty look.

I pulled her a little closer, laughing to myself about what a menace she was to others. Hopefully we'd get to the bar, only a few more blocks away, without injuring anyone. "Think you could ever see yourself living here?" I said it casually, but in reality I was dead serious and anxious to hear her answer. This woman had my heart and I wanted to get to know her better.

She turned to look at me. "I think so. For the first time since my parents died, I feel like I could finally leave Oklahoma."

I knew all about her fears of leaving her state and that this was a big step for her. "That's great."

A couple of blocks later, I led her into the lobby of a hotel. She turned to me in confusion. "I thought you said we were going to a bar."

"We are. It's on the top floor of this hotel." We walked to the elevators and got on when the doors opened.

"Oh." She leaned in and whispered to me, "I thought you were getting a hotel room."

I turned and gave her wink. "Why, when we have a perfectly nice one back there that Alicia is willing to vacate for us?"

She giggled and leaned into my arm. I could have sworn she rubbed the side of her head up and down against my biceps, but then the elevator opened at our floor.

The hostess seated us at a quiet table in the corner of the indoor lounge. We could see the sweeping views of

Manhattan through the panoramic windows. Kimmie gazed around the sleek room, her mouth slightly open, as she took in the beautiful modern interior before letting her eyes settle on the glittering lights of the city through the windows.

"Matt. This is gorgeous. And so glamorous." She looked around one more time before focusing on me. "I know I keep saying this, but I can't believe I'm here. This is definitely not cow country."

I laughed, leaning back in my seat to watch her enjoyment and delight. "There's not a cow in sight."

Someone came over just then and asked if we wanted tap or sparkling water. "Just tap is fine," Kimmie said, when I turned to her in question.

Once he left, we picked up the cocktail menu and studied it.

"Oh my god." She dropped her menu and looked at me.
"What?"

"The prices," she whispered to me.

I looked at the menu and laughed. "I guess this is more expensive than Oklahoma?"

"Um, yeah." She picked her menu up again.

I smiled at her. "You are absolutely delightful." I was used to women who had grown so immune to their families' wealth that they wouldn't blink at paying these prices for a drink. And this bar wasn't even that expensive.

"I hope you mean that as a compliment." She raised her eyebrows at me over the menu.

"Of course. What are you thinking of?"

"Maybe the Gibson? I like the sound of the name." She put the menu down.

Once we ordered, she went back to staring out at the skyline. "Do you think it's too late for me to start over?"

"What do you mean?" I wasn't sure what she was referring to.

"I mean, I had wanted to come to New York for college. I never did and ended up not doing anything much for the past decade." She turned to meet my eyes. "Do you think I could really come to New York at thirty years old and start a whole new career? Maybe even go back to school?"

I reached across the table to take her hand. "I think you can do anything you set your heart to. And thirty is young. I know people who have had career changes in their forties." I pointed to myself. "Look at me. I had a big career change last year."

We broke apart when the waiter came back with our cocktails. I lifted my drink, some sort of whiskey concoction, and clinked it against her glass. "Cheers to us. Two people who met on the internet, got to know each other despite some misunderstandings, and are right now having their second date, which might end up back at her hotel room, hastily vacated by her best friend."

"Matt." She sputtered out a laugh, almost spilling her drink. I wiggled my eyebrows at her to let her know I was joking. We both took a sip, and when we put our glasses down, I was smiling so wide my cheeks hurt.

"What are your dreams?" she asked. "I know you followed your instincts and became a firefighter despite your father's wishes. But what do you want from life?"

Besides having my mother back? I didn't say this out loud. I looked into her eyes and decided to tell her the truth. She would be going home in two days so I didn't have time to play games. "I want a family. Kids or no kids is fine. I want to find someone that I can go through life with. If she wants kids, that's great. If not, I'm fine with dogs. And if she wants them and we can't have them for some reason, then there are other ways to have kids. None of it is a deal breaker. But she has to be the right person."

She blinked at me. "Wow. I wasn't expecting you to say that."

"What about you?"

"You mean kids? Or someone to go through life with?" She took a sip of her drink and then cupped her chin in her palm, one elbow on the table.

"Both." I watched her face. Normally, I wouldn't bring up something like this on a second date, but I felt like we'd known each other for a while. And this wasn't a usual situation where I was dating someone who lived in the same city.

"Definitely the someone to go through life with. And I always thought I would just have kids." She gave a little shrug. "Kind of a default reaction, I guess. I think knowing I'm adopted, I want to make sure I'm ready and that I'm with someone that I can raise kids with." She cut her eyes to me. "You know?"

I nodded. "Tell me more about Ruby. I guess she's not really Russian?" My eyes twinkled at her.

Her mouth quirked. "No, she's not Russian and her last name isn't Chenapov."

I tried to keep a straight face but I couldn't. Kimmie narrowed her eyes at me before continuing. "It went so much better than I thought. I think a part of me has been afraid to meet her all these years." She sat back and told me about Ruby, how her mother, Kimmie's grandmother, hadn't known that Ruby had been pregnant and given her baby up for adoption.

"Was her mother upset?" I couldn't even imagine.

"Yes. She said she would have helped Ruby raise me." A faraway look came over Kimmie's face. "Ruby had thought her parents would have been horrified. Good Taiwanese daughters do not have one-night stands and then get pregnant when they aren't married. But my grandmother—" She broke off. "That sounds so strange to say. But anyways, she said family is everything and she would have helped out. My grandfather died a few years back."

"Can you imagine if Ruby had kept you? You would have had a whole different life." I picked up my drink and took a sip.

"I know. But I can't imagine not having my mom and dad as my parents, so I guess everything did work out for a reason." She gestured to me. "What about you? What was your mom and dad's relationship like?"

I played with my glass. "I thought they had a great relationship. They fought, like any couple, but they always seemed in tune with each other." I drew my eyebrows together, thinking of the man my father had become ever since my mom passed away. "My father changed after she died. She was always able to make him laugh. He was much more serious than she was, but she'd tease him and make him do things he wouldn't normally do."

"Like what?" Kimmie's focus was on me, and it made me feel good.

"Swim in the freezing-cold ocean, go on the roller coaster, go out to dinner without a reservation." I laughed. "My father is a very regimented person. He likes routine and order, following the rules. And my mother didn't." My expression sobered, thinking about the man he'd become. "He won't talk to me about her. At all. Every time I bring her up, he tells me we will not discuss her."

"Why is that, you think?" There was sympathy on Kimmie's face. I'd told her briefly about my father's refusal to talk about my mother.

"I think something happened between them before she

died. It doesn't make any sense that she was driving to the Hamptons by herself. She'd never done that before. I think . . ." I trailed off. I'd never spoken out loud my suspicions to anyone, not even to Nana.

"What do you think happened?" Kimmie asked softly.

"Either they got in a fight, or something happened that upset my father and maybe she didn't tell him, or he found out something she was trying to keep secret . . ." I breathed out a sigh. "I don't know. But I think something happened and he won't talk about her because whatever it was, it was bad."

"Oh, Matt." She reached out and touched my hand. I laced my fingers with hers, and it was exactly what I needed at the moment. Kimmie understood. She always had. This woman got me like no one ever had.

We didn't say anything for a while, just sat there, our hands intertwined on the table while we held our drinks with the other. If you'd ever have told me I would be perfectly content to sit in silence, sipping drinks with a woman at a rooftop bar, I'd probably have laughed. I hated uncomfortable silences. I usually tried to fill them, especially when I was on a date, hoping to make a good impression. But here I was, perfectly fine being quiet and absolutely falling for the woman across from me.

The waiter stopped by our table, forcing us to reluctantly unlink hands. "Want another round?"

"Kimmie?" I looked at her.

"Sure." I could tell she didn't want to leave yet either.

"Can we take it outside?" I asked the waiter. It would be a little cool, but there weren't many people out there and I suddenly wanted to stand at the top of Manhattan with her. "Is that okay?" I turned to Kimmie.

She nodded and the waiter said he'd be right back with our drinks.

"You'll be warm enough?" She had on a heavy cardigan sweater that she'd worn over her light blue blouse and jeans.

"If not, I've got you to keep me warm, right?" She looked surprised by what came out of her mouth and giggled.

That laugh. "I'll keep you warm, don't worry."

The waiter returned with our check and drinks.

I took care of the bill and then we carried our drinks outside. It was a clear night and we could see most of the Manhattan skyline. We walked around the corner to a high table and stopped next to it. Most everyone who was outside was in front of the main bar. I raised my eyebrows at Kimmie and she nodded, putting her drink down. I put an arm around her and drew her into my side as we stared out at the twinkling lights of Manhattan. She leaned her weight into me and my heart, which had been frozen since my mother died, began to thaw.

She sighed. "In this moment, right here on this rooftop with you, I can so clearly see myself living here."

"It's not too late. FIT has continuing education classes that you could take, even for credit if you wanted them." Without meaning to, I ran a hand through her thick black hair.

She grimaced and pulled away slightly.

"What? Did I hurt you?" My hand stilled in her hair.

"No. I just don't like my hair. It's so thick and coarse and when it's humid out, it expands by two hundred percent."

I let out a bark of laughter. This was why I loved being with Kimmie. "What are you talking about? Yes, your hair is thick, but it's gorgeous. It's not coarse at all. And I'd love to see you with humid big hair."

She looked up and scoffed. "No, you wouldn't. I literally look like I stuck my finger in a socket."

"Kimmie, Kim. You are the best." I stroked her hair again and she stilled under my hand. "This is why I love—" I cut myself off. Oh, shit. What had I almost said? I didn't want to rush things if she wasn't ready.

Kimmie stared up at me, her eyes wide. Her lips parted and my gaze went right to them. My breath caught when she turned so that she was fully facing me and put her other arm around my waist. The wind blew her hair gently, lifting it up and away from her head. Without realizing it, I was leaning down while she reached up, and then our lips pressed together and she sighed against my mouth.

Nothing had ever been as good as this kiss, this woman in my arms. I gently cupped her face with one hand, while the other rested lightly on her back. I focused on her and her alone, not caring if the entire world came crashing down around us.

She pulled me into her slightly and I deepened the kiss. Everything faded away until there was only me and Kimmie, alone on this rooftop on this magical night, and I knew I held the woman of my dreams in my arms.

THIRTY-ONE

Kimmie

I practically floated home that night. I had never been kissed like that in my entire life. The two serious boyfriends I'd had, the few casual dates who had kissed me, they all paled compared to that kiss. How had I lived this long without Matt's kiss? He made me feel like the most special person in the whole wide world, like I was the only one who mattered to him. I felt cherished and loved, even though it was too soon to use that word. I didn't want to be away from him for even one moment.

But reality eventually crashed down when we got back to the hotel. I don't even remember leaving the rooftop bar. I will always remember that place. If I could, I'd erect a plaque there that read, "Kimmie and Matt Kissed Here."

"We're back," I said, disappointment heavy in my voice.

"I'll walk you to your room." He squeezed my hand, which was enfolded in his, and I just wanted to stay at his side for as long as possible. I was already bereft, feeling the loss of him once he left me.

We walked into the lobby and onto the elevator. We

had the elevator to ourselves, and Matt pulled me close, kissing me again. All I could feel was his touch, his hand lingering at my waist and the sweet taste of his lips. I didn't want him to stop.

But too soon, the elevator dinged and we stepped out. He walked me to my door and we just stared at each other.

"Alicia did say we could have the room." There was a hint of a smile on his lips, but his eyes burned in question.

"I know." I swallowed, as reality continued to crash my romantic party. "But we have that meeting with your father tomorrow and . . ." I was conflicted. I really wanted him to come in, but at the same time, I was anxious about the meeting and it felt rushed.

"It's okay, Kim." I loved it when he called me Kim. And when he called me Kimmie. "I'll wait until you're ready."

This man melted my heart in so many ways, and I had no words. But he must have known because he leaned down and gave me a soft kiss on the lips before leaning his forehead against mine. My heart almost exploded out of my chest.

"Thank you." That was all I could manage.

We stayed like that for another moment before we broke apart and he gave me one last kiss on the lips. "Sleep well. We'll convince my father tomorrow."

"Okay," I whispered, and put my key card against the lock. With one last lingering look, I walked in and shut the door, leaning against it with a sigh.

THE NEXT MORNING, I woke up to Alicia sitting on me.

"Why am I in this room and why are you without

Matt?" She bounced up and down, making my breath puff out with each movement.

I groaned, trying to push her off me. "Get off! I can't breathe."

"Kimmie, where's Matt?" She rolled to the side so that she was lying in the bed next to me.

"He dropped me off and went back to his apartment." I yawned and looked at the clock on the night table. "Why are you up so early?"

"I couldn't sleep. We have to be ready." She sat up, tucking the pillow behind her. "What happened last night?"

I reached for my phone, and when I saw the time on it, I gasped and shot straight up in the bed. "Alicia! It's nine thirty. We're supposed to be at Robert's office at ten."

"What? It's only eight." She pointed at the clock on the nightstand.

"Well, it's wrong. Look." I threw my phone at her as I jumped out of bed and ran into the bathroom to pee and throw water on my face. Shit, shit, shit. How had we overslept?

"Oh, no!" I heard Alicia wail.

We literally ran around like chickens with no heads for the next twenty minutes, frantically trying to look presentable. Alicia only had time to put on light makeup and I just barely got myself dressed and my hair tamed into a high ponytail before we had to leave to get to Robert's office.

As we ran down the street, no coffee or food in our stomachs, we looked at each other, the panic evident in both our eyes. We made it to the building with two minutes to spare, then took turns punching the elevator button. Why was it that elevators were always waiting when you didn't want them, but when you needed them, they were at the very top of the building?

By the time we got up to Robert's office, we were both panting for breath and exactly two minutes late. Sarah greeted us, looking in amusement at our disheveled state.

"They're in the conference room. You remember from yesterday?" She pointed behind her.

We nodded and with a last deep breath fast-walked down the hall. As soon as we entered, Matt jumped up and came toward us. "Everything okay?" he whispered.

I gave him the thumbs-up while trying to smooth down the red sweater dress I'd pulled on over black leggings. Robert greeted us and then we all sat down. I placed my shaking hands in my lap, praying with all my might that everything would work out.

Matt cleared his throat and turned to his father. "Dad, there's something we need to tell you." He launched into the speech he'd prepared as Alicia and I held hands.

When he was done, there was silence in the conference room. Robert literally went quiet as he stared at each of us in turn, with his gaze resting on me last. After what felt like two hundred hours, he finally spoke, pointing to me.

"Let me get this straight. You're actually a meme and you're not Kim?" His face was stern and I gulped.

"No, I am Kim. But I don't look like her." I pointed to Alicia. "I look like me." And I pointed to myself, feeling idiotic.

Robert held up a hand. "First, what exactly is a meme?"

Alicia and I stared at each other, wide-eyed, as Matt explained memes to his father. Oh, no. I just had the biggest urge to laugh. I could feel Alicia shaking beside me as the absurdity of the situation hit us. We were sitting here, waiting to hear the fate of our careers, and Matt was explaining what a meme was to his father. I bit my bottom lip hard, trying to keep it in. Alicia was now doubled over, holding her stomach as if she had a stomachache, but I knew better. I knew she was dying from laughter, clutching her middle to contain her mirth.

Matt glanced at us as he finished his explanation, a frown on his face. And that's when Alicia lost it and let out a hoot, which she quickly covered up with a moan.

Robert shot to his feet, rushing to her side. "Are you okay?"

Alicia gasped, gulping for air, which was a mistake because she choked and started coughing.

"Matt, get her a glass of water." Robert gestured to the pitcher of ice water on the side and Matt rushed over.

Meanwhile, all I could do was sit there, watching as my dreams probably evaporated with each gasp from Alicia. Robert was so not going to want to go into business with two women who had completely lost their shit. This was it. The end of my dream of living and working in New York City. I covered my face with my hands, shoulders slumped in defeat.

What felt like hours later, I felt Matt's presence next to me. He gave my shoulder a squeeze and I finally took my hands away from my face, looking up at him in question. He pointed but didn't say anything.

I followed the direction of his finger and saw Robert and Alicia talking on the other side of the table. I hadn't even heard Alicia get up to join him. And Robert was calm. He listened as Alicia explained that the video wasn't my fault, that I was the least likely person to ever want a video to go viral. She told him that I had wanted to die and move to another planet when I found out my co-worker had posted the video and it had gone viral. And how I didn't want it to have anything to do with my Etsy shop. Everything I'd earned from my Etsy shop had come from the brand itself, and not from the viral video.

I could have kissed Alicia right then and there. But I contained myself, sitting on my hands, with Matt by my side as we watched Alicia wind down her defense of me.

"This is very unusual." Robert turned to me. "I don't know what to say. What's going to happen when everyone finds out who you really are? And they will find out."

I nodded miserably. The bubble of hope I'd had watching Alicia talk to Robert popped.

"But her lie is exactly what makes her perfect for Endless's brand." Matt spoke up.

Robert held up a hand. "I understand that. And I applaud your actions," he said to me. "But how do we make the Endless customers understand that?"

"What if we have Kimmie announce publicly on her social media platforms the truth?" Matt asked and I shot him a grateful look. "PR can help us figure out how to phrase it so that everyone understands it was all a mix-up and she just wanted to keep that meme away from her brand."

"How would we do that?" Matt's father looked at each of us in turn. "To some, maybe most, she'll still come across as having lied."

"I think if we tell the truth, most of her audience will be loyal to her. Someone put a video of her up without her consent; it went viral, again without her consent. She didn't tell anyone who she is because she's a private person and didn't want it to taint her Etsy shop." Matt spoke with a quiet confidence that I wished I felt. Because right now, I tended to agree with Robert. People would think I was a liar who just wanted instant fame.

After a long silence, Robert finally spoke. "I need to think about this. And speak to our people."

My heart sank. Alicia walked back to my side as the three of us faced Robert.

"I understand," I finally said. "It would be an absolute dream to work with Endless. But I get that you don't want to jeopardize your company."

"I'm not saying no. I just need to see how we can present this, if it would work." He looked me in the eyes. "I still believe in the collaboration. It's just going to be more complicated than I thought."

I nodded, misery flooding my heart. Matt reached out to touch me on the arm.

"In the meantime, Alicia." Robert turned to her. "I think we should still get some photos of you, in case we decide to move forward."

"Yes." Alicia stood.

"Okay, I'll get back to you soon." Robert nodded at me.

Alicia gave me a hug, squeezing me tight, before she followed Robert out of the conference room.

"That didn't go so bad." Matt took me in his arms, and I turned my head so that my cheek was against his hard chest.

I took comfort in the warmth radiating from him and in the way his strong arms were wrapped around me. If only I could just enjoy being with him. I breathed in the scent of him, running a hand over his biceps.

"You don't think that was bad?" I said into his chest.

"At least he didn't yell or say no immediately. Trust me, that was pretty good for my father." Matt rested his chin on the top of my head.

I buried my face in his chest. "Okay."

"You're meeting Ruby in Chinatown?" he asked.

I nodded. "But first I'm meeting my friend Mila Yang for a quick coffee."

"I want to start talking to our team here, but maybe I'll meet up with you later?" His hand stroked through my hair and I never wanted him to stop.

"Want to go to Chinatown with me and meet Ruby? We can find some baos." I suddenly wanted him to meet my birth mother.

"Are you sure?" He looked down at me and I smiled, reaching a hand up to his cheek.

"Yes. I want you to meet her. That is, if you do. I just want to spend as much time as I can with you." I couldn't believe I was saying this to a man. I wasn't usually this bold, especially after really only the second day meeting him in person. But nothing about the situation with Matt was normal.

"That sounds great. If Ruby doesn't mind."

I pulled out my phone and texted Ruby, who answered right away. I looked up with a smile. "She said she'd love to meet you."

"And then we're having drinks with Nana." Matt's eyes sparkled at me. In our three-way text when we were trying to figure out when I could meet Nana, she had suggested drinks.

Having Matt's young woman in New York warrants day drinking in my book, she'd texted, making me laugh. I already loved Matt's grandmother, and I hadn't even met her yet.

"I can't wait." I smiled at him and he gave me a light kiss on the lips. We broke apart and headed out of the conference room for the elevator.

THIRTY-TWO

Matt

"Here, try this one. It's the char sui bao this bakery is famous for." Ruby handed Kimmie and me each half of the bun that she'd broken apart.

We took it from her as we strolled down the sidewalk on Mott Street in Chinatown. We'd had lunch earlier at a dim sum restaurant, but after walking around Little Italy and part of Soho, we were hungry again.

"This is so good." Kimmie's eyes rolled back and the look on her face had me pausing with the bao en route to my mouth. I wondered if this was what she looked like when she was coming. Such a blissed-out, happy expression. I couldn't take my eyes off her face and I was suddenly aware of my pants getting uncomfortable. I tore my eyes away and shook my head. I could not be having sexual thoughts about her while on a crowded street with her birth mother.

Kimmie looked over at me. "You haven't tried it yet? It's so good."

I gave her a weak smile and quickly shoved the white fluffy bun filled with roast pork in my mouth. And then I understood why Kimmie's eyes had rolled back. It was good. "This is amazing," I said, when I could talk.

Ruby smiled at both of us. "I also got a chicken bao and a pork and vegetable one for you to try."

"I can't believe how many great restaurants there are down here." Kimmie took another bite but her eyes were on the Asian stores and restaurants lining both sides of the narrow street, teeming with people.

There was so much to see, from the tourist stores selling "I Love NY" merchandise and souvenirs to the tiny Chinese shops selling everything from slippers to step stools and lucky cat figurines. There were bakeries bursting with Chinese breads, cakes, buns, sesame balls, and egg tarts crammed between restaurants, and Asian grocery stores and fish markets that left a malodorous stink as we walked by. I'd been to Chinatown before, but now, seeing it through Kimmie's eyes, it was as if I was seeing it for the first time with her.

"If I lived in the city, I'd be trying a new place every time I came here." She looked over at me. "I'd be down here every day. I have to drive a least an hour to Tulsa just to find Asian groceries."

Ruby's eyes went to Kimmie. "Are you thinking of moving here?" Her tone was casual, but I saw the way her throat moved when she swallowed, as if the answer was important to her.

"I've always wanted to live here. Matt knows." Kimmie smiled at me. "I've been thinking about it . . . ." She popped the last of her bao in her mouth.

"If you do, I can show you around, take you to all my favorite places." Ruby flushed and looked away. "That is, if you want me to."

Kimmie touched Ruby's arm briefly. "I'd love that."

They exchanged a look and I smiled. I should have felt like an interloper, yet, it was right for me to be here with Kimmie and her birth mother. Ruby had made me feel welcome and Kimmie was obviously delighted for us to meet.

"Hey," Kimmie suddenly said. "My friend Mila is a dancer and she lives in Manhattan too." She looked at Ruby. "I should introduce you. I think she's having a hard time." Kimmie's expression darkened. "I saw her right before we came down here and I think all the rejections are getting to her."

Ruby nodded. "I get it. Dancers don't get paid very well, there's always competition, and it's expensive to live here." She shuddered. "I remember all those cattle calls. Maybe I can help her, if just as a sounding board."

"That would be great." Kimmie gave her a grateful smile.

When it was time to say good-bye, they both got emotional.

"Well." Ruby looked at Kimmie and I could see the way her eyes took in every detail of her daughter. "I'm so glad we had this time together." We were standing by a subway entrance.

"Me too." Kimmie's chin wobbled and I wanted to pull her to me, but I knew this was between her and her birth mother.

I walked away to give them privacy. After a minute, I heard Ruby calling my name and looked up. "Take care of her, okay?"

"I will." I walked back and gave Ruby a hug, before she turned and disappeared underground. My head swiveled to Kimmie. "Okay?"

She nodded but blinked rapidly. I held her hand and when she took a deep breath and nodded again, we walked the few blocks to the bar where we were meeting Nana.

NANA WAS ALREADY THERE, standing outside waiting for us. Her face lit up when she caught sight of Kimmie.

"You are just absolutely adorable. And what a great dancer. That video was a hoot!" She held out her arms and Kimmie let go of my hand to hug Nana.

When I'd told Nana about how Kimmie didn't look like Alicia and was really Let Her Rip, she'd cackled. She'd seen the viral video and really admired Kimmie for standing up to her boss. She even knew what a meme was, when my father hadn't.

Nana pulled back, eyes roaming over Kimmie's face. She nodded and then looked over at me. "Matt, she's a good one."

"So, you're not mad at me for not telling Matt what I looked like for so long?" Kimmie bit her lip.

"Oh, honey, life is too short to be mad. It sounded like a series of misunderstandings and it all worked out, right?" Nana let go of Kimmie to give me a hug and a kiss.

We walked into the trendy bar that Nana had heard about and I was surprised at how nice it was. From the outside, it looked like a dump. Trust Nana to find the latest gems in the city.

The two of them dominated the conversation while I sat back watching them. I didn't mind. I was happy that they got along so well, that Nana was just as taken with Kimmie as I was. Both of them were having cosmos, "the perfect girly day-drinking choice," as Nana phrased it. I was having one too, and they'd teased me about "the hot firefighter with the girly drink."

"Everything worked out with your father?" Nana looked over at me, and I realized I'd missed most of the conversation. I was just so happy that the two women who meant the most to me in the world, now that my mom was gone, were getting along so well in person.

"I hope so." I set down my drink. It was a bit sweet for my liking, but I wanted to have the same cocktail as them.

Kimmie told Nana about the meeting. "I hope Robert will decide to partner with me. It would be such a dream come true." She glanced over at me. "And I'm thinking of moving to New York if the deal goes through."

Nana clapped her hands. "Wonderful. I'll have you both over for dinner next time you're here." She handed her phone to me. "Matt, take a picture of us."

They held up their cosmos and, giggling, mugged for the camera. I looked through the pictures and stopped at one that caught my eye. They had goofy smiles on their faces, which were slightly turned toward each other. But it was their eyes that got to me. There was fondness there, and respect. And love. My nana approved of Kimmie. I looked at them, swallowing the lump in my throat as I handed Nana's phone back to her. I wished my mom was here too. She should have been sitting here, squealing over the pictures the way Nana and Kimmie were, trying to decide which one to post on Nana's Instagram.

HOURS LATER, Kimmie and I left a little ramen place by my apartment and walked out into the cool night. The temperature had dropped while we were in the restaurant and Kimmie shivered next to me.

"That was seriously one of the best meals I've ever had," she said, and then laughed. "I've eaten so much great food here."

"Not sad you missed Nobu?" I took her hand. Kimmie had asked if it was okay with me that we gave the Nobu reservation to Alicia and Hana. Alicia had been dreaming of going there for years.

"Nope. I'm not really into expensive fancy places. And besides, if I do move here, we can go another time, right?" She flashed me a smile.

I pulled her into my side, dropping a kiss on the top of her head. She wasn't like any of the women I'd been surrounded with my entire life. Women who cared about status and only wanted to date me for my money. I'd come to realize this when my mother died. Suddenly, it was like a light had gone off in my head and I'd seen my life for what it really was: a privileged white man making more money than I needed and surrounded by superficial women who didn't want me for me, but only for the status I could afford them. That was why I hadn't dated much in the past three years. And that was why I knew I was falling in love with Kimmie. She was everything real and true about life, and I suddenly couldn't imagine my life without her.

"Matt?" She touched my arm. "Are you okay?"

I shook my head and focused on her. "Never better." I stopped walking and pushed a strand of hair back behind her ear. "I'm going to miss you when you leave tomorrow."

She made a face. "I'm going to miss you so much too."

I put both arms around her and she said into my chest, "I don't want to leave yet."

I held her, right there on the streets in Manhattan, and could literally feel her heartbeat thump through my body.

"I want to be with you all night. We don't have to do anything, but I don't want to leave you at the hotel." I pulled her in even closer, hoping she wouldn't say no.

"Or something might happen?" Her teasing tone lightened the mood and her grip tightened on me.

My entire body relaxed. I didn't have to say good-bye to her yet. "Do you want to go back to my apartment?"

"Yes. More than anything." She lifted her head and I leaned down to kiss her.

"Okay," I said when we pulled away.

We were only a few blocks away from my place and we walked slowly, since Kimmie stopped every few steps to look at everything. Her phone dinged, and when she read the text, she laughed and showed it to me. It was from Alicia.

I'm sleeping in Hana's room if you want to come back here with Matt. Wink, wink.

"Tell her it's safe. She can stay in your room."

Kimmie's thumbs were already flying. She looked up from her phone. "We'll meet them for breakfast tomorrow?"

I nodded. Breakfast, and then the company car was taking them to the airport. I had decided to go see them off. I could already feel how empty my life would be once Kimmie went home.

When we got to my building, the doorman opened the door for us.

"Hello, Matt West." Mrs. White was sitting on a couch in the lobby with her two dogs. She turned to peer curiously at Kimmie. "And who's this?"

"This is Kimmie." I made the introductions.

"Oh." Her face lit up. "Your girlfriend?"

I turned to catch Kimmie's eyes and, at her amused smile, said, "Yes."

"It's so nice to meet the young woman responsible for making Matt West glow." Mrs. White reached out a hand and Kimmie took it and gave it a squeeze before turning to me.

"I had no idea my boyfriend glows." She gave me a mischievous grin.

I groaned. "I do not glow."

They both said at the same time, "Yes, you do." And then they turned to each other, mouths open in surprise.

"I like this girl, Matt West," Mrs. White said to me. She turned to Kimmie. "Your boyfriend saved my dogs once. Good man, that one." She pointed at me.

"I know." Kimmie was practically beaming at Mrs. White. "You love dogs." She stopped and laughed. "Well, obviously. But Matt said you complained about a beagle in the building?"

I pinched Kimmie on the arm lightly. I couldn't believe she was asking Mrs. White about that. She pinched me back. Hard.

"It wasn't the beagle I complained about, but the owners." Mrs. White leaned closer. "They're so rude. Never pick up after poor Bailey and the one time I saw them leave the poop on the sidewalk and said something, the woman actually cursed at me."

"Oh." I raised my eyebrows. Maybe I'd judged Mrs. White unfairly. I'd thought she was complaining about the beagle's weight.

"Have a good night, you two." She gave me a pointed

look. "And don't worry, these walls are thick. I would know. My family owns this building."

"Oh my god," I muttered under my breath. She didn't just go there.

Kimmie pealed out a laugh.

"Wait, your family owns the building?" I hadn't known that.

"Yes." She leaned closer and said in a mock whisper, "How do you think I got to keep these two? When my husband died, these two became my companions."

I chuckled, and after we petted Milly and Mickey, we said good-bye to Mrs. White and headed for the elevators.

We didn't speak when we got to my apartment. I didn't even turn on the lights. Our coats came off and we came together like magnets attracting. One of my hands cradled the back of her head as I angled down to her, capturing her lips in a kiss. Her hands stroked me, my other hand cupped her ass, and somehow, we made it to my bedroom and onto the bed. As our clothes came off and I felt her bare skin against mine, I felt more alive than I could ever remember. It was as if the world had burst into Technicolor. She had the softest skin I'd ever felt and I ran my hands all over her body, wanting to know every inch of her. The past three years of sadness fell away and my entire being was focused only on this woman in my arms. Kim. Kimmie. She sighed against my mouth and I was lost.

When we were lying side by side, both out of breath from the best sex I'd ever had, I turned to her and said, "I'm crazy bao you."

She burst out laughing, the laugh that had driven me crazy before I'd ever met her. I gathered her in my arms until I was spooned around her. She gripped my forearms and wiggled her ass until it was pressed right up to my cock, her laughter waking it up again. I buried my face in her neck, kissing a sensitive spot there until she was no longer laughing.

I never wanted to let her go. I'd never been surer of anything in my life. She was everything to me.

Instagram Post

2,045 likes

mycraftybaokim New York City was beyond my dreams. I may soon have some news to share, related to my trip. Stay tuned! And was I glad for my large, roomy tote bag from My Crafty Bao. It held everything I needed for the day; my laptop, water, a notebook, plus everything I always carry.

Pick a tote that says YOU. Who are you? Are you athletic, and want bold colors, sporty images, or geometric designs? Are you soft and feminine, leaning toward flowers, pastels, and sweet images? Or are you fun and flirty and like things like hedgehogs, umbrellas, beach scenes, or wine bottles? Or are you none of the above and have your own ideas? Whatever your style, I have a tote bag that will fit your personality. And if you don't see a fabric that you like, I'm also open to custom orders and can find a fabric you're looking for.

Don't be afraid to show who you are and send me pics. I love seeing everyone's personalities.

Be bold, be daring, be you.
xo, Kim

VIEW all 95 comments

melissabegood35 Did you get a pastrami sandwich? How come you didn't post a pic of yourself with the tote? Why just your products lately? And what's the big news? ● ●

gretchenbanks33 I love love love these tote bags! I'm going to order one. I just can't decide which one.

melissafoster You are so inspirational. I cannot wait to hear your news. I bet it's something big!

peytonwilton1 Are you for real? How can any one person be so perfect? Hope you went shopping at Bloomingdales.

ambersmalley8 (in response to peytonwilton1) I bet you she's not real. No one is that perfect. She's a fake. I've said it before.

melissafoster (in response to ambersmalley8) Why are you even still here? Go hate somewhere else! We don't need you here if you don't believe in Kim.

matte194nyc

ambersmalley8 (in response to melissafoster) You suck. Byyyeeee!

melissafoster (in response to ambersmalley8) Real mature.

leahknowsbest: (in response to ambersamlley8) You're probably a bot. Or a very jealous person.

tomkennedy I was glad to find your shop before, but now my girlfriend wants everything in your shop for

Christmas so I'm basically giving you all my money this holiday season. Thank you for making me broke.

Kimmie

I missed Matt so much. It'd been a week and a half since I got back from New York City, and the safe life I was used to in Oklahoma had turned so bland and dull. I missed the hustle and bustle of the city, the diversity of people, and all the food I could have just by stepping foot outside. And most of all, I missed Matt.

We'd talked and FaceTimed every day, often long into the night in bed until one of us got sleepy. I couldn't stop thinking about him, about his body and reliving the night we'd spent together. I didn't know sex could be so good. It wasn't awkward at all. We fit together like we'd been made for each other. I couldn't stop thinking about him and I had basically decided that I was moving to New York. Because Robert had told me before the weekend that Endless was going ahead with our collaboration.

I yawned as I poured another cup of coffee. It was Monday morning and I was trying to force myself to establish a work routine. Since I worked from home now, it was so easy to fall into the lazy habit of staying in my pj's all day. I'd tried to establish a regular schedule, which said I should be finishing breakfast now and getting ready to start working in my sewing room.

I sewed through the day by myself. Alicia was at the diner and Hana was writing. I stopped for a quick lunch of leftovers from the weekend. When my cell rang, I was surprised to see it was two thirty in the afternoon.

It was Matt.

"Hi." I couldn't keep the happiness from my voice.

"Hi yourself." His deep voice sent a thrill through me. "I just got out of a meeting with the PR team and they think you should just be candid and explain what happened. Just be you."

"Yes. I agree." My palms got sweaty thinking about it. I'd have to out myself as Let Her Rip. But hopefully, most people would understand why I had wanted to keep my identity secret.

"Our lawyer is working on the contract and will send it to your lawyer later today. My father also wanted to know if you've thought about which products you want to have with Endless exclusively." Matt's voice was so professional right now as we talked about work. I loved this side of him. Just like I loved every side of him.

"I think definitely the double-frame purses and wristlets. They're a pain to make because I have to glue in the frame. It'll probably go much faster mass-produced." That was one aspect of the double-frame purses that I hadn't liked. The industrial glue I used was strong and I had to wait hours after applying it to allow it to get tacky, before I could put the purse into the frame. I can't tell you how many times I'd applied the glue and then forgotten about it, only to find it hours later, the glue too hard to insert the purse into the frame. I'd have to pry the glue off and start again.

"That's good. They're unique, and I know they'll sell well." Matt's voice changed then. "I miss you."

"I miss you too. When are we going to see each other again?" I didn't want to sound needy but the reality was, I *was* needy. I needed Matt. He was like a drug I didn't know I needed until I'd had a shot, and now I couldn't live without it.

"I hope soon. I'll come visit you once I figure out my

schedule." We'd talked about him flying here if he could get a few days off in a row.

"This is torture. Me being here. You there." I took a breath and then said what had been on my mind for the last few days. "I really think I'm going to move to New York. Not just for you, but to go to FIT and be a New Yorker. Plus, Endless is there, and Ruby. I don't want to be in Oklahoma anymore. I love my home state, but I think it's time I moved on."

"You know I would love that."

We were both quiet, thinking about the possibilities. And then Matt said, "I have to go. I'm working at the firehouse tonight."

"Okay. Say hi to Frank for me." I couldn't help the laugh that escaped. Matt had told me Frank hadn't stopped talking about me since our meeting. He was also sucking up to Matt now, which was a huge change.

"I'll be sure to tell your real boyfriend that." Matt laughed.

After we hung up, I decided to go to the diner since it was usually slow at this time of day. I didn't want to be by myself anymore.

"HOW ARE we going to tell everyone that Let Her Rip is actually mycraftybaokim?" Alicia slid onto the stool next to me. The diner was mostly empty, only two tables and a lone man at the other end of the counter. Violet was helping her parents in the kitchen and popped out every once in a while to talk to me when Alicia was busy.

"I'm going to make an Instagram reel and TikTok and just tell the truth. Explain how it wasn't me who made that video viral. And then announce the partnership with Endless."

"That sounds too simple." Alicia frowned at me.

"It is, but again, sometimes, the truth is the best way." I shrugged. "I know there will be people who won't believe me and will hate on me, but I hope most of our audience will understand."

Alicia stared at me for a moment. "I'm glad this is finally coming out. I'm really excited about the collaboration with Endless." We'd talked about it at length when we came back from New York. How we would make it an equal partnership—maybe even change the Etsy name to Our Crafty Bao.

"Me too. And I think I really want to move to New York City." My heart tripped just saying that out loud.

Alicia angled her head toward me. "I'm so glad you're finally getting out of Oklahoma. It's a great state, but you've been wilting here. With the Endless deal, we'll both be able to afford to move. I've been thinking about it too."

My eyes widened. "We can get an apartment together!"

"You wouldn't move in with Matt?"

I shook my head. "It's too soon for that."

Violet walked up to us, carrying a plate. "Here, my father wanted you to try this and see if you like it." She placed the plate in front of us and I saw it was some sort of quiche.

Alicia picked up the fork Violet handed her and took a bite. "Yum. I love the mushrooms."

I took a bite and nodded in agreement. "Yes."

Violet looked back and forth between us. "Okay. I'll tell him." But she didn't leave. She was staring at us.

"Everything okay at school?" I asked her, remembering how sad she'd been about not having any friends at school the last time I'd seen her.

She nodded. "I think so. I think I know how to finally make those girls like me. Thanks to you." She gave me a shy smile.

"Don't try to please them, okay, Violet? Just be you." I was worried about her. I knew how she felt, since I'd gone through the same thing in high school. High school sucked big-time.

"Thanks, Kimmie." She turned and went back into the kitchen before I could say anything else.

Alicia turned to me. "What was that all about?"

I shrugged. "I think she's having trouble at school."

We stared after her for a moment and then turned back to our conversation, both excited about everything that was happening. This collaboration with Endless was going to change my life.

THIRTY-FOUR

Matt

"Your girlfriend might really move to New York?" Nana placed a pitcher of fresh-squeezed lemonade on the table in her apartment. I'd come to Brooklyn after leaving the fire-house this morning to visit her.

I knew I had a goofy grin on my face but I couldn't help it. I'd just finished catching Nana up on the latest with Kimmie, and how my father wanted to move ahead with the collaboration, calling the collection Crafty Bao for Endless.

"She's talking about it." I still got a thrill whenever I thought of Kimmie as my girlfriend.

Nana sat down across from me. "It's good to see you so happy. I can't wait to see her again."

"I'm going to visit her, maybe next week. If you can believe it, Frank actually said he'd switch tours with me. He's completely obsessed with Let Her Rip." I poured a glass of the lemonade and placed it in front of Nana before pouring one for myself.

Nana grinned. "I guess you have Kimmie to thank for Frank being nice for once."

"Yeah. I have Kimmie to thank for a lot of good stuff in my life right now." I paused, thinking about seeing her again. The past week and a half without her had been endless.

"She showed me her sewing table the last time we Face-Timed. I think that's the one thing she's going to miss about leaving her childhood home." Nana took a sip of her lemonade, her eyes twinkling at me over her glass.

"Wait. What? You FaceTime with her?" I put my glass down and stared at my grandmother.

"Of course. You don't think I was going to let you date someone without getting to know her better?" She waggled her eyebrows at me.

I looked at Nana in disbelief. "So she is perfectly fine FaceTiming with you, but it was like pulling teeth to get her to FaceTime with me?"

She gave a self-satisfied smile. "I guess she likes me better."

I burst out in laughter. "Nana. Really?"

She put her glass down and gave a shrug. "Can you blame her?"

I shook my head at her. "Nana, Nana."

"Matt, Matt." She copied my movements and then got serious. "Really, I'm glad everything is working out for you. And that your father is on board."

"Kimmie's going to make the video today. She'll release it once the team has reviewed it. And that will also serve as an unofficial announcement that Crafty Bao is coming to Endless." I sat back in my chair, a smile on my face. "My father and his team have been working to launch it with some of the pictures they took of Alicia when she was here. Along with the bao stuffed toy."

Speaking of which, I'd forgotten I'd brought one for

Nana and reached down for the backpack I'd dropped next to my chair. I took it out and handed it to her. "This is for you."

"What is this darling thing?" She took it and admired it. It was the medium-size bao, about the size of a cantaloupe, and so soft and squishy.

"It's one of the prototypes Dad had made up."

"It's adorable! People are going to go nuts over these." She squished it and then hugged it to her. "Thanks, Matt. My own bao." She put it down and picked up her phone. "Here, take a picture of me with it. I want to post it to Instagram."

I laughed as I took her phone. "Okay, but don't mention what it's for yet. It hasn't been announced formally."

"I won't." She held up the toy and I took a few pictures.

I handed her back the phone and watched as she looked through them and selected one to post. But then she gasped. "Matt. Have you seen this?" She pointed at her iPhone.

"What?"

"Matt." Her voice was more urgent this time and she held out her phone.

I gave her a puzzled look, wondering why she seemed so concerned, and then grabbed her phone. It took me a moment to understand what I was looking at. But when understanding dawned, I shot to my feet.

"Oh, shit." How the heck had this happened?

Kimmie

"Kimmie, are you home?"

I was in my sewing room working on orders when I heard the front door slam and Alicia yelling for me.

"Up here." I stepped on the pedal and my sewing machine roared to life, sewing together the seam in a matter of seconds. And that was all it took for Alicia to run up the stairs, because when I looked up, she was in the doorway, out of breath and her eyes wild.

"Did you see it yet?" she asked, breathless.

"See what?" I put the piece I'd just sewed together aside and picked up another one.

"Oh my god, Kimmie. Get on your phone. Look at your Instagram. I don't know how this happened. But everyone knows." She walked to me and picked up my phone and handed it to me.

I took it from her, my forehead furrowed. "What are you talking about?"

She pointed and I opened my Instagram app, taken aback when it said I had thousands of notifications. "I haven't posted anything lately. Did someone tag me?"

"I think so. I didn't have time to go through all of them." She waited as I scanned through some, and then my breath caught and my mouth opened.

"What the—" I looked up at Alicia. "Who outed us?"

"I didn't." Alicia held up her hands. "I swear."

"No, of course not. I know you wouldn't." But someone had. I opened my Twitter account and noticed that #letherrip was trending again. I was trending. Because someone had told the world that Let Her Rip was the person behind the My Crafty Bao shop and accounts, which had been getting so popular lately.

"Oh, shit." This was really bad. Just when I thought we'd finally figured out how to handle that video, this had to happen. I was going to make my own video today. I'd been going over what to say in my head. Who had done this to us?

Alicia sat down in one of the chairs and pulled out her own phone. "I'm going to see if I can figure out who leaked this."

"I need to call Matt." As if he knew I was thinking about him, my cell rang.

I picked it up after the first ring. "Matt."

"You saw it." His voice was rushed.

"Yes. Who did this? What happened?"

"I was about to ask you the same thing." He paused and I heard someone in the background saying something to him. "I'm with Nana. She's the one who told me."

"I have no idea, Matt. I was just about to record my own video." I sat back in my chair, closing my eyes for a moment. "This is bad, isn't it?"

He sighed. "Yes. It doesn't look good. We had wanted you to be the one to tell everyone, to be authentic and real. Now, because someone decided to tell everyone, it'll look like you're trying to cover your ass."

I sat up. "Does your father know yet?"

"I don't know. I called you first." He sighed. "I guess I need to call him."

"Oh, no." I slumped back in my chair. "Why is this happening? That video has been screwing up my life ever since it went viral, and it's still messing everything up. We were so close." I moaned, one hand up by my face.

"Kimmie." Alicia's voice had me looking over at her. "It was Violet."

"What?" It took a moment for my mind to switch gears. "What was Violet?"

"She's the one who outed you all over social media. Said she overheard us talking at the diner and wanted to be the first to let everyone know that Let Her Rip and My Crafty Bao are the same person."

My face fell as understanding dawned. *Violet* had outed me? Why? Did she hate me?

Just then, Matt cursed. "My father is on the other line. I think he knows."

"Oh my god. Everything is falling apart." I closed my eyes and once again cursed the existence of that viral video.

Matt's voice was tense. "I'll call you back." And he hung up, leaving me to stare at Alicia.

THIRTY-FIVE

Matt

I called Kimmie as soon as I got off the phone with my father. We were fucked.

"What did he say?" Kimmie didn't even bother saying hello.

"He's furious." I let out a sigh, my ears still ringing from my father's loud voice. "He thinks you guys leaked it without getting the okay from PR."

"We didn't—"

I cut her off. "I know. I told him that. That you would never do that."

"Now what?" Her voice was so defeated I wished I was there to take her in my arms and comfort her.

"Now we wait for my father to calm down." I knew him. There was no sense in talking to him when he was livid. "And then we'll figure out damage control. I need to get on social media and see what the reactions are."

"If I didn't like Michelle so much, I swear, I'd be tempted to sue her right now for putting up that damn video." Kimmie's voice was heated. "It's done nothing but cause my life hell. I don't understand why people want their videos to go viral."

"I know. But suing her is not going to help. You might have to come to New York. Work with our team to figure out what to do." My heart lifted a bit at the thought of seeing her again, even if it was for something like this.

"Does your father even still want to go ahead?" I understood Kimmie's concern. Nothing had been signed. And knowing my father, there was a very real chance that he'd back out. He hated being lied to, even though Kimmie hadn't done it.

"I don't know." I had to be truthful with her. "But I'm going to do everything I can to figure this out and see if we can convince him that you're still a viable brand for Endless."

"What should I do?" I hated the helplessness in her voice.

"Nothing for now. Lie low, don't answer any of the comments. I'll touch base in a bit." Good thing I didn't have to work at the firehouse today. There was no way I could scroll through social media like I needed to if I was working.

"Okay." She sighed. "I guess I'll just hide out and keep sewing."

"Yes. It's all going to be fine." I had the biggest urge to tell her I loved her, but I didn't want the first time to be over the phone and when she was so worried.

"Thanks. Let me know as soon as you know anything." We said good-bye and hung up.

I walked to my desk in the corner of my living room and opened my laptop. I got to work, pulling up all of Kim's social media sites on my computer, iPad, and phone.

Kimmie

Alicia and I sewed in silence for the next hour. There was nothing to say until Matt told us how bad the damage was. Alicia had started tracking the comments but then stopped because she could see it was getting to me. I wanted to look for myself, but I didn't know if I could take it if people were being mean. This was why I hated attention. Why couldn't someone who *wanted* to go viral have done so instead of me?

After an hour, the silence got to be too much. I needed to distract myself. "How are things with Todd?"

Alicia gave me a smug smile. "Good. I'm not ready to get in a relationship again after being with Josh for six years, but Todd is a good distraction. He's so good in bed. And his penis . . ." She rolled her eyes as I scrunched up my nose.

"Ew. Don't say that word." She knew I hated it.

"What? Penis?" Alicia wiggled her eyebrows at me.

"Stop!" I shrieked, putting both hands over my ears.

"You are so juvenile. That's what it's called. A penis. What do you want me to call it? Ding-dong?" Alicia was doing this to distract me, and it was working.

"I don't know, 'peepee,' or 'thing' sounds good. Or 'cock' or 'dick.' Just not the p-word."

"Penis, penis, penis. How is Matt's penis?" Alicia sang, acting like a teenager.

I could be just as bratty as Alicia. I stood up, took a cushion off the couch, and swatted her over the head with it. With a scream, she put her hands over her head and ran and got another cushion and then we were hitting each other. I swatted as hard as I could, trying to work out all the nervous tension in my body. It felt good, and Alicia got in a few whacks herself, before we both collapsed on the couch and surveyed the mess we'd made. Paper pattern pieces had floated off the sewing table from the breeze caused by our pillow fight, and random pieces of fabric littered the floor.

"Things have to work out with Endless," Alicia said once we'd caught our breath. Our eyes met for a moment in panic. "I want to move to New York with you."

There was so much riding on this partnership. If it didn't go through, I wouldn't be able to afford to move to New York. And the thought crushed me. To be so close to finally living out my dreams, in the same city as the guy I was falling in love with, doing what I loved and working with a huge company like Endless . . .

I stood suddenly, unable to sit still. "This can't fall apart. It just can't." I looked at Alicia, anguish flooding my body. "I want this so bad. Now that I got a taste of what life could be like, I don't think I can return to what I was doing here in Oklahoma." I started pacing around the sewing room. "I wasn't really living. I was just existing. I want so much more. I want Matt. I want life in the city. I want to eat all the foods and see all the things in New York. I want to be around creative people, building the brand I started here, sending it out into the world. I want our baos to give other people happiness." I stopped and turned to Alicia. "It can't fall apart. It just can't." The last words came out in a whimper.

Alicia stared at me. I knew she wanted this as badly as I did.

We heard the front door open downstairs. "Kimmie, are you home?"

"We're here." Both Alicia and I ran down the stairs to meet Hana. One look at her face and I knew she knew.

I threw myself on the couch in the living room. "You saw."

She nodded. "It's all over town. Michelle was the one who told me."

"Michelle?" Damn that girl.

"I ran into her on the street. She is beyond sorry for the mess she's caused you." Hana sat next to me.

I rolled my eyes. I was trying very hard not to blame Michelle. But how could I not?

"Anyways, I've been following all the reactions, and it's not bad at all." Hana stroked my hair. "People are rallying behind you."

"What, really?" I sat up. "They're not calling me a liar?"

"Well, some are." Hana shrugged. "But most are understanding. When Violet posted about it, she told everyone that you hadn't known someone took that viral video. That you're a private person and didn't want that meme associated with your store. She essentially said what you were going to tell everyone anyways."

"Why is the hashtag trending again though? Does Violet have a lot of followers?" I hadn't wanted to see all the comments and reactions so I hadn't looked up the original post.

"She doesn't. But she commented on your most recent post and I guess your followers saw it and it blew up from there."

I covered my face with my hands. "I hope Robert gets that I had nothing to do with this. The last thing I would do is to bring more unwanted attention to myself."

"Have you talked to Matt?" Hana asked.

I nodded. "He's doing damage control with his father. Said I might have to fly to New York."

"That's a good idea." Hana nodded back at me.

"You need to fight for this, Kimmie," Alicia said. "I know Endless hates this kind of publicity, but the collaboration is too perfect for them to just let you go over something that's not your fault."

"I know." I sighed but then brightened a bit. "I guess the silver lining is that I'd get to see Matt again."

"Yes. See, look at the positive." Hana patted me on the shoulder just as my cell rang.

"It's Matt." I picked up the call, holding my breath that he had good news.

"Kimmie, can you come to New York?" Matt got right to the point.

"It's bad, then?" I couldn't breathe.

"My father has calmed down a bit. But he's still upset by all the publicity you're getting that we can't control. I told him people are actually rallying behind you. That it doesn't have to be a bad thing. You're getting a lot of publicity that could be good for Endless in the long run, especially because you didn't generate all this interest." Matt's calm voice slowed the pounding of my heart and I closed my eyes, taking a big breath.

"So, what happens now?"

"He wants to meet with you and the whole team. Figure out how to proceed if we proceed." Matt paused and took a breath. "But I think you need to post a video now. Be authentic, tell the truth, from your point of view. I've been studying the comments and posts and the majority of people are behind you. They love you. I think if you speak up now, it will go a long way toward damage control."

"Does your father want me to do this?" I sucked in a breath.

"He doesn't know. But I have a gut feeling about this. If it works, it will show my father how people look up to you and are supporting you." When I didn't say anything, he said, "Don't give up, Kimmie. I believe in you."

He believed in me. Even after everything that had happened, Matt believed in me. My eyes prickled and I swallowed as my gaze swung to Hana and Alicia. They'd both told me they believed in me too. Now it was just a matter of whether I believed in myself. I'd done nothing wrong (well, except letting people think Alicia was me). I'd been caught in this viral video that was not my doing. I hadn't sought out the attention, nor had I posted the video or encouraged the following in any way.

My dreams were important to me. I didn't want to live by myself in the middle of nowhere anymore. I was ready to believe in myself.

"Okay," I said into the phone. "I'm going to make a video now and then I'm getting on the next plane to New York."

THIRTY-SIX

Instagram Reel / TikTok Video

[VIDEO OF KIMMIE TALKING, with background music]

"Hi, everyone. My name is Kimmie Park. A lot of you know me as Let Her Rip. And I'm also Kim from My Crafty Bao. My life kind of blew up when that video of me went viral. I'm a very private person and I was mortified. I wanted to move to another planet. Because I had no idea someone had taken that video and then posted it. And no, I'm not mad anymore at the person who did that. She meant well and had no idea it would go viral.

"I don't crave fame. I don't even have a social media presence under my own name and only got one because of my Etsy shop. When I posted that first picture of my best friend, Alicia, I had no idea people were going to think she was me. It was an honest misunderstanding. But I didn't correct it because I didn't want to associate that meme with my Etsy shop. It's the one thing I'm really proud of, and the merchandise I make and the posts I put up are all me, the real me. If it weren't for that viral video going around, I would have told everyone that the pictures I posted weren't me. But I couldn't. I didn't want to taint my shop with a meme.

"I'm here to say I'm sorry for misleading all of you. But I hope some of you can understand why I did it. For someone who does not crave the limelight and who hates having people talk about me, this video has made my life difficult. I didn't post pictures of Alicia intending to lie to anyone. And I was about to tell everyone the truth, but someone told you all before I could. I wish I'd gotten the chance to tell you myself first.

"So this is me. My name is Kimmie Park and I've decided to stop being embarrassed about that video. Because the thing is, I meant everything I said. That was me. I make mistakes just like everyone else, I lose my shit sometimes, just like everyone else, and I get embarrassed, just like everyone else. But I've realized I need to own it. The good, the bad, the embarrassing, they are all me. Behind that meme is a real person. Me, Kim. Kimmie.

"I'm not hiding anymore. I'm ready to claim me. And finally live by my signature to be daring, be bold, be me. [Smiles] And I wish you would all delete that damn video so I never have to see it again.

That's it. Be daring, be bold, be you.

(COMMENTS HAVE BEEN *disabled*)

THIRTY-SEVEN

Kimmie

Matt picked me up at the airport the next day. He jumped out of an SUV and, after giving me a quick kiss on the lips, threw my suitcase in the trunk as I got into the passenger side. There were cars all around us, honking and angling for space to pick up passengers. Matt pulled away as I sat and drank him in, my body literally humming to be so close to him again. I leaned in and inhaled the fresh scent of his aftershave and his own special Matt smell, which I would have recognized with my eyes closed. Once we were exiting the airport, he reached out an arm and I snuggled into his side.

"You're here." He grinned at me before turning his eyes back to the road.

"I am. Thanks for picking me up." I hadn't known he had a car in Manhattan. He'd told me it was really his father's, but since his dad rarely drove it, Matt used it when he needed it.

"That video you made was so real." His hand stroked

my arm, sending shivers up and down my spine. "I was right. People are completely rallying behind you."

I made a face against his biceps. God, his arms. I could feel the hard ridges of his muscles against my cheek and I sighed. I'd spoken from the heart in that video, and to my relief, the reactions had been mostly positive. I'd disabled the comments for the video, but people were talking about it on their own accounts.

"Do you mind if we stop at the firehouse before going to my apartment? I have to pick something up from my locker." He glanced at me as he merged onto the highway.

"Of course not." I put a hand on his thigh, needing to touch as much of him as I could. "Is Frank working today? I could give him a thrill and dance for him."

"If Let Her Rip twerked for him, I think he would fall at your feet and give you anything you wanted." Matt laughed. "He's mellowed ever since finding out I'm dating Let Her Rip, so thank you for that."

"No problem." I gave him a cheeky grin.

He squeezed my shoulder. "It's so good to see you."

"You too. I can't wait to get this meeting with your father over with tomorrow." On the plane ride here, I'd resigned myself to whatever happened. If Endless decided I was too much of a risk and didn't want to partner with me, there was nothing I could do about it.

"Everything's going to be fine. I can feel it." He flashed a smile at me and we kept the conversation light for the rest of the ride to the firehouse.

He found a parking spot around the corner. When we got out of the car, I spotted a gray-and-white dog huddled against a building. Some sort of pit bull mix, it wasn't very big and was so skinny I could see its ribs. I let out a gasp and Matt followed my gaze.

"Oh, poor thing." I walked toward the dog slowly, not wanting to scare him (or her).

Matt came to my side and we both crouched down a couple of feet in front of the dog. "Come here, buddy," Matt said, holding out a hand.

The dog half stood and I saw she was a female.

"I think he's a she," I said.

"Doesn't matter." Matt looked at me with a smile before turning back to the dog. "She can still be buddy, right?

"Yes, you're right." My heart gave a thump, watching the tender look on Matt's face as he inched closer, his hand still held out.

The dog sniffed his hand and then licked it. Matt picked her up, the dog trembling so hard that Matt looked like he was shaking too. And my heart melted. Not just at the dog, but at the man holding the dog. He was like my wildest wet dream. (Yes, my wet dreams were sometimes G-rated and filled with dogs.) I wanted him. I wanted to *be* the dog. I had never been jealous of a dog before. And a poor, neglected one at that. I'd sunk to a whole new level. I wanted to snuggle next to her in Matt's strong arms and have him focus those eyes on me too.

The dog turned, and when her soft brown eyes met mine, I sank again. Man and dog, I wanted them in my world more than anything I'd wanted in a long time.

I crouched down at their side and slowly reached out to pet the dog. Her tongue stuck out and I was a goner, just like the first time I'd seen Matt's pictures with Cleo. The dog picked her head up off Matt's shoulder and moved as if she wanted to come into my arms. Matt loosened his grip and she literally crawled into my waiting arms. I looked up at Matt, my arms full of this poor neglected creature, and my heart was lost. She gave a sigh and rested her head against my shoulder. She probably weighed around thirty pounds and should have been heavy in my arms, but she felt so light.

I petted her head while Matt ran his hand down her body.

"She needs food and water." Matt pointed to some cuts on her face. "Someone or something got her."

"Poor baby. It's okay, we're going to take care of you now." I felt around her neck. "She doesn't have a collar."

"We'll take her to the firehouse and get her cleaned up and fed." Matt reached out to take her from me and then stood. "Someone either abandoned her or she's a stray. The firehouse will call around, see if anyone has lost a dog, but I doubt it. Judging by her condition, if someone had lost this dog, I wouldn't let them take her back."

I got up too and we walked the short distance to the firehouse. One of the guys saw us coming and alerted the others, until most of the eleven guys on duty were gathered around us. A few called out greetings to me and my face warmed, surprised they remembered my name. Frank came out from the kitchen and his face lit up when he saw me.

"Let Her . . . I mean, Kimmie." He ran a hand through his hair, his face turning red. "So great to see you. I thought you went home."

"I did. I'm back here on business." I gave him a smile and he leaned to give me a kiss on the cheek. "We found a dog." I gestured to her, lying on a blanket that someone had found. Another guy had given her a plastic container of water and someone else came out of the kitchen with a leftover hamburger. We all watched her gulp it down, and the way she devoured it hurt my heart.

"Matt." I tugged on his hand. "I want that dog." Which was completely irrational. I still lived in Oklahoma.

He met my eyes. "I know. I do too. But my building doesn't allow dogs over twenty-five pounds. She looks like she's about thirty, and once she gains weight . . . plus what would I do with her when I'm here overnight?"

Frank squatted down to rub the dog on the head. "I know we're supposed to return lost dogs, but if anyone tries to claim this dog, I'd take them out. No one treats a dog like this and gets them back."

"What are you going to do with her, then?" I looked around.

"We'll probably call Animal Control to come get her." I thought the man who said this was named Bill, but I wasn't sure.

"No." I shook my head. "Can't someone here foster her? Or get her into a rescue or something?" I turned to Matt again. "Can we keep her somehow?"

"I . . ." He was at a loss for words, but I could see the way he was looking at the dog.

"I'll take her for now." We all turned to Frank, who stood up. "I live with my parents in Queens and they have a fenced backyard. We can watch her until she gets adopted."

The guys around me all started talking at once.

"Frankie, I didn't know you still live with Mommy and Daddy!"

"Aw, how sweet, our Frankie boy lives at home."

"Hey, Frank, does Mummy still do your laundry and wipe your ass?"

Frank held up his hands. "Yeah, yeah. Break my balls. But I'm saving a lot of money to buy my own place."

Matt clapped him on the shoulder. "I had no idea you were an animal lover."

Frank nodded. "Animals are better than people."

"They are," I said, and Frank turned red again when I smiled at him.

The other guys drifted away, but Frank stayed by our side. "You want the dog?"

"I wish." Matt looked deep in thought and then he turned to me. "Mrs. White, who you met, might be able to convince the board to let me have a dog over twenty-five pounds. Maybe we'll call her an emotional support dog or something, for the brave, heroic fireman that I am."

I gave him the side-eye and he turned up a hand.

"What?" he said. "I'm not above using my fireman status for something like this." Then he dropped his hand. "But even if I could get the board to approve her, there's still the problem of where she'd go when I have to be here overnight."

I knelt down and the dog looked at me with those big brown eyes, so much trust in them even though she should have been wary of me. She licked my hand, and as irrational as I knew it was, I literally felt like I was meant to have this dog.

"She can stay with me on the nights when you're at the firehouse," I said without looking up.

"What? Kimmie, you live in Oklahoma." Matt's voice was confused.

I looked up. "I'm moving to New York. If things don't work out with Endless, I'll just find another job here." Our eyes held, and then with a hoot of happiness, Matt pulled me up and into his arms. I wrapped my arms around him, not caring that we had an audience. And when he lowered his lips to mine, I heard Frank say, "Um, okay, I'll give you two some privacy." And then it was just Matt and me, together again, and he was kissing me as if it was the most important thing in the world to him.

MATT HAD to literally peel me away from the dog. I hadn't wanted to leave her there. He was going to talk to Mrs. White as soon as we got to the apartment.

By the time he drove up to the building, it was dinnertime. My stomach growled as Matt put my suitcase on the sidewalk. "I'm going to park and I'll meet you inside?"

I turned my face up for a kiss and then grabbed my suitcase. "Oh, look, Mrs. White is in the lobby." I pointed through the glass door.

"Perfect. I'll join you as soon as I can." He brushed a thumb over my cheek and my knees literally weakened. I couldn't wait to get him inside and out of his clothes, to feel that magnificent body against mine.

Matt got back in his car and the doorman opened the door for me. I thanked him and then walked over to Mrs. White.

"Hi, Mrs. White." I greeted Mickey and Milly, who gave me polite licks.

"Matt West's girlfriend who makes him glow," Mrs. White said, and the two of us dissolved into giggles. "Are you visiting again?"

I sat next to her. "Yes. How've you been?"

"Never better." She turned so that her body was angled toward mine. "I just had my annual physical and the doctor says I have the heart of a fifty-year-old. Must be all the walking I do with these two." She gestured to her dogs.

"That's great." I widened my eyes at her. "I wish Matt had a dog. He could use the company when I'm not here. You know, being a firefighter, it's very stressful and he sees some awful things sometimes. It would be so much better for his mental health if he could come home to a loving dog."

Mrs. White nodded at me. "He should get a dog."

I looked down, a sad look on my face. "He fell in love with one this afternoon. A stray we found on the street. She was so skinny and was shaking, but she let Matt pick her up. Those eyes. We want her so much."

Mrs. White looked around. "Where is she? We allow dogs in this building."

I gave a sigh. "But only up to twenty-five pounds, Matt said. This dog is probably thirty pounds now. And once she gains weight, she'll be more."

Mrs. White turned to me, and without seeing her face, I knew she was studying my profile. "You are a very clever girl, aren't you?"

I shot a look at her from the side of my eyes. "What do you mean?"

Matt walked into the lobby just then, and Mrs. White's face lit up. "Matt West. I was just telling your girlfriend how clever she is."

"She really is." He came to my side but halted when he caught the way Mrs. White was looking at him. "What? What is it?"

"Your job is very stressful, isn't it, Matt West? The things you see. I think you could use an emotional support dog." Her eyes gleamed as she nodded at Matt.

He nodded back. "Yes, very stressful. It sure would be nice to come home to a dog." He shook his head. "But I can't get one. Who would watch her when I'm at the firehouse overnight? Kimmie's going to move to the city soon, but until then . . ."

At that, Mrs. White stood up. "Why don't you bring the dog by tomorrow and we'll see if she gets along with Mickey and Milly? If she's as sweet as Kimmie says, she can stay with me on the nights you work."

"What?" I jumped off the couch. "You would watch the dog?"

"The dog is over thirty pounds though," Matt put in.

"If Mickey and Milly approve, I'll make sure the board makes an exception for one of New York's bravest. Besides, what's a few extra pounds? We can't give the poor girl a complex just because she gains weight." Her mouth twitched.

Matt and I stared at each other. Holy shit, I hadn't expected Mrs. White to watch the dog. I'd thought maybe Frank could keep her until I moved to New York. We both turned to Mrs. White at the same time.

"Thank you," we chorused together, then caught each other's eye and burst into laughter. Mrs. White joined in, and soon people were staring at us strangely as they walked through the lobby.

THIRTY-EIGHT

Matt

I didn't want to get out of bed the next morning. I opened my eyes to see Kimmie in bed facing me, curled up on her side with her hair spread out on my pillow. Our legs were intertwined and I swear, I never wanted to leave this bed. It was hard to believe that it had only been six weeks since I first DMed Kimmie on Instagram. So much had happened since then, and if anyone said to me that it was too soon to know if you were in love, I'd tell them they were wrong. Because I knew without a doubt that I was in love with this woman. I watched her sleeping peacefully for another few moments before she stirred.

One eye opened and she smiled when she found me watching her. "Good morning, Matt."

I loved that. I fucking loved how gravelly her voice sounded first thing in the morning and how she gazed at me, half asleep but with a smile as if the sight of me made her happy. How had I gotten so lucky?

I leaned in and gave her a kiss on the lips. She swatted me away.

"Ew, Matt. I have morning breath. Don't get too close."

I laughed. "I don't mind. And I have morning breath too. Do you think I'm gross?"

She lifted her head and her hair fell around her shoulders. I loved her hair. I didn't know why she said she hated it. "Nothing about you is gross."

I reached for her but she turned her head to look at the time on the cable box. She sat up and flung back the covers. "We have to get up. I'm not going to be late to this meeting with your father."

I fell back against the mattress with my eyes closed, stifling a moan of disappointment. I wanted to stay in bed all day with her. The last thing I wanted to do was be in a meeting with my father and everyone else involved in this project. But then she pulled on my arm and I opened my eyes and saw the look on her face. This meant the world to her. I couldn't let her down.

"Okay, I'm up. Let's get them." I got out of bed but grabbed her before she could go into the bathroom. "One last kiss for good luck?" I pulled her close and she melted into me until we fit together perfectly. And she tilted her head up, meeting my mouth, morning breath be damned.

AN HOUR LATER, we sat in the conference room with my father and eight other people. I sat next to Kimmie, facing my father, his assistant, Tina, the PR and marketing team, two members of the board, and our lawyer. I turned to Kimmie and almost laughed out loud when I saw that she looked like she was about to pee her pants. I gave her an encouraging smile. We were ready. We had her audience behind us.

My father cleared his throat, signaling that the meeting was starting. I stood and clicked on the projector, showing the data I had gathered. This was the way to Robert West's heart. Pure, undiluted data.

"As you all have seen by now, Kimmie's video from yesterday went viral. People love her, are backing her and rallying behind her. They see themselves in her. She is real to them. And you can see by the graph I made that while there are some who criticize and condemn her, ninety percent of the people who have commented are behind her." I stopped to let it sink in, especially for my father.

"Yes, her viral video and this latest debacle are not what Endless is about and do not fit into the culture of Endless. But Kimmie, the real live person sitting in front of you"—I gestured to her—"and Kim, the person behind the My Crafty Bao shop and brand, are exactly what Endless needs. Her products are what Endless customers will go crazy for." I held up all three sizes of the prototype baos, one after another. "This is what Endless is about. Her personal connection to baos, to her parents who are no longer with her, her commitment to keeping that viral video away from her brand. This is the real Kim. She cannot be held responsible for other people's actions. And she has proven that she does not crave the spotlight. Together with her best friend, Alicia, Kimmie and My Crafty Bao would be an incredible asset to Endless."

I sat down and faced my father.

He looked from Kimmie to me, and I could practically hear the breath Kimmie sucked in and held. But then my father smiled. He actually smiled.

"I agree with everything Matt just said. Support is pouring in for Kimmie." He stood and clicked something, and the images on the screen changed. It was a picture of

Alicia holding one of my double-frame purses. "Look at these sample pictures we had taken of Alicia." He clicked through a few more and I heard Kimmie catch her breath beside me. Because the pictures were amazing. Alicia's smile, the look on her face as she faced the camera dead on while displaying Kimmie's merchandise, was mesmerizing. And once we got pictures of Alicia with the stuffed bao toy, it was going to be even more epic.

A murmur went up from everyone gathered. They could feel it. This was going to be big. I knew everyone was picturing the bao on different merchandise, and the reaction from our customers. Not to mention Kimmie's hundreds of thousands of followers.

Finally, after a few minutes when everyone was speaking at once, my father turned his attention to Kimmie. "Your honesty and realness have won over your audience. And us here at Endless. We'd be honored to carry your brand."

Kimmie gasped and her hands flew to her mouth. She stared at my father. He gave her a nod, and she nodded back. She turned to me, joy in her eyes, and I smiled at her, so big I could feel my cheeks aching.

"Thank you, Robert. You have no idea what this means to me." Her eyes were shining. "I'd like Alicia to be an equal partner with me. She is the face of my brand, along with her brilliant mind, and I couldn't have done it without her."

"Of course." My father stood. "In fact, I want to offer her a mentorship of sorts. We could really use her mind and enthusiasm here."

"I can't speak for her, but I have a feeling she's going to love that." Kimmie stood too, and my father walked around the table so that they could shake on it. Everyone started talking, and as the team stood and surrounded Kimmie, congratulating her, I stood back and watched her accept their congrats. She was the one glowing now. Not me.

THIRTY-NINE

Kimmie

I decided to stay in New York City for the next two weeks, not going back to Oklahoma until right before Thanksgiving. I needed this time with Matt, time to really get to know him in person and see him, be able to touch him. I put my Etsy shop on vacation again.

As soon as the meeting was over, Matt and I had driven to Frank's house in Queens to get our dog. We already thought of her as ours, even though we didn't have a name for her yet. She perked up as soon as she saw us.

I fell on my knees and wrapped my arms around her and she licked my face.

"She's been eating a lot. I had to give her a little at a time so she wouldn't choke." Frank leaned down and rubbed her on the head.

"Thank you for taking care of her." I beamed at Frank and he ducked his head and blushed.

Matt clapped Frank on the back and I was glad to see that they were getting along. Maybe my meme had some good consequences, after all.

"You should post a picture of you and the dog." Frank turned to me.

"That's a great idea." This could be my first Instagram post as myself (not counting the video I'd just made apologizing for the misunderstanding). What better subject than my new dog? I beamed at Frank and he blushed again as I handed him my cell so he could take a picture.

We drove the dog home. I was already starting to think of Matt's apartment as home, even though I planned to get my own apartment. Or one with Alicia if she really moved with me. Mrs. White had told us it was okay to have the dog in Matt's apartment while she petitioned the board on our behalf.

"I think she needs a bath." Matt said, once we were back at his apartment.

"We should take her to the vet too. Make sure she's okay." The dog sat in front of us, one ear sticking straight up and the other down, as if she was listening to our conversation.

We went into the bathroom and Matt picked her up, placing her in the tub. We'd stopped at the pet store next to Matt's building and bought everything she'd need, including dog shampoo. She'd picked out a stuffed toy herself. I used the detachable shower head to wet her down as we talked about names.

"How about Bella?" Matt asked.

I wrinkled my nose. "She doesn't look like a Bella." She licked my hand, which I took as agreement.

"Ember?" I suggested, rubbing shampoo into her fur.

"Cute, but I don't think it fits her." Matt cocked his head as he studied the dog. "Blaze?"

I laughed. "That's a very fireman choice." I turned to the dog. "Blaze? Is your name Blaze?"

I used the showerhead to wash the soap suds off her. She stood quietly, as if enjoying her bath. I ran my hand up and down her body until all the soap had washed out.

Matt helped me pick her up and put her on the bath mat, where she stood still as we rubbed her down with a towel. "She's gray and white. What does that remind you of?" Matt asked.

I studied her. "Smoke? Ashes? Cinder?"

"Cinder. Hm." Matt studied her. "What about Luna?"

The dog's tongue came out as she panted, and I swear, there was a big smile on her face.

"Luna it is," I said, and wrapped my arms around her.

THE NEXT TWO weeks were some of the best of my entire life. It was a whirlwind time, exhausting, but it filled me with so much energy. We spent time with Ruby and her fiancé, Eric, and introduced her to Mila. We had dinner with Nana in Brooklyn and also saw a Broadway show with her. And I met Matt's friend Jason and his family for brunch, where Jason teased me about taking them to Smokies for barbecue. Matt and I also went apartment hunting, which made the move seem even more real. I was literally bursting with happiness and loved everything about New York City.

A few days before I was supposed to go home, we went for a walk in Central Park with Luna. It was a sunny, if cool, day in November, the week of Thanksgiving, and my happiness was too big to be contained indoors. Luna had really come out of her shell in just the short time she'd been living with us. She'd jumped and barked as we put her harness on, and then bounded for the front door. Once outside, she ran the whole way to Central Park with us flying behind her.

We slowed our pace once we were in the park. Matt took my hand, the one that wasn't holding Luna's leash. I looked up and found him gazing at me.

"Happy?" he asked.

I nodded. "It's hard to believe that two months ago, I didn't know who you were."

"And now . . ." He stopped walking and so did I. "I love you, Kimmie Park."

I didn't think I could be any happier than I already was. I was wrong. This, hearing Matt tell me he loved me, was beyond anything I could have imagined.

"I love you too, Matt West." I leaned into him and right there, in the middle of Central Park, with Luna patiently waiting at our side, he kissed me so deeply that I saw stars.

I floated home on a high. I was going back to Oklahoma in two days. And then I would start packing and decide what to do with the house. I thought I'd rent it for now, since I didn't know if I could really sell it. I hoped Alicia decided to move with me. Robert had offered her a paid mentorship position at Endless, in addition to working on our line. If she did, we could get a bigger place. Everything was falling into place. As awful as that viral video and meme had been, I couldn't deny they had brought me great things too. They had brought me to this point in my life.

"What do you want for dinner?" Matt asked when we were back in the apartment.

I was sitting on the floor, wiping Luna's paws with a baby wipe. It was incredible how dirty they got from the streets of New York City. "Let's stay in tonight. Order something?" I wanted to snuggle up on the couch with Matt and Luna. "Maybe watch a movie?" I wiggled my eyebrows and reached over to squeeze his biceps. "And other things?"

He laughed, and when I stood up, he grabbed my butt. He'd told me the first time we'd slept together how much he loved my butt. I turned and ran my hands over his chest. I loved his body so much and couldn't imagine how I was going to survive being separated from him in the short time it would take me to go back to Oklahoma and pack.

He pulled me close and kissed me, one hand cupping my ass. When we came up for air, I whispered, "I think dinner will have to wait a bit." I ran my hands up his muscular back and then down again, slipping my hand into his pants, feeling his taut buttocks. I couldn't believe this was all mine. He was already hard against my front and I wanted nothing more than to be in bed with him right now.

My cell rang.

"Damn." My head swiveled to where I'd left it by the front table, but Matt turned my head back to him.

"Ignore it," he said. Which was good advice, since it stopped ringing.

But then it started again, and something in its ringtone made me freeze. A tingling went through my body and I was suddenly alert, my eyes focused on my phone. I pulled away from Matt and answered it before it stopped ringing.

"Kimmie." It was Alicia and she sounded like she'd been running.

"What's wrong? Are you okay?" I knew instinctively that something was wrong.

"It's Hana. She got hit by a car while crossing the road. She's in the hospital. I think she's going to be okay but you need to come home."

My eyes rounded and I lost my grip on the phone. It crashed to the ground as I stood there, unable to move.

FORTY

Matt

I watched as all the blood drained out of Kimmie's face and she dropped her phone. I was by her side in seconds.

"What is it? What's wrong?" When she didn't answer, I picked up her phone. "Hello?"

"Matt. Kimmie needs to come home. Hana's in the hospital." Alicia explained and then I told her we would call her back when we knew what flight we were on.

Because I was going to Oklahoma with Kimmie. She still hadn't said a word.

"Kimmie, it's okay." I held her by her upper arms and looked into her eyes. "She's stable—the worst of it is a broken leg and pelvis. She's going to need surgery but it's not life threatening."

Kimmie stared at me for another moment and then she finally opened her mouth. "It's my fault. I left her and this happened. Just like my parents. They went to do something they'd always wanted to do and they died."

I shook my head. "No, Kimmie. It's not the same. It's not your fault at all."

Her eyes widened and she suddenly sprang into action. "I need to go home. Now. Where's my suitcase? I need to call the airline. Maybe I can fly standby." She turned around in a circle and Luna came up to her, putting her paws on Kimmie.

"I'll call the airline while you pack." I pulled her into my arms, and after resisting for a moment she collapsed against me. "I'm going with you. It's going to be fine. Okay?"

"You're coming with me?" Her voice was so small and lost that it made my heart constrict.

"Yes." I let go of her and walked to my computer, flipping open my laptop.

She finally calmed enough to start packing, and I went online. Five minutes later, I cursed. There didn't seem to be any flights out tonight. I went to different airlines and discount sites.

"Did you find anything?" Kimmie stopped shoving her clothes into her suitcase to look at me.

"No, but I'm still looking." Fuck, there was nothing. It was almost seven at night. I knew Kimmie was going to worry until she saw Hana with her own eyes.

After another five minutes, I had to admit defeat. The earliest flight I could get was at six thirty tomorrow morning from LaGuardia. I booked it and then turned to Kimmie.

"We have to wait until the morning. But I got us on the first flight out. It gets into Oklahoma City at eleven tomorrow morning, with one connection."

Kimmie looked up from where she sat next to Luna, her arms around the dog. "It's two hours home from there."

"Hana's at a hospital in Tulsa." Alicia had told me on the phone. "Is that closer?"

"Maybe by half an hour." The defeated look on her face made me feel like I'd failed her.

"I'm sorry, that was the earliest flight I could find. We could go to the airport and try to get on standby, but I think that's going to be more stressful for you, waiting at the airport. Plus we'll get there in the middle of the night and they probably won't let you see her. It's probably better to wait until the morning."

"I know." She hugged Luna, who turned and licked her face. "I need to call Alicia back."

"Why don't you do that and I'll order dinner? We'll have to go to bed early to get to LaGuardia in the morning."

"What are we going to do about Luna?"

I thought for a moment. I could ask Mrs. White, but since I didn't know how long I was going to be gone, I didn't want to burden her with three dogs for an undetermined amount of time.

"I'll call Frank. See if he can come tomorrow and pick her up." His parents had fallen in love with Luna too and said she could stay over anytime.

Kimmie nodded and with one arm still around Luna, called Alicia back.

WE FINALLY MADE it to the hospital just after two thirty the next day. We rushed up to the floor where they told us Hana was. Alicia met us in the waiting room. Kimmie dropped her purse and ran at her friend, who caught her. Alicia whispered something to Kimmie and then looked up at me.

"She just got out of surgery a little while ago. They had to put a rod in her femur. We should be able to see her soon." She was rubbing Kimmie's back as she spoke.

"This is all my fault." Kimmie lifted her head. "I got

cocky. I thought I could move to New York. And then this happens."

"Hana's accident is not your fault." Alicia's voice was fierce. "A man was making a left turn when Hana crossed the street. She was in his blind spot and he didn't see her. It was an accident."

Kimmie shook her head so that her hair flew around her face. "It is my fault. I need to see her."

"You will, soon." Alicia and I exchanged a look.

Kimmie sank into a chair, dropping her head into her hands. Alicia and I sat on either side of her and we waited in silence until someone finally came to tell us she could see Hana.

Kimmie jumped up and followed the nurse back, leaving Alicia and me behind.

"Thanks for coming with her."

"Of course. She was too upset." I gave Alicia a worried look. "She blames herself."

"I know." Alicia flopped back in her chair. "I thought she'd gotten over the fear of leaving home. She was so happy the last few times I talked to her, deciding to move to New York." Her brow furrowed in concern. "I hope this doesn't make her change her mind."

My heart stopped at the thought. "I hope not." I sat next to Alicia and we didn't talk again until Kimmie came back out, twenty minutes later.

I stood as soon as I saw her. "How is she?"

"She's okay. Still a bit out of it. But the doctor says she'll be fine." Kimmie looked between me and Alicia. "She'll have to stay in the hospital for at least a week or two."

Alicia turned to us. "How did you get here?"

"I rented a car," I said.

"I have to get back. I'm supposed to work at the diner tonight." Alicia turned to Kimmie. "Will you be okay?"

She nodded. "I have Matt. He can drive me home later. I just want to spend some time with her once they get her into a room. They won't let me stay overnight."

Alicia gave us both a hug and then she left. I held Kimmie's hand as we waited. Neither of us spoke, but she leaned her head on my shoulder. When we were finally told Hana had been transferred to a room, we took the elevator to Hana's floor.

Kimmie knocked on the door lightly before stepping into the room. "Hana." Kimmie walked to her aunt's side. I hung back.

Hana was propped up in bed and smiled wearily when she saw us. Her face was bruised and swollen. "You're still here."

"Of course I am." Kimmie sat in the chair next to the bed. "How do you feel?"

"Sore. Like I got run over by a car." Hana tried to laugh but winced in pain. I saw the way Kimmie's eyes widened in panic.

"I'm sorry," Kimmie said.

"Why are you sorry?" Hana's gaze went from Kimmie's to mine in question.

"It's my fault. Your accident. I left home and something bad happened to someone I love." Kimmie bowed her head so that her hair swung forward, hiding her face.

Hana gave me a quick look before turning to Kimmie. "No." Hana's speech was slow, probably due to the anesthesia, but I could hear the fierceness in her words. "This is not your fault. Maybe my own for not paying attention before I crossed the street."

Kimmie picked her head up but didn't say anything. I

saw the doubt in her eyes and knew she would blame herself, no matter what anyone said.

"I'm serious, Kimmie. You going to New York had nothing to do with my accident . . ." Hana paused to catch her breath. "Just like your parents going on that hiking trip had nothing to do with their accident." Hana directed her gaze at Kimmie. "Okay?"

Kimmie's chin wobbled and I knew she was holding back tears. "Okay. But I'm here now. You're going to need help once you get out of the hospital and I'm going to help you."

Hana sighed. "I can't deny that I'm going to need help, but it doesn't have to be you."

Kimmie flung out a hand. "If not me, then who? You're not married and you don't have kids. Your parents are in Korea. I'm the logical person."

Hana gave her a look. "You might find it hard to believe, but I do have people who could help if I need it."

Kimmie shook her head. "It doesn't matter. You took care of me when I needed it, and now I'm going to take care of you."

Hana yawned then and put a hand over her mouth. "I'll be fine. Please don't worry."

Kimmie set her jaw and I knew she was going to worry anyway. Then she asked, "Do you need anything from home? I can pick it up and bring it to you."

Hana leaned back against the pillows and closed her eyes. "Maybe a few things. But you can bring them tomorrow. It doesn't have to be today."

"I want to come back. I can keep you company. Get you pain meds if the nurses are too busy. I'll take care of you." She leaned down and put her cheek against Hana's hand. Hana stroked Kimmie's hair.

Hana dictated a list and Kimmie wrote it down. When the nurse came in to shoo us out, we decided to go home. Kimmie was quiet for the first ten minutes of the hour-long ride, seemingly lost. But then she turned to me and said, "You know I can't go back to New York with you."

I took my eyes off the road for a second to look at her. "I know. She's going to need your help if she's stuck in the hospital for at least a week."

"That's not what I meant."

The quiet resignation in her voice had the hairs on the back of my neck standing up. "What do you mean?"

She shook her head. "Hana is going to need help, even when she gets out of the hospital. She won't be able to get around easily. She won't be able to walk on that leg for a while, and once she can put weight on it, she'll be on crutches. I need to stay."

I glanced at her. "Okay. I'm glad you're here to help her. We'll just push your move back a bit until she gets on her feet."

Kimmie shook her head again. "No, Matt. You're not getting it. I can't move to New York. Don't you see?" I looked at her, wondering if I should pull over. I had a sinking feeling in my stomach, and my heart jumped into my throat.

"I know this isn't good timing, but once Hana has healed and can get around easier, we can—"

She cut me off. "No, Matt. I can't move to New York. It's my fault this happened. I know you don't understand, but this fear I had of leaving home was very real to me. It's why I didn't apply to FIT back in high school and why I've stayed in the house I grew up in all these years. Hana's accident just proved to me that I can't leave. I can't move to

New York. Not now, or ever. I can't lose someone else I love."

I took my eyes off the road and saw the tears rolling down her cheeks. I felt for her, but I felt like my heart was breaking too. "What about me? Don't you love me?"

She turned to me, not bothering to wipe the tears off her cheeks. "I do, Matt. I do, so much. But it feels selfish. I love you so much and I can't imagine not seeing you every day, being with you and Luna. But if I moved, I'd never forgive myself if something else happens." She put a hand on my leg. "I know it doesn't make sense to you. It doesn't make sense to me either. But it's a feeling I have and—" She broke off and looked away.

A lump formed in my throat. I reached down and took the hand she'd put on my thigh and kept it there as I drove her back to her house. Neither of us spoke, but I could feel both of our hearts breaking just a bit with each mile we passed.

FORTY-ONE

Kimmie

Two days later, I stood with Matt in the parking lot of the hospital. It was Thanksgiving Day and he was flying home this morning in time to have dinner with his father. He was driving to Oklahoma City from here, having already said good-bye to Hana and Alicia. Hana was doing much better and I'd been driving back and forth to spend the day with her before going home at night and snuggling with Matt, trying to absorb his being into mine, tracing my hands down his body, trying to memorize him for when he was no longer here with me.

Because no matter what he said to me, my irrational mind had already decided. I couldn't leave Oklahoma. I had to stay, to get Hana back on her feet, and to help her when she came home from the hospital. And after that, I would stay here, safe in my parents' house, just like I was meant to be all along. The brief foray I'd made into life in New York City wasn't realistic. It was a dream, and dreams killed you or someone you loved in real life.

The wind blew around us, making my hair fly into my

eyes. Matt reached over and smoothed it back, and then reached out to take me into his arms. The minute he pulled me against his chest, I let out a sob. I hadn't wanted to cry. I didn't want to make him feel bad. It hurt, physically hurt my heart, to say good-bye to him. But I couldn't move to New York and he couldn't move to Oklahoma. He was an FDNY firefighter, something that meant the world to him, and I couldn't ask him to give that up, not after everything he'd been through to get to this point.

"Kimmie." He waited until I looked up at him. "I'm not letting you go so easily. I'll wait for you. Wait until you're ready."

"Matt." My voice was thin, because it was taking all my strength to stick to my resolve. "You can't. It's not fair to you, because I physically don't think I can go to New York."

Just the thought sent terror through my heart, every time I thought about how I almost lost Hana. If the car had been going a little faster, or if Hana hadn't seen the car at the last minute and tried to get out of its way . . . My whole body trembled and Matt tightened his arms around me. How I was going to miss these arms. I cried harder, thinking of how lonely my life would be, now that I knew what life was like with him in it.

"I don't care what's fair or not. I'll come visit when I can, and I'll wait for you to be ready to come back to New York." He leaned down until his forehead was against mine. "I love you, Kimmie Park, and I'm not going to let you go."

I took in a shuddering breath. "It's not going to work, Matt. I have to be here and you have to be there. We should just end things now."

"No." His forehead pressed against mine a little harder. "No. You're not going to get rid of me this easily. Luna's not going to let you go either. I have to go back to work, but we'll figure this out."

He pulled away to look at me, and then touched me on the face with one hand. I closed my eyes, wanting to remember everything about this moment. When his lips touched mine, my eyes flew open and stayed open, wanting to take in every detail of him even though I couldn't see much this close up.

When we pulled away, I gave him a sad smile. "Thank you for coming home with me."

"Always." He gave me one last kiss and then straightened. "I should go."

"Okay." I nodded, even though I wanted to fling my arms around him and beg him not to go. Not to leave me.

He opened the car door with our hands still linked and then we finally let go when he got in. With one last look at me, he started the car and pulled away, leaving me there in the parking lot, tears running down my face while I wondered if I'd made a mistake.

THREE MISERABLE WEEKS LATER, I was making breakfast for Hana, who was sitting at the dining table with her laptop, her bad leg propped up on a chair because it ached when she let it hang down. She'd ended up having to stay in the hospital for two weeks, so had only been home for a week. We were figuring things out. We moved her down to the guest room that Alicia had been using, and Alicia moved upstairs. I knew it was frustrating for Hana not to be able to do the simplest things like taking a shower by herself, but she didn't complain. She'd been writing a lot. When I wasn't helping her out, I was sewing up a storm in my sewing room. Good thing I had so much time to sew because I'd literally gotten around four hundred orders in the last month. I'd hired Hallie from Rip's store to help me, on top of Alicia and Hana.

"Kimmie." I looked up at Hana's voice. "Out with it."

"Out with what?" My hand stilled over the "special eggs" I was making in the pan. It was basically a Taiwanese omelet that Ruby had taught me how to make, with sauteed garlic, scallions, and pickled radish. There was a pot of congee—rice porridge—on the stove, and I'd already set out the sides of rousing (pork floss), pickled cucumber, fermented bean curd, and wheat gluten on the table in front of Hana. Ruby had taught me about this traditional Taiwanese breakfast, and the one advantage of driving to Tulsa every day to visit Hana was that I'd stocked up on a lot of Asian groceries.

"You've been moping for weeks. What's going on?" Hana fixed me with eyes partly narrowed.

"Nothing's wrong. Everything's fine." I tried to inject cheer into my voice as I turned back to the eggs.

"Stop." Hana's voice was so stern it made me look up. "I'm not stupid."

"I . . ." I looked away, back at the eggs, and scooped the spatula under the omelet to take it out of the pan and onto a waiting plate. I brought it over to the table and sat down, looking at Hana.

"Kimmie. Something's up. What is it?" Hana's voice gentled, but she was giving me that look that I knew meant business.

My shoulders slumped. "I told Matt I couldn't move to New York."

"Why?" Hana's voice was incredulous. "It's your

dream. Matt's there. Luna. What are you doing in Oklahoma?"

"Taking care of you." Even as I said it, it sounded stupid to me. Hana would heal soon, and then she'd be off again, traveling and writing. Alicia had accepted Robert's offer of the paid mentorship and was making plans to move to New York. And I would once again be stuck here. Alone.

"I'm going to be fine. Yes, I need physical therapy and I might not be running any marathons soon, but I'm going to get back to my life." Hana didn't take her gaze off me, and I looked down, unable to meet her eyes.

Because a part of me agreed with her. Was I being stupid, or delusional, thinking my decision to move to New York was responsible for Hana's accident? But then I'd think about actually moving to New York and my entire body would seize up. The fear, that ice-cold fear, would wash over me, knowing that if I did, something else was going to happen to either Alicia or Hana. Or even Matt. That I'd bring whatever it was that made dreams die with me and it would affect Matt, hurt him. And that was enough to keep me where I was, even as I berated myself for being stupid.

When I didn't answer, Hana spoke again. "How does Matt feel about all this?"

"He calls and texts every day. He says he'll wait for me to be ready to come to New York." I met Hana's eyes. "I can't do that to him. So, I stopped answering his calls and texts last week. On my birthday." He'd called to tease me about turning thirty and had sent me a stuffed dog that looked like Luna in the mail. And it'd hurt so much that I couldn't answer him.

"Kimmie." Hana pressed her lips together, hard.

"I don't know if I'll ever be ready. I can't let go of this

fear . . . Ever since my parents died, I've had this belief that dreams kill you. And . . ." My voice wobbled and I had to take a breath to keep talking. "My dreams were all coming true. Despite the Let Her Rip video, the hiccup with Matt when he didn't know what I really looked like, the whole thing with Endless, I had a glimpse into what my life could be like. And I loved it. I wanted to live in the same city as Matt. As Luna. As Ruby. I wanted to work at Endless instead of doing it remotely, and keep sewing for my Etsy shop, take classes at FIT. I was going to have it all. And then you had the accident and reality crashed in. Dreams kill you. Or they kill someone you love."

"Kimmie." There was so much love in Hana's voice that the tears threatened again. I thought she was going to say something kind and loving, and I braced myself for the tears to come. But what she said was, "I love you, but you are the stupidest idiot I have ever met."

My mouth dropped open and the tears dried up.

"You have a wonderful man who loves you, who forgave you when you finally told him the truth about who you really are, who fought for you at Endless and has been by your side, even flying to Oklahoma with you when I had the accident. He calls you every day, and because of some superstition that you brought on yourself from your parents' death, you've decided you don't deserve happiness and would be better off here in Oklahoma all by yourself? I'm sorry, but that's just idiotic in my book."

"But you're alone. You don't have anyone either." I couldn't keep the hurt from my voice. Hana had never spoken like this to me before.

"How do you know I'm alone?" Hana turned and practically glared at me.

"I . . . You never talk about anyone . . . I've never met

anyone . . ." I couldn't form a complete sentence, still taken aback that Hana had called me idiotic.

"I don't talk about it because it's my private business." Hana's expression turned fierce. "I have . . . people that I love and see at different points in my life. I'm not like everyone else. I don't crave a monogamous relationship with just one person. There's a woman I love that I spend time with whenever I'm in Asia. And a man I see when I'm in Europe." She turned her face away. "I don't talk about it because it's not conventional. But it's my life and I chose it. I want to be free to do what I want, when I want. But that doesn't mean there aren't people who are special to me."

I didn't think my mouth could drop any more open, but it did. I stared at my aunt and realized we never really knew anyone else, no matter how well we thought we did. There were parts of me that Hana would never know about. And parts of her I'd never know about. And I realized it made me love her even more. She lived life on her own terms, without regard for what anyone else thought of her. I stood and went behind her, wrapping my arms around her.

"I love you," I whispered into her ear. "I love you so much. You mean so much to me."

She put her arms around mine and squeezed. "And I love you too. Which is why I need to kick you in the butt when you deserve it." She twisted around until she faced me. "Don't lose Matt because of some neurosis you've built up from your parents' death. Talk to a therapist if you need to. But don't lose that man because you're being an idiot."

I smiled, even as I felt like crying. Because even though I knew her words were true, that fear in my heart was still there. I didn't know if it would ever go away. But Hana was right. I'd fucked up, letting Matt go. I needed to call him and tell him I was sorry.

"I . . ." I stopped and swallowed. This was hard for me to say. "I think I want to talk to someone." Hana had made me see a therapist when my parents died, but I hadn't liked the woman and stopped going after a few months. I'd had an aversion to therapy ever since. But I think I was finally ready to talk to someone. To get help for my hang-ups from my parents' death.

"I'm glad." Hana gave me a gentle smile and then slapped the table. "Okay. I've said my piece. Now can we eat? I'm starving."

I laughed and let go of Hana to spoon a bowlful of congee for her before going to my room for my phone. I'd eat later. I needed to call Matt first. And then I was going to look for a therapist. Because maybe talking about my fears with a professional mental health counselor would help me get over this and I *would* find the courage to go back to New York.

But when I turned on my phone, I saw that I had a lot of notifications on Instagram. I'd gotten used to posting something about myself every two or three days and realized I didn't mind sharing parts of my world. I still couldn't believe the following I'd built up, especially when Endless had officially announced our collaboration a week and a half ago. My heart had ached when it happened, because I'd thought I would be with Matt, celebrating with champagne. Instead, I was in Oklahoma, spending all day with Hana in the hospital and then coming home to an empty house because Alicia was out living her life.

I opened Instagram first (yes, I was procrastinating; admitting I was the stupidest idiot wasn't easy). And saw that I had a DM from frankiefdny374. I sat up. That was Frank from Matt's firehouse. He'd started following me as soon as he knew who I really was and we'd liked each other's posts but he'd never DMed me. My heart rate picking up speed, I read his message.

Kimmie, I thought you'd want to know, but Matt had a near miss at a job today. He's fine, but I think he's a bit shook. I don't know what happened between you two, but he's looked like hell since he came back from Oklahoma. Sorry if I'm overstepping but thought you'd want to know.

My heart stopped. I sat on the couch for a few seconds, my breath coming fast as my mind whirled. And I knew what I had to do.

FORTY-TWO

Matt

I was fine. The beam that had fallen had only grazed my shoulder. They'd checked me out at the scene and declared me fit, but still put me on medical leave for at least a week. I hated it because I was fine.

My father came to my apartment with a carton of chicken soup from PJ Bernstein's. It was something my mom always got for me when I was sick. Thinking about her, coupled with the near miss at work yesterday, hardened my resolve to have it out with my father once and for all. If this job had taught me anything, it was that we never knew when each day would be our last. I was lucky this time, but I might not be the next time. That was the reality of my job. And I was going to finally find out why my father wouldn't talk about my mother with me.

My father stood awkwardly by the front door after I'd opened it. "Here." He held out the soup and I took it from him.

"I need to talk to you. I need to know why you won't talk about Mom." I didn't waste time on small talk.

I saw the way his face hardened, and I knew he was going to say the same thing he'd said every time I tried to talk about my mother.

"No, Dad. I'm not going to let it go. I need to know what happened that night. Why she was driving to the Hamptons by herself." I put the soup on the coffee table and then faced him, my hands in fists by my sides.

"Matt, I told you, I don't want to talk about her."

I got in his face. "Well, that's no longer good enough for me. I need to talk about her. I want to talk about her. I need to understand what she was thinking that night." I pointed at him. "Tell me now. I'm not going to let it go. I need to know. Why won't you talk about her?"

The last few words ended in a shout. I'd never raised my voice to my father before. We stared at each other, and then all of a sudden, his face cracked.

"Because it's my fault she died, okay?" The words shot out of his mouth like bullets. "Is that what you want to hear?"

I stared back at him, eyes wide in shock. "What're you talking about?" This was the last thing I'd expected him to say.

He met my eyes briefly before looking away. "We got in a fight. She was upset. Said she was going to the Hamptons house." He looked down but I could see the anguish in his eyes. "I didn't stop her, even though I knew she hated to drive at night." He folded his arms over his chest. "I even thought to myself, good, let her go. Let her cool down and give me some peace and quiet." He took a breath and seemed to sag in front of my eyes. "I got what I wanted, didn't I?"

"Dad, no." I didn't know what to say.

But it was like the floodgates finally opened and my dad

kept talking. "She wanted me to work less. Had been asking me to cut back for months. That night, she told me she couldn't take it anymore. She wanted a divorce."

My mouth dropped open. My mother wanted a divorce? But I'd always thought they were so happy together. How could she have been so unhappy and I didn't know?

"I thought she was just emotional, that she wasn't serious. And I let her go." He brought a hand up to his forehead and rubbed it. "I let her go. And she got in that accident and she was gone. She died angry at me."

"Oh." That was all I could say.

"That's why I can't talk about her. If I had stopped her from leaving, she wouldn't have been on the 495 that night and caught up in that horrific crash. She wouldn't have died like that, all alone on a highway."

My nose stung and my eyes grew hot. I couldn't speak. I could only stare at my father.

"I didn't want a divorce. I loved her. Loved her so much. I didn't know she was so unhappy. And I let her go and she died." His voice cracked and he looked away again.

I finally found my voice. "It's not your fault, Dad. It was an accident and she was there at the wrong time. Mom wouldn't have wanted you to blame yourself." As the words came out of my mouth, I knew they were true. Whatever had happened between them, she would never have blamed him for letting her leave.

"Do you blame me?" My father's voice was gruff. "I know how close you were to Lily."

"No," I said, and realized it was true. "It's not your fault. And Mom still loved you. Remember what the firefighter who was with her at the end said? She wanted us to know she loved us. Remember? 'Tell Robert and Matthew I love them.'"

My father stood there, still by the front door, and just looked at me. Whatever had happened between them, whatever the reason she'd said she wanted a divorce, I knew she wouldn't want him to blame himself.

I walked to him and embraced him. "I love you, Dad. Mom did too."

His arms came around me and he held me for a moment. When we parted, I could see by the way he was swallowing and blinking that he was trying to get ahold of his emotions.

"Thank you," he finally said.

"Can we talk about her now? Remember her? How much she loved us."

He paused and then nodded. "When you told me you were going to be a firefighter, all I could think was that I was going to lose you too. That's why I was against it. Not because you weren't working at Endless anymore."

I stared at him, realization dawning. I never thought about what me working for the FDNY meant to him. "I'm sorry."

"I'm proud of you." He turned to the front door as he said that and opened it. "I'll see you, Matt."

And he left and I let him. I stood still for another few minutes, letting what happened sink in. And then I knew what I had to do. Kimmie hadn't returned any of my texts and calls in the last week. I knew she was trying to cut me out of her life, but after hearing about what happened between my parents, I knew I couldn't let her go. Nana had told me to follow my heart when I'd finally told her that Kimmie wasn't moving to New York and wouldn't talk to me. Nana had looked at me with those wise eyes and said,

"If she's the one for you, then nothing else matters. You'll find a way to work things out. Follow your heart."

I was going to do that. If Kimmie wouldn't come to New York, then Luna and I were going to move to Oklahoma to be with her. I would find a job there, maybe join the fire department, or find something else to do. Because what mattered was her. Not a job, or the city where I grew up. I'd ask Frank to watch Luna for me while I flew to Oklahoma to tell Kimmie in person that we were moving there.

I stopped and laughed, thinking how Frank had become a friend, someone I trusted with Luna, someone who would cover for me. With my mind made up, I pulled out my suitcase and started packing.

FORTY-THREE

Kimmie

I stared out the windows of the taxi as the familiar buildings of Manhattan came into view. My heart lifted and I knew I'd made the right decision. How had I been so stupid these last few weeks? Why had I let a superstition that I'd developed when I was sixteen morph into something so big that it'd kept me from the man and the city I loved for almost a month? Alicia and her mother promised to help Hana while I was gone and they'd all practically shooed me out the door and to the airport.

I couldn't wait to surprise Matt at his apartment. Frank had told me Matt was on medical leave, so I was hoping to catch him at home. My heart hammered wildly in my chest, imagining his reaction and hoping he hadn't given up on me yet. As the taxi got closer to his apartment, I realized how stupid this plan was. What if he wasn't home? What if he wasn't happy to see me? I should have called first.

The taxi pulled up to the building and my heart threatened to jump out of my chest. I paid the driver and tipped him when he took my suitcase out of the trunk. As I rolled it to the front door, Junior opened it for me.

"Kimmie! I haven't seen you in a while." He greeted me with a big smile.

"Good to see you, Junior." Once I was in the lobby, I stood there, uncertain. "Um, do you know if Matt's home? I, um, came to surprise him."

Junior gave me a puzzled look. "He left this morning. With a suitcase. I think he was going on a trip or something."

"What? Where?"

"He didn't say where he was going." Junior gave a shrug.

"Oh, no." I knew it. I should have called. What if he had a new girlfriend already and was going to visit her? What if he'd left the country for a while? My mind spiraled at all the possibilities and I had no idea what to do.

The elevator dinged and I looked up to see Mrs. White with Mickey and Milly coming off the elevator.

"Kimmie! I wondered what happened to you. Matt West looked so depressed the last few weeks."

She walked to me and we hugged. I petted her dogs as I tried to figure out what to do. Call Matt? Head back to the airport and go home? But I didn't want Oklahoma to be my home anymore. I wanted . . . Matt.

My shoulders sagged and Mrs. White patted my back. "It'll all work out, whatever it is."

I gave her a weak smile. "Thanks, Mrs. White. Do you know where Luna is?"

"I think she's with Frank." Mrs. White gave me a look. "Matt's been so helpful around my apartment, doing things for me that I can't do myself, in exchange for having Luna stay with me when he's at the firehouse overnight."

My cell rang just then in my hand. Seeing it was Matt, my heart lifted.

"Matt?"

"Kimmie. Where are you?" Matt's voice brought tears to my eyes. I'd missed talking to him every day.

"I'm in New York. Standing in your lobby with Mrs. White. Where are you?" Mrs. White was listening to my end of the conversation and gave me an encouraging nod.

Matt laughed, a joyful sound that made me bite my lip. "Kimmie, I'm at your house with Hana."

"What? In Oklahoma?" I walked to the couch and sat down in shock. "What are you doing there?"

He was still laughing. "I came to find you. Hana almost had a heart attack when she opened the door to find me on the doorstep."

"Oh my god. And I came to New York to find you." A giggle escaped and I put a hand up to my mouth.

"I'm sorry, Kimmie," Matt was saying, as I tried to control my emotions. "I should have been more understanding about your fear of leaving. I was selfish, thinking you had to move for this relationship to work."

"No, Matt. I was selfish. I let my fears that I developed as a sixteen-year-old completely obliterate my common sense. Hana made me realize what a stupid idiot I was being. I'm going to see someone, work this out in therapy. Are you okay?" My heart pounded so hard that I had to put my hand over my chest.

"I'm fine. You're more important to me than a job. I came here to tell you that Luna and I are moving to Oklahoma. I'll find another job. Maybe with a fire department here, or work for my dad remotely." He rushed on, as if wanting to get all the words out. "It doesn't matter. As long as we're together, it doesn't matter where we live."

I sank back against the couch, feeling faint. Mrs. White was staring at me, but all I could think was that Matt was willing to give up the FDNY for me. "You would do that? Leave New York and your job?"

"Yes. I wanted to tell you in person." He laughed. "But it turns out you're not here."

"And I came here to tell *you* in person that I'm moving to New York. That I'm so sorry for the last few weeks and my freak-out."

There was silence for a moment, and then Matt and I burst out laughing at the same time. I laughed so hard that tears came to my eyes, and I knew Junior and Mrs. White were staring at me but I didn't care. Matt wasn't mad at me. He was in Oklahoma and I was in New York. I laughed even harder.

When we finally calmed down, Matt spoke first. "Stay there. I'm going right back to the airport now and getting on whatever flight I can back to you. Put Junior on and I'll tell him to give you the key. Want me to tell Frank to bring Luna to you if he can?"

"Yes. I've missed her so much." I stood to give Junior the phone, and after Matt spoke to him, Junior handed the phone back to me. "I'm so sorry, Matt. I've been so stupid."

"No more apologizing. I'll let you know what flight I get on." He paused and then said, "I love you, Kimmie Park. I'm coming for you."

"I love you too, Matt West. I'll be waiting." And with tears streaming down my cheeks, I hung up.

Junior handed me the key and with a last smile at him and at Mrs. White, who was beaming at me, I went up to Matt's apartment to wait for him.

HOURS LATER, I sat on the couch, Luna cuddled up next to me. Frank had driven her into Manhattan and I'd met him downstairs so that he didn't have to try to find a parking spot. Our reunion had been so joyful. Luna recognized me right away, as soon as I opened the back door of Frank's car. She whined and jumped all over me, licking my face and butting me with her big head. I'd looked up to see Frank smiling at us.

"Thank you so much for driving her in."

He gave a shy smile. "Anything for you, Let Her . . . I mean, Kimmie."

I gave him a teasing look. "For all that you've done for Luna and for me, you can call me Let Her Rip if you want."

We smiled at each other and then he said, "I didn't know you planned on flying to New York without telling Matt. When Matt told me he was going to Oklahoma, I thought the two of you had talked. I would have stopped him if I'd known you were on the way here." He'd laughed at us. "You guys are like that couple in that short story, 'The Gift of the Magi.'"

He'd blushed again and I narrowed my eyes, wondering how I could let him know how grateful I was to him for letting me know about Matt. Then I knew. Holding Luna's leash tightly in my hand, I started twerking, dancing to a beat in my head. Frank froze, but then he started clapping his hands in time to my movements. Luna jumped around me and we danced together on the street as Frank clapped and hooted, beaming at me.

I smiled now thinking about it as I rubbed Luna's back. Matt should be here soon. He'd called an hour ago to say he'd just landed. I'd spent the hours while he was in the air getting acquainted with New York again. Luna and I had taken a long walk, going up and down the Upper East Side, looking into shop windows and stopping so Luna could say hello to other dogs. We'd gone to Central Park, which I'd missed. With each step I took, my body became more alive. I'd missed this, all this walking and activity. I'd missed the energy and the way adrenaline pumped through me, making me feel like I could accomplish anything.

I'd ordered Thai in, eating with Luna at my side as we watched a reality TV show. And I took a shower and made sure I shaved, my body trembling at the thought of finally being with Matt again.

When he texted that he was five minutes away, I jumped up, clipping Luna's leash on. The elevator came right away, and within minutes we were on the sidewalk. And as if we'd timed it, a car pulled up and Matt got out of the back seat.

"Matt," I called, and ran toward him, Luna at my side. He looked up and caught me, and then my arms were around his neck and his around my waist. He hugged me, hard, as if he wanted to meld my body into his, and then he was crushing his lips to mine. There was nothing gentle about the kiss. We were back together again, where we belonged.

EPILOGUE

EIGHT MONTHS LATER

Kimmie

The front door slammed and Alicia came running into our apartment.

"It's about time. I thought you forgot about the dinner tonight." But then I noticed she was already dressed in a stunning hot-pink dress with spaghetti straps that floated around her. "You look great."

I was wearing a little black dress, a staple in my New York City wardrobe. I had a whole bunch of them in different styles and fabrics. The one I had on was sparkly and made me feel like a jewel.

"Thanks. I had to do a promo piece for our new line at Endless and they let me keep the dress." She grinned at me. "I love this job."

Alicia had moved to New York with me a little less than eight months ago. I'd eventually move in with Matt, but for now, I loved having Alicia for a roommate. I no longer felt as alone as I had in Oklahoma before I became Let Her Rip. We had our own lives, but I could also count on her when I needed her. And the nights Matt was at the firehouse, Luna stayed with us and she completed my heart.

I'd come first and stayed with Matt until we found the perfect apartment for Alicia and me. It was in the Seventies between First and Second Avenues and was a true two-bedroom. It was only a few blocks from Matt's apartment and we'd gone crazy decorating it. It looked like Pottery Barn had eaten Urban Outfitters and threw up a boho-chic baby, but we loved it.

Our Crafty Bao line at Endless had taken off. In the first week of the launch alone, they sold out of the bao stuffed toys. The merchandise with the baos on them and the double-frame purses flew off the shelves. Robert had contracted with us for a new line for each season. Alicia was now the face of the entire brand, her picture all over our social media and advertisements, as well as doing promo pieces and appearing on TV, podcasts, and other media outlets. I was happy as the designer behind the brand. We'd kept our Etsy shop for now, changing the name to Our Crafty Bao. And I'd been posting pictures of my life in New York City on my social media. It turned out people couldn't get enough of Matt's and my story, along with Luna. I didn't post often, since I still liked to keep most of my life private, but when I did, it was always well received.

"You ready to go?" Alicia linked arms with me.

Robert was hosting a dinner to celebrate our collaboration. Crafty Bao was now their top-selling brand and we were in demand. At the rate we were going, Alicia and I talked about closing our Etsy shop, but for now, I still enjoyed sewing at night, a way to decompress from the busy days. The classes I was taking at FIT inspired me, and I had so many designs in my head, just waiting to be let out.

"Let's go." I grabbed my purse and keys, and we headed

out into the hot August night. Matt was meeting us at the restaurant, since he was coming off a tour at the firehouse. He was no longer a probie and had gotten his company badge seven months ago. I was so proud of him.

We took the subway down to the Fifties, where Robert had rented a private room in a restaurant for the occasion. When we walked in, I took a moment to take in all the familiar faces. Robert was there with his assistant, Tina, as well as Sarah from the front desk. There was our whole team, the PR and marketing people, the lawyer and Marie, the intern who had been assigned to me and Alicia. Ruby and Eric were there, standing next to Matt and Nana, all beaming at me proudly. And there was Matt, looking so hot I wanted to jump him right then and there and tear his clothes off.

The only person who was missing was Hana. She was currently living in Thailand, researching her next book. She'd told me a bit more about the woman, Seri, who was more than a friend. Maybe one day I'd get to meet her. But for now, Hana was happy doing what she loved the most, and I would see her soon, when she came to New York next month.

Matt walked over to me and gave me a kiss. I smiled against his lips as I always did, grateful I'd come to my senses and hadn't let this man get away. My therapist and I were unpacking all my fears stemming from my parents' death and being adopted, and I felt stronger emotionally every day. I'd ended up renting out my house in Oklahoma and would probably eventually sell it. It had been sad to sort through Mom's and Dad's things that I'd kept in the house all these years, but it had also been cleansing. I felt lighter, freer to be me and no longer burdened by the fear that my parents' death had brought out.

"You look gorgeous, Kimmie," Matt said to me.

My cheeks heated. He still had the power to make me blush. "And you look extremely hot, fireman," I teased. "Catch lots of underwear today?"

He threw back his head and laughed. "There's only one person I want throwing their underwear at me."

He took my hand and we greeted everyone. Ruby hugged me. We'd gotten close over the past few months.

Waiters took our drinks order and we sat down, as Robert stood to make a speech, congratulating us on our accomplishments. Everyone raised their glasses and we drank to the success of Crafty Bao and Endless. And we all laughed when the first course came out, a variety of baos to be passed around the tables.

Then Matt stood up. "I want to make another toast. Almost a year ago, I slid into Kimmie's DMs, and it was the best shady move I'd ever made."

Everyone laughed and I looked up at him. I hoped he wasn't about to embarrass me.

"Before I knew what she looked like, I pictured her as kindly, grandmother type."

I swatted him on the side. "Hey," I said, causing everyone to laugh again.

He smiled down at me. "Then I thought she looked like Alicia." He gestured over to Alicia, who waved. "But that image never went with the voice I got to know for a month before I finally met Kimmie in person. And when I saw her for the first time, it was like my heart knew. This was the person I'd been talking to for the past month, who knew more about me than anyone, even though we'd never met." He paused and raised his eyebrows. "It was awkward, to say the least, because at the time, I thought she was Alicia, Kimmie's best friend."

He leaned over and took my hands, forcing me to stand up. What the heck was he doing? He knew how much I hated being the center of attention. I gave him a desperate look and made to sit down, but he was still holding my hands and I stumbled on my heels, nearly toppling over before Matt's strong grip righted me. My cheeks burning, I glared at him.

"This is the perfect example of the real Kimmie. She may trip on her own feet, stammer when talking to people she doesn't know, or walk into walls, but she's also the graceful twerker from that viral video and the brilliant mind behind Crafty Bao. She's also the best dog mom to Luna, and a loving niece, daughter, and best friend. And I couldn't imagine my life without her."

Before I understood what was happening, Matt handed me a plate with a gua bao, a Taiwanese bun that opened like a clamshell, on it.

"What's this?" I looked from the bao to Matt. It didn't look like there was anything in it. "Where's the filling?"

"Open it." Matt's eyes danced and I could feel everyone staring at me.

I reached over and opened the bao and found a beautiful diamond ring snuggled in the center of the white fluffy bao. Matt picked up the ring and dropped to a knee next to me. "Kimmie Park, I'm crazy bao you. Will you marry me?"

My mouth dropped open in shock and my hands flew to my face as I stared at Matt. I heard murmurs around me, but I could only look at this man in front of me.

When I could finally move, I placed a trembling hand on his cheek. "Matt. A thousand times yes. Yes, I'll marry you."

Matt rose, taking me in his arms, and kissed me as if we were the only two people in the room. When I looked up to see our friends, family, and colleagues clapping and whistling, for once, I didn't mind being the center of attention. Especially when Luna appeared out of nowhere and ran to our side, and I saw Alicia holding up her phone. She had Hana on FaceTime, and Hana had tears running down her cheeks as she blew me a kiss.

My heart was full. I was so loved and no longer alone.

ACKNOWLEDGMENTS

For my first three books, I have always thanked my agent, Rachel Brooks first, and this book is no exception. She spent over eighteen months with me on this and there are no words to describe how much I value her wisdom, advice, encouragement, and the way she is always ready to go to battle for me and my books. Thank you, Rachel and Book-Ends Literary Agency, for always having my back.

Thank you to Sean Walsh for illustrating the most gorgeous cover, and capturing the essence of Kimmie and Matt. Jim and I are in awe of your talent. Thank you to Janice Rossi, who had no idea when she wandered into my fitness class, that she would one day be roped into designing this beautiful cover. Thank you also to Eileen G. Chetti for the thorough copyedit of the book.

To my FDNY husband Jim, thank you for answering my numerous questions about life as a FDNY firefighter. When he got tired of my questions, he handed me off to his friend and fellow firefighter Mike Waterman. Thank you, Mike, for reading the fire department sections and setting me straight on details. Any mistakes are my own.

Special thanks to Kimberly Packard and Sarah Echavarre Smith, who both guided me through the self-publishing process and answered my never-ending questions. Thank you also to Tif Marcelo for commiserating with me when I needed it. Thank you to Anita Kushwaha, Samantha Verant, and Delise Torres for always reading and supporting my work, and to my hardcore Berkletes friends, especially Tracey, Ali, Lauren, Amy, Nekesa, and Sarah Elizabeth for reading and providing blurbs. I love you all!

And as always, thank you to Jim and Lakon for putting up with my writing frenzies and to my dogs, Lokie, Mochi, and Cash (and Pinot in heaven) for being the best writing companions ever.

ABOUT THE AUTHOR

Lyn Liao was born in Taiwan and moved to the States when she was seven. She also writes thrillers and upmarket fiction under the name Lyn Liao Butler.

Before becoming an author, she was a professional ballet and modern dancer, and is still a personal trainer, and fitness and yoga instructor. When she is not torturing clients or talking to imaginary characters, Lyn enjoys spending time with her FDNY husband, their son, their three stubborn dachshunds, sewing for her Etsy shop, and trying complicated yoga poses on a stand-up paddle board. So far, she has not fallen into the water yet.

facebook.com/lynliaobutlerauthor

twitter.com/lynliaobutler

instagram.com/lynliaobutler

tiktok.com/@lynliaobutler